Gaia Hunted

A Novel

J.R. Walcutt

Spirit Warrior Press

2019 Spirit Warrior Press Trade Paperback Edition

LIBRARY OF CONGRESS CATALOGING-IN-PUBLICATION DATA
Gaia Hunted : a novel / Jason Walcutt
ISBN 978-1-7327583-1-5
eBook ISBN: 978-1-7327583-0-8
1. Urban Fantasy—Fiction.   2. Legends and Mythology—Fiction.   3. International Thriller—Fiction.

Printed in the United States of America

Spirit Warrior Press
www.spiritwarriorpress.com

To Drappie and Lala

CHAPTER ONE
City of Peace

It is an irony that I can be surrounded by thousands and still feel utterly alone. I thought coming here would shake things up. But as the crowd of strangers grows and presses the air out of me, I feel like I'm drowning in people. A vampire with translucent skin and bloody fangs holding the hand of a seminude cowgirl in heels pushes past me, almost knocking me to the ground. I wrap my hands around my worn tote bag, shivering in my thin, and in retrospect, poorly chosen Wonder Woman costume. Why did I come to Salem on Halloween?

I'd been in my apartment, feet on the couch, laptop resting on my knees, eating Reese's Pieces out of a bowl and feeling sorry for myself. Hearing groups of rowdy children scampering outside, I'd sequestered myself in my living room with the lights off and the blinds closed. Only two months had passed since losing my teaching job. The last thing I wanted to do was interact with children.

But hiding out wasn't me, so I pulled an old Halloween costume from college out of the depths of my closet, wiggled into it, and took small pride in the fact that it still fit. Then I grabbed a tote bag, filled it with the rest of the Reese's Pieces, and left the apartment.

Now here I am.

Desperate to escape the throng of partygoers, I step onto a side street and run into Aladdin's Jasmine.

"Hey! Watch where you're going!" the girl cries, sweeping aside her hip-length wig of black hair. "You scuffed my shoes."

Looking down, I see that her blue slippers are, in fact, smudged and say, "Sorry, didn't mean to."

She takes a pull from a neon-green vape pen and exhales out her nostrils. "People today, they have no manners."

"I couldn't agree more," I reply, turning to walk away.

The next moment, we're shoved to the side of the street by a group of Kim Kardashian wannabes who strut past. "Clear the way," says a girl wearing only a miniskirt and bra.

"Well, that proves our point," I say.

Jasmine rubs her shoulder and shoots the group a murderous look. "I hate those types of girls."

I glance pointedly at her ballooning, shimmery blue pants and matching halter top, complete with ample cleavage.

She notices my expression and crosses her arms. "First off, my costume is awesome." She tosses back her black mane. "And second, I highly doubt they're in costume." She nods at me. "What's your name?"

"Mattie."

"I'm Alice."

"Well, Alice, it was a pleasure meeting you." I turn to leave and see hordes of costumed strangers swaying to a rock band of mummies playing Donovan's "Season of the Witch." A creeping sadness comes over me. I'm ready to go home.

"I hate crowds," says Alice.

"Me, too," I spot a gap in the crowd. "Got to go."

But as I turn, she says, "Holy shit, what's that on your face?" She reaches up and tucks a lock of my hair behind my ear.

I step back surprised and brush away her hand.

"Whoa," she says. "Sweet birthmark."

The birthmark is a skin discoloration in the shape of a jagged crescent moon. "You think? I usually try to hide it with my glasses."

"Hey, you should be proud of that mark."

"Why?"

"You just should be." She keeps staring at my face.

We press against the brick wall of a building to avoid being trampled by a gaggle of tweens carrying brooms.

Alice takes another pull from her pen.

"Listen," she says. "I have to give you a psychic reading."

"You're a psychic?"

"One of the best in the world."

"Yeah, and I'm Marie Antoinette."

"Have you ever had a reading before?"

"No," I reply.

"Why not?"

"Because I don't believe in any of that stuff."

"I don't really care if you believe in it."

"I should be going—"

"Hey, wait. I'll show you how good I am." She closes her eyes and presses the back of her left hand to her forehead. "You came here alone."

Well, that wasn't too hard to figure out.

"You live in Cambridge," she continues.

My jaw drops a tad, but then I remember that my tote bag reads "Cambridge Public Library" on the side.

"Yep, you got it. You're a real phenomenon." I break away from her and head back onto the main street.

But when I spin around, I see something that sends chills rippling across my skin. Maybe fifty feet away from me is someone wearing the mask of a bull—except there's something not quite right about it.

The twisted, moving face has a bristling snout, jagged horns, and black olive-pit eyes, which stare into oblivion. Hanging around the person is a brackish green aura resembling exhaust belched from an old pickup.

"What the hell . . ." I whisper, an ice cube of fear skittering down my spine. I rub my eyes. This can't be real.

The next moment, the bull mask dissipates like an ocean fog, and I can make out the man beneath—ink-black hair molded into a widow's peak, cheeks sunken like a bayou swamp, smoldering brown eyes.

A hand squeezes my elbow, and my pulse rockets. I jolt, twist around. Alice. I sigh, my heart still rattling. Then I blink, uncertain if this woman is also a hallucination.

When I glance back, the man is gone. He never looked in my direction, but for some reason, I'm sure he was searching for me. I'm reminded of my dreams, dreams always forgotten, always just beyond my grasp—dreams that have haunted my waking life, my lost dreams. I let out a ragged breath.

"What's wrong?" Alice looks around, frowning, eyes narrow. "What did you see?" Her tense voice does little to soothe my nerves.

"I – I –" I turn back to where the man had been. But all I find are crowds of Frankensteins, fairies, and vampires. "I'm OK," I reply, voice shaking. "I saw some freak in a costume."

The slight flicker of her eyes shows she's not convinced. Her face remains grim.

"Let's get off the street. Too many assholes out here."

I close my eyes and take a calming breath to subdue my hammering pulse. I need to leave the overcrowded street. I need to forget about the deadened expression in the man's eyes.

"OK," I concede with a nod. I'll give her ten minutes. By that time, I'll feel better.

Alice grabs my hand and guides me through the throng.

CHAPTER TWO
Gaia

We enter a crowded magic shop off the main drag. Shelves overflow with precious stones, books about alchemy, and artifacts ranging from miniature skulls to crystal balls. The smell of sandalwood incense and moss-scented candles overpowers my nose. Navigating around a curio cabinet filled with voodoo dolls, we pass a gigantic mirror bordered with grinning blue gargoyles.

I catch a glimpse of my reflection. My French braid has come undone, and strands of chestnut-brown hair have gone off on wild orbits. Try as I might to tame it with products, my frizzy hair has a mind of its own. My green eyes stand out more than usual. A glow surrounds the buckshot spray of freckles on my cheeks. Maybe I'm kind of excited about learning my future.

Alice leads me past the shop's clerk—a hobbit-sized man dressed in a kimono, standing vigilant at the cash register and eyeing a large, loud group of teenage boys.

"Steve. My booth is occupied in case anyone comes by."

The man grunts.

A cloth-enclosed cubicle stands at the back of the shop. Once inside, Alice closes a scarlet curtain. She climbs into a high-back chair with velvet armrests and gestures for me to sit on the metal foldout chair across from her.

Alice lays her hands on the round wooden table, palms facing up as if making an offering.

"So, first I'll tell you about your past and present. Then we'll take a look-see at your future. Sound good?"

I shrug, my initial excitement tempered by a burst of skepticism. She might as well be offering me an all-expenses-paid vacation to Paris. I'm suddenly struck by how ridiculous this situation is.

"How does this work, exactly?"

Alice moves her head in circles, as if preparing for a round of calisthenics. Her vertebrae pop, and I wince.

"Simple. Place your hands on top of mine. I'm going to hold your hands and feel your energy."

"My energy?"

"You know, your *Qi*, your life force. Every living creature is bursting with it. I feel that energy and interpret its meaning."

"Sure—" That was a real SAT answer to the question of how to be a psychic. "What should I do?"

"Relax and don't worry. I'm good at this."

Relax? I can't remember a time in the past ten years when I've *relaxed*. I've been shuffling from one activity to the next—from school to clubs to sports. And when I started teaching, I was putting in twelve-hour days.

I stare at Alice's open palms as if they are mousetraps, and purse my lips as I remember my latent fear of fortune-tellers. A part of me doesn't want to know my future, or at the very least, the future a psychic might tell me. Won't this knowledge somehow influence my life? Will I subconsciously follow a path ordained by someone else?

Finally, I place my hands on top of hers. She grasps them, and warmth and calm flow through me. The back of my neck tingles as all the hairs on my arms stand on end.

After a sharp inhale, Alice flutters her eyelids. She lets out a deep breath, and her eyes snap open. "Oh, crap," she mumbles. "You just lost your job."

I feel the blood drain from my face, and I am as exposed as a nudist in a hailstorm. I hadn't told her that. I hadn't told anyone, except Patrick, that my career as a teacher had hit a huge pothole. "How do you know that—" It's not a question.

Eyes quivering, Alice continues. "You were a teacher—a middle school teacher. But they let you go."

My stomach drops like a roller coaster dip. I got the pink slip in August from the charter school where I was teaching. It was my first job after graduating from college. They said it was budget cuts. "How?" I whisper to myself.

"So alone," Alice murmurs. "You've felt so alone. Your dad left when you were young—your mom, she's gone far away. It's been only you in this world."

I'll need a jack to lift up my jaw.

"No wonder you came here. You have nothing left to lose, and you're at the point where you need answers. But to what questions? What is it that haunts you? You're different, but there's something more."

My heart pounds against my chest, and my insides twist.

Go now, I think to myself. But it's like I'm watching a car crash in slow motion. I can't turn away.

"You've felt alone your entire life. Something has been missing. Something so essential and crucial that you can't think of going on without it. Your search has finally brought you here."

Goose bumps stud my skin as she creeps closer to a truth that has frightened me my entire life. My throat is as dry as a winter wind.

I fear that Alice is going to trespass into areas of my mind that I dare not tread, but she pulls away. Emerging from the hypnotic state, she lets go of my hands and blinks, then gives her whole body a little shake like a wet dog. Nostrils flaring, she inhales on her vape and grins. "Not bad, right? I told you I was good."

I'm cold all over as though I have snow stuffed under my skin. I'm too shocked to reply, so I nod my head. My leg muscles tense. I'm ready to jump up and run away, but I'm glued to the chair. Some part of me yearns to continue down this rabbit hole. Maybe I'll finally find the answers to the questions that terrify me. "Yeah." I exhale and feel some color return to my cheeks.

Noticing my reaction, Alice smirks and takes another puff from her vape. "I think we're on the right track," she says. "Now, let's check out your future." She grabs my hands again, and her eyes flutter as she enters a new trance.

Something is different this time. The air changes. Alice's face transforms to a blank slate. Her eyes roll up inside her head until all I see are two white globes. Is she having a seizure? But the rest of her body is as still as a marble bust.

Her hands tighten on mine, and nails dig into my skin. I've joined her in the trance. I can't cry out or even open my mouth.

When she speaks, her voice is empty and hollow. It's not her voice. It's as if someone else is speaking through her:

"The Mother, the life-giver
The Father, the life-taker
One touch to save the earth
Two touches to give the birth
Endless lives, undying soul
Pay the price, suffer the toll
In this lifetime, always asleep
In the next, many will weep
The power she holds will be the end
Her lost love will make all ascend
Black is the heart of evil feared
The Earth Goddess will be revered."

Alice snaps her eyes open, revealing round saucers of dilated terror. Her hands, still clutching mine, begin to shake.

"Holy shit," she says. "You're her."

That's when I realize it. The air hasn't changed—Alice has. Gone is the snarky Disney princess. Her face droops—some truth pressing down on it.

I pull away, uncertain about this changed person. I force a smile to mask my fear. "So," I begin, "what's my future?"

"It can't be," Alice says. She shakes her head like she's resisting an assault.

"What can't be?"

"I didn't actually think you would be her," she says, still not really talking to me. "I thought this was a test, but you have the mark."

"The mark?" Out of some base instinct, I touch the jagged crescent moon birthmark on the side of my face.

"This is fucked up," Alice whispers.

"What are you talking about?" I glance to the curtain—the exit. "You're scaring me."

"The v-v-vision," she stutters. "I've never had it before."

I throw a wary gaze at her and think about the poem she recited.

"What does the poem mean?"

She thrusts forward, and her eyes tighten to small aqua blue marbles. "It means only one thing." Alice's voice drops to a whisper, and a faint smile appears on her lips. "You're her. You're Gaia."

"Gaia," I repeat, feeling my brow furrow.

Suddenly, it all makes sense. The girl's face twists with fervor and flushes with excitement. I let a stranger, likely mentally ill, take me to a secluded place. This was a bad idea.

"I don't know what you're talking about." I break away and stand up.

"Wait, wait, wait," Alice pleads, desperation crawling in her voice, her eyes wild. "You're the Goddess. You don't understand now, but you will. I need to get the others."

"I don't want anything to do with the *others*," I say. "I'm leaving."

"Don't go!" Alice screams, hysterical. She clamps down on her mouth, surprised at her own outburst. "Please, wait. I can explain everything."

"No, I think it's best that I leave." I step toward the curtain.

Alice grabs my wrist so hard it hurts.

"Stop. Wait. Please," she begs. "We gotta conduct the ceremony."

I stare into her wild eyes and my voice hardens. "No, I *have* to go." I yank my hand away.

Alice falls to her knees, cups her hands, and begs. "Please stay. Please! Don't go."

"No way," I say with a caustic tone. I pull aside the curtain and storm out of the shop, past the artifacts of the occult and the confused tourists, out into the bustling streets. As soon as I'm outside, I'm running.

"Don't leave!" she screams, chasing after me. "You're her."

I push my way into the crowds to disappear. But even when I'm a block away, I hear Alice's scream, like a faint wind on the back of my ears.

"Gaia!"

CHAPTER THREE
Alone with Tear Drops

I stumble through the streets, needing to escape, needing to forget. *"Gaia,"* I whisper to myself. A shiver runs across my skin like fingernails along the side of my neck.

What was she talking about? Gaia. My thoughts race.

Gaia is someone from Greek mythology—something to do with Captain Planet. But beyond that, I would need Google.

A cold wind billows among the throngs, and they release a collective shivery moan. I cross my arms at my chest.

That's when I remember the man with the head of a bull. Was he real or my imagination? Somehow he's connected to Alice's psychic reading. Is he someone from my lost dreams? Is that even possible?

I shake the thought away. I've had enough. I want to go home to Cambridge and forget this horrible night. Coming here was a mistake.

Making my way back to the main square, I find the number of people has tripled. It's like a scene out of a Kubrick film—drinking, debauchery, and desire.

A tipsy SpongeBob SquarePants jostles me, spilling a beer down the front of my costume. He slurs an apology and stumbles away.

My world clouds in hues of red and black, and the evening's sharp air doesn't register on my burning skin. I march toward the train while wringing out my shirt. I toss my tiara on top of an overflowing trash can. The muscles in my back are so tight I have an urge to scream. It's as if a Band-Aid was ripped off, exposing a raw wound to the air. I don't even resist the dam of tears as they run down my cheeks.

I shoulder- and hip-check my way out of the masses and finally get onto an open side street. The air there is easier to breathe.

Up ahead, a pack of five young men approaches. They're costumed like early-nineties rappers decked out in baggy pants, oversized parkas, and obnoxious jewelry. The man in front, who can't be older than twenty-two, has a fake teardrop tattoo under one eye, a shaved head, and a meaty round face.

As I'm passing, Tear Drop leers at me, and makes a kissing sound.

"Hey, sweetie," he says. "Why you so sad? I'll make you feel special." His lecherous smile transforms my insides to lead. His friends titter like a clique of high school girls.

My skin feels all dirty. I know I should ignore him, but I'm sick and tired of people like him. I give him the finger.

"Screw you!" I shout.

My words stun Tear Drop for a few seconds, then his face breaks into an ugly grin that sends a ripple of fear through me. I hurry away not waiting for his response.

I get some distance from the city center and the crowds, and I stare at the sky. The moon is bright and full, but thick, fast-moving clouds invade from the ocean, obscuring the horizon.

Why is everything crumbling around me?

Ever since my mom left a year ago, I've felt lost. She re-married a professor at another school, who turned out to be a prepper and insisted they had to live in the middle of Wyoming to wait for the upcoming economic apocalypse. My mom went along less for the dire predictions and more for the chance to live and work on a farm.

I had lived with my mom my entire life, but she said that I needed to learn to live without her. I could always visit, but Wyoming might as well be Ulaanbaatar. For the past two years, I've been going through the motions—wake up, brush my teeth, go to work. When I was fired, it barely registered because I felt so empty inside.

I find my way to a warehouse area next to the water. I think this is the way back to the train, but I'm not sure. My mind is not in the right place. As I turn a corner, an eighteenth-century ship with three large masts looms at me from across the water. It bobs in the choppy waves next to an earthen jetty. A strong breeze makes the boat creak and my body shiver.

At the far end of the jetty, a small white lighthouse flashes its beacon across a bay of black water. Up in the sky, the moon stares down, casting an ethereal glow. It occurs to me that I'm alone, and I must have taken a wrong turn. I check my watch. If I hurry, I'll be able to make the next train back to Boston.

When I turn around, I stop in my tracks. A cold sweat breaks across my skin, and my heart begins to race.

Tear Drop and his gang are walking straight toward me. He catches me eyeing him and flashes his creepy grin.

I search for anyone to help, but I'm still alone. The gang is blocking my path. I'm not leaving the same way I came in. I spin around and walk across an empty parking lot to a self-storage building.

Glancing over my shoulder, I see the men increasing their pace. I walk faster as well, hoping there is someone inside the dimly lit building. I yank on the door, but it refuses to budge. I pound on the glass, but empty silence is the only response. My pulse continues to race like that of an animal that knows it has become prey.

I rush over to the water and climb up onto a grassy embankment. The men close in within ten feet of me.

"Leave me alone!" I shout. "I don't want any trouble."

Tear Drop doesn't break his stride. The group continues to advance.

On the distant jetty, I see people walking. I let out one high piercing scream, but none of them turn toward me. It's Halloween—half of Salem is screaming.

I keep backing up. Now the shadows of the storage building hide us. My thoughts spiral to dark places and nausea churns my stomach.

To one side, the frigid waters swirl. They convulse and heave, lapping over the earth and stopping within a few inches of my feet. I take a step to the rocky edge. A wave hits my feet and turns my toes to ice cubes.

Should I swim for it? I ask myself. I doubt I'll make it more than a few feet before I freeze and drown.

Finally, I gather all my courage and take a deep breath. I spin and stand my ground.

"Get out of here!"

Tear Drop steps up to me and shoves me hard. I crash to the ground and pain sears up my arms as they break my fall. My heart slams against my chest as I lie there in the dirt. I scramble to my feet, but I don't have anywhere to go.

I scan the men's faces and find Tear Drop smiling.

Suddenly, I'm falling. It's as if someone's dropped the floor beneath me, and I'm tumbling down. My mouth dries up like a desiccated rose, and I can't swallow. I want to scream. I want to fight. I want to shout. I want to tear my hair. But instead, I freeze. I realize I'm living a nightmare.

Tear Drop advances with outstretched hands, but before he has me in his grip, a woman's voice rings out like a klaxon.

"Stop!" Her low voice carries the authority of a police officer.

To my surprise, Tear Drop stops and turns around. The voice compels and constrains him like iron manacles. Staring beyond the gang, I brush the hair from my eyes and find two women watching us. One of them is Alice.

"I'll be with you in a minute, princess," says Tear Drop.

"Let her go now, asshole," Alice replies, her clenched knuckles white.

Beside her stands another woman, propped up on a gnarled wooden cane, with long gray hair tied into a ponytail that flows down her back. Her umber eyes pierce mine, and she wears a red hooded cape and a flowing skirt. The wrinkles on her face outnumber the rosary beads around her neck.

Tear Drop nods at the smallest gang member, who wears a black hat with a big gold dollar sign on it. "Get them out of here," he instructs him.

Dollar Sign nods and steps forward, but then pauses. "She's an old lady."

"I don't care if she's your goddamn grandmother," Tear Drop sneers. "Get them the fuck out of here."

The old woman stares at him.

"Why don't you get rid of us yourself?" she says to Tear Drop. "If you're such a big man."

"My pleasure." Tear Drop snorts. The next moment, he rushes toward the old woman with a fist pulled back, ready to strike.

As he gets within a few feet of her, she raises her hand. In the darkness, she holds something. The next moment, orange spray shoots out from her hand and hits Tear Drop in the face.

Tear Drop screams and paws at his eyes; he collapses to the ground and convulses. "It burns! It burns!"

The woman lifts her cane, and without a moment of hesitation, brings it crashing down on Tear Drop's skull. There is a loud crack like a watermelon being split in half. His whole body slumps.

The other gang members stare slack-jawed. One of them tenses, maybe thinking about attacking, but the old woman turns to him with her hand outstretched, holding the can of mace. "If you want to end up like your friend, now is the time to strike. But I suggest you bring him to a hospital immediately. Hopefully, he won't have too much more brain damage."

The remaining gang members exchange wary expressions. Then, on an unspoken cue, two of them crouch, lift Tear Drop, and carry him off. All the while, they shoot nervous grimaces back at the woman, whose eyes and hand never waver for a second.

"Yeah, that's right assholes!" yells Alice. "Keep walking."

When they leave, I let out a breath I hadn't realized I was holding. My pulse makes a clobbering clamor in my chest, and my eyes follow the gang as they disappear around the building.

"Mattie," Alice finally says. I twitch as if awoken from a nap. "Are you OK?"

My hands hurt a bit, and I'm shaken and every muscle in my body is tense. But otherwise fine. "I'm fine. Thanks for helping me."

"It's what we're here for," Alice says. There's a long pause before she adds, "We've been searching for you."

I remember the psychic reading, and a pearl of discontent swells in my stomach. "Listen, I appreciate your help. But please leave me alone. I want to go home."

"I'm sorry I scared you earlier. I didn't mean to," Alice says and then glances at the other woman whose face is like a bullfrog—bulbous and serious. The older woman stares at me with a steely gaze.

"Whatever," I say. "It's in the past."

Alice presses her hands together. "Please, Mattie. Try to understand. I never thought I'd actually find you. To meet you before was a shock."

"A shock?" I let out an incredulous laugh. "Who are you kidding? I'm normal. There's nothing strange about me," I say.

"And you're crazy if you think there is."

Alice takes another step forward. She is close enough to touch me if she wants to.

"There are things we need to tell you."

"Enough!" I say, startled by my own voice. "I should never have trusted you." My hands clench into fists, and my tight shoulders square like a bull ready to charge. "Leave me alone." I'm going home, and I'll be damned if I am going to spend another second with these women for the rest of my life.

As I walk past them, the old woman speaks. "I know you're scared and hurt."

"Yeah, I got assaulted by Vanilla Ice. I'm going to call the cops."

"I'm not talking about those cretins. I mean your real pain."

My eyes waver, and I stop. "What are you talking about?"

"I can feel your loneliness." The woman scrunches her nose. "It radiates off you. Whatever has happened to you, I'm sorry." With slow steps, she approaches me and then, to my surprise, she hugs me.

Her warm body pulls me into a loving embrace. I know I won't be able to muster the anger to challenge her. She might be small, but weakness is not one of her attributes. My hard shell cracks.

After everything that has happened today, all I want is to be held by someone. I break down and sob into the woman's shoulder. I don't know how much time passes. At some point, the woman wraps a wool shawl over my shoulders.

"I'm sorry," I say, sniffling. I stare up at the bleary stars twinkling behind the clouds. "I'm not in a good place right now."

The old woman caresses my arm. "No, Mattie. You're exactly where you should be."

I shake my head. "I don't understand."

She looks up to the huge round moon, which breaks through the clouds and illuminates the bay in iridescent silver.

"You will."

"What are you talking about?"

Her smile is one of the grandmothers I never knew. "I know it's difficult, but I need you to trust us."

"Why should I?"

"You're Gaia," Alice interrupts.

The older woman shoots her a quick, reprimanding glance that silences her.

But it's too late. The damage has been done, and I've already regained my skepticism.

"That again." I pull away from the older woman. "I don't even know what that means."

"Yet." She gives me a stern look. "You will."

"Fine. Great for me. But guess what? I don't want to know."

The older woman continues as if I had not said a thing. "It's scary. But it's always important to know the truth about your-self."

"What truth?" I counter.

Her grin deflects my skepticism. "I know you. I know that you're different."

"Fine, what do you know?" I challenge.

There is a long pause in which she looks as though she's siz-ing me up for a boxing match. "You dream, yet you don't dream."

I jerk to attention as fast as if someone slammed their heel onto my toe. "How do you know about my dreams?"

"Don't you find it strange," she asks, "that every night you go to places you know you've been? You meet people who are fa-miliar. You experience things that happened in a past you can't recall. But when you awake, you can't remember any of the de-tails. You're left with only a faint sense that something amazing has passed."

The chill returns to my body. What the woman has described is how I have felt every morning of my entire life. "How do you know?" I ask in a wavering whisper.

"I know because I know the truth about you."

"And what's that truth?" I swallow hard. My eyes are focused and unblinking.

"Come with me." The woman turns and gestures for me to follow. "I will show you."

Alice and the older woman walk back toward town.

I remain fixed in place with my hands clenched into fists. Somehow, they got me hook, line, and sinker. "How can I trust you?" I ask. "I don't even know your name."

The older woman spins around and smiles. "My name is Gertrude." She bows, and says, "Look at us, Mattie. I'm dressed like a witch, and Alice looks like a cartoon character. You can't seriously be frightened of us?" Gertrude's smile masks a secret. "Besides, we're not here to harm you." She walks away from me again. "Just the opposite. We've been put here for one reason."

"What's that?" I shout to her back.

I catch her reply on a warm burst of wind that hits my face. "For you."

CHAPTER FOUR
Witch House

I race after the two women, mind still spinning. There is so much they haven't told me. "How do you know about my dreams?" I ask after catching up with them.

Gertrude's head swivels, and I catch a glimmer of concern in her expression. "Not here," she says, her eyes narrowing. "We'll talk somewhere else."

"Where?"

"Somewhere safe."

"Safe?" A shiver ripples through me, and I know it's not from the brisk air. The throbbing pain in my arms is an all-too-vivid reminder of Tear Drop and his gang, but I don't think Gertrude is worried about them. I pull her shawl tighter around my shoulders. "Are we in some type of danger?"

Gertrude folds a grin like an origami crane. "Of course not. I didn't mean it that way. Salem is a pleasant town during the day, but this time of year, well, as you have seen, the trouble-makers come out." There is a frenetic tension in the way both women scan the streets.

What are they searching for?

Gertrude grasps my hand, squeezes it, and pulls me along.

All I can think about are my dreams, and the fact that I have a disease and only I know it.

Every night of my entire life, I enter a deep sleep and have vivid dreams. But, when I wake up, I can't remember any of them. Sometimes after waking, a dream is so close, so tantalizing. It's on the tip of my tongue. Yet, when I am about to remember it, the details wither away like dying flowers. Vestiges of the dreams do remain like fossils buried in the ground. Certain words and pictures resonate with me. It's kind of like déjà vu. I imagine a wall in my mind that blocks dreams from my conscious thoughts.

Dreams are said to be the relief valve for the subconscious. When deprived of dreams, people go insane within a matter of days.

Almost no one believed me. From an early age, I learned it was better to hide this fact rather than have schoolchildren think I was odd, or strange, or call me a weirdo. The few friends I had would dismiss my condition as insignificant because even when someone says they can't remember their dreams, in truth, how could that be?

My mom was the only one who believed me, and she brought me to a string of psychiatrists, psychologists, and doctors to see what was wrong. She wanted to help me. They never found anything. Even the professionals thought I was making it up.

In my heart, I know something is wrong. My lost dreams have haunted my existence. I know they contain secrets, and if I could only remember them for *one* night, maybe I will feel like everyone else. Maybe I'd be normal and not feel so alone anymore.

We continue downtown through the partygoers, all the while remaining silent. Halloween banners and cardboard cutouts of pumpkins flutter in the breeze. Arriving at a residential area, Gertrude leads me to a 17th-century house—dark and deserted.

It has a steep-pitched roof and half-dozen gables. A sign in front of the house reads *The Witch House*.

Not a good sign.

I rip my arm free from Gertrude's grasp.

Alice runs into me. "What's wrong?" she asks. Her voice is tense. She looks back and forth with anxious energy, peering into the darkness.

"What's wrong?" I repeat in disbelief. "I was attacked, and now a woman dressed like a witch is escorting me to god-knows-where. Nothing's wrong. Yeah, everything is fine and dandy." This has gotten too weird.

"She ain't a witch," Alice says.

"I don't care," I snap back. "Listen, I'm not going in there until you tell me about my dreams, and if you don't, then I'm going home."

Alice shoots an anxious look to Gertrude, who replies with a nod. The old woman's eyes pierce mine with unwavering intensity. She stands silent for a moment.

"Have you ever considered the possibility that your visions aren't actually dreams?" she asks.

"What are you talking about?"

Gertrude's hand tightens on her walking stick and her features sharpen. "I have a question for you." She tilts her head and asks, "Do you believe in an afterlife?"

"Ugh," I groan. "Are you guys religious or something?"

Gertrude's eyes bulge wide, and her nostrils flare. "We're nothing of the sort!" The woman exclaims, pounding her walking stick into the ground. "Questions about the afterlife are not a matter of religion. Everyone dies, and everyone must ask, 'What will happen next?'"

I fall quiet. "I asked you a question, young one." She prods her cane at me.

I stare down at my purple Converse, avoiding her eyes.

"I don't know," I mumble.

"You don't know, or you've never asked before?" Gertrude probes like a Spanish inquisitor.

I exhale and turn away. "Yeah, sure," I answer. "I believe in an afterlife."

"Well, what happens in your afterlife?"

"It's really not one of my more pressing life concerns," I say, rolling my eyes.

Gertrude snorts. "The young always have more pressing concerns," she replies with a derisive sneer. "At my age, death is a daily reminder from every ache to every rattling cough. Death is as natural as birth. It is what happens after death that preoccupies my waking life."

"OK, fine," I throw my hands into the air. "What happens in the afterlife?"

Gertrude reveals a taunting smile. "You're a smart young woman, so I assume you don't believe in pearly white cloud kingdoms and a bearded old man."

My response is a shrug.

"You've read about reincarnation?"

"Yeah, sure. You're born, you die, and you come back to life as a squirrel or a rock."

The old woman winces as if I poked her in the side. "Well, yes and no. I believe that when you die you come back to life as a new person. This means that Alice and I and everyone else in the world have lived hundreds, thousands, maybe even millions of past lives."

"So, you think I've lived hundreds of lives?"

"Correct." The old woman brightens at my amazing logic abilities.

"What does this have to do with my dreams?"

Gertrude's smile wanes, and she leans toward me. "You're different than Alice and I. Because you can remember all your past lives."

A shiver of nervous fear slides across my skin. I may have underestimated the depth of crazy that's standing in front of me. "That's ridiculous. I can't remember any past life."

"True," she says. "You can't now. But what do you think are your dreams? Those aren't dreams. They are memories from past lives."

"*Right*," I say, recoiling from them. "This was a mistake." I spin on my heels ready to run, but Gertrude's grasp holds me in place.

"It sounds strange," the old woman acknowledges. "But ask yourself, isn't it stranger that you can't remember any of your dreams? Isn't that impossible?"

My muscles tense, ready to rip myself free and run, but Gertrude is right. For my entire life, I've felt that there was something wrong with me. Now, these women are giving me an explanation—albeit a bat shit crazy one.

Gertrude's grip on my arm loosens. "We want to help you remember your past lives."

"How?"

"We know how to break down the wall that is blocking your memories."

The image has powerful resonance for me. It's the same one I used to describe my disease.

"You can do that?"

"Only if you trust us," Gertrude replies, letting go of my arm.

"I don't know." Now that I'm free, I'm trapped in place.

A masterful saleswoman, Gertrude takes a step back and makes a gesture with her hands. "If you want to go, then go. But know that you'll live the rest of your life being ignorant of your true self."

I bite my lower lip and hope I'm not making a huge mistake. "I'll come with you, but if this gets too weird, I'm out of here."

Gertrude's grandmotherly smile re-emerges. "Of course, dear. Of course. Come. Come. Let's meet the others." She approaches the door of the Witch House, raises her twisted cane, and knocks on a door three times. The door opens a second later, and light blinds me.

Once I recover my sight, I find a rustic room painted the color of ash. Tourist pamphlets, souvenirs, and advertisements hang from a display. The knot-studded hardwood floor creaks under my footsteps.

A plump, middle-aged woman with chipmunk cheeks wearing an elven green cloak greets us with a palpable nervousness. "We've been waiting for you, High Priestess."

My eyebrows jump. "High priestess," I mouth without saying the words, casting a skeptical glance toward Gertrude.

The old woman's nostrils flare and her eyes bear into the woman. "No need for the titles, Olivia," she scolds. "Is everyone prepared?"

The anxious woman gives a sharp tug to her long ponytail. "Indeed, High Prie—I mean, Gertrude." She points to an adjoining room. "The portal is prepared, and the priestesses are gathered." She hesitates; her eyes drop down to her yellow felt slippers with imprinted kittens. "Except one. We're still waiting for Tatiana."

"Where is that blasted woman?" she asks, her voice slicing. "We can't conduct the Ascension without her."

Now my head spins. Priestesses? Portals? Ascension? Who are these people?

"I know, High Priestess," Olivia slips, her eyes seeking approval. "I've sent a message. She should be here soon."

Gertrude's face softens to a frown. "We can't delay the ceremony. The moon is at the right position. We have only a few hours, and if we miss this window, we will have to wait a whole month."

That's when I notice Olivia staring at me as if I'm Lady Gaga. "Is this—is this—is this really her?" Olivia stammers, lower lip trembling, and her index finger quakes at me.

"Of course this is her," Gertrude replies. "Pull yourself together, Olivia. This is what you've been trained for."

Olivia presents me with a deep bow. She grasps my hand and kisses it. "It's my greatest joy to meet you, blessed goddess—"

With her cane, Gertrude raps Olivia on the head with a slight tap. "Enough, you're scaring the poor girl."

My mouth hangs open. The old woman exhales, impatience growing on her face.

"Olivia, go with Alice to the portal and notify the other priestesses that we will begin soon."

Alice escorts the awestruck woman into the next room.

I eye the other room with wariness—the one with the portal. "I'm not going in there until you tell me what's going to happen. What's an Ascension?"

Gertrude's eyes level toward mine. "The Ascension ceremony will help you remember your past lives. I know you don't fully understand, but you will. Everything will become clear. We are here to help you realize your true self."

The part of me that says don't take candy from strangers is telling me to run. I stand silent and still.

"OK, but if this gets sexual, then I'm out of here."

Gertrude erupts with a deep belly laugh and pats me on the shoulder. "No need to worry. We only perform conception ceremonies in the springtime." The old woman takes my hand and guides me, dazed, into the next room.

In the adjoining room, dark, heavy curtains black out the windows. Hundreds of red candles light up the room, and flickering shadows dance upon the walls. The earthy smell of incense hits my nose. Hardwood furniture lines the outer walls leaving an open space in the middle of the room where a pentagram has been drawn on the floor in white chalk. Ten women, most middle-aged or older, stand dressed in brown, gold, and green cloaks. All have free flowing hair and awed faces. As soon as I enter, they fall silent and stare at me.

I pat down my disarrayed hair, feeling self-conscious. I've

never liked being the center of attention.

I look anywhere but their faces, and my eyes land on the only guy in the room. He's tall and kind of cute. He reminds me of one of those smooth-faced, scrawny Youtube personas, who make snarky comments while playing video games. He stands awkwardly against the back wall, his longish brown copper hair hanging over his eyes and skinny arms crossed across his Adventure Time t-shirt. Inscribed on his right arm, I see an elaborate tattoo of a whale.

A door slams and my attention is pulled to the other side of the room as a woman, a little older than myself, saunters in. She wears a bright crimson cloak like Red Riding Hood. Her black hair has a streak of silver running through it. She wears a black leather corset, which is rather ridiculous.

Gertrude gives the woman a disapproving stare. "You're late, Tatiana."

"My apologies, High Priestess." The woman's fiery eyes flare up.

"Assume your role. We will begin now."

The clicking of her red high-heel pumps echoes throughout the room as she walks through the pentagram. I swear that she shoots me a laughing look.

"Mattie, let me introduce you to your priestesses," Gertrude begins. "These women have pledged themselves to serve and protect you at all costs. For thousands of years, the traditions we know have been passed down from one generation to the next. Our whole lives have been devoted to one task: your Ascension."

I fidget at the hem of my blouse and stare at the floor.

"But it is ultimately your choice whether or not you undergo the Ascension. We cannot force you. It needs to be your decision. This choice holds both good and bad. Having knowledge and awareness of your past lives can be a heavy burden to bear. Many of your past lives were nightmares ending with gruesome deaths. But others were filled with love, wisdom, compassion. You will become aware of them all.

"The world needs you now. It needs you more than at any point in history. You are incredibly special, but you will only realize this after you Ascend. Dark days are coming and only you, Mattie, only you, Gaia, will be able to lead us down the path that will bring light to this darkness."

"Gaia," I whisper as a shiver courses through me.

"I have said my part and done my duty. What do you say, Mattie? Do you trust us? Do you trust yourself? Will you take part in the ceremony? Will you Ascend?"

I stare in disbelief at this strange woman whom I had met only an hour ago. No one—except my mom or my dear friend Patrick—has shown me such respect and admiration. The fact remains: these women were kind to me when I needed it the most. The least I can do is repay their kindness by taking part in their silly ceremony.

One part of me knows the truth. I'm not special. I'm nothing more than a single, unemployed middle school teacher. But a voice deep inside of me pleads for me to push on. I need to know what is at the end of this tunnel.

I finally break the long silence.

"OK," I reply. "Yes."

Several women sigh as the room fills with a sense of relief. Joyful smiles burst upon their faces.

"Thank you, Goddess," Gertrude whispers. Her eyes are filled with thanks and love.

CHAPTER FIVE
Ascension

Gertrude raises her cane and pounds it on the worn floorboards. "Let the ceremony begin," she intones.

Silence fills the room and my pulse hammers. A chill trickles down my back navigating the rivulets of cold sweat on my skin. What the hell did I sign myself up for?

Gertrude takes my hand and escorts me to the center of the pentagram. "Stand here, and we will do the rest," she says. She turns halfway but pauses. She reaches over and caresses my cheek as a mother would her daughter. Her mouth parts to tell me something—maybe a warning, but she hesitates and backs away.

The women form a circle, and their stares trap me in place. The skinny man with the brown hair melts into the shadows of the room, only the whites of his eyes visible in the flickering candlelight.

Olivia, head bowed and holding a silver goblet, approaches Gertrude. The cup, filled to the brim with a dark liquid, is large enough to hold a whole bottle of wine. The old woman grasps the vessel and takes a gulp. She wipes her mouth with a white handkerchief and passes it to the next women. The goblet snakes around the circle of women. After all have taken a sip, Gertrude offers the goblet to me.

I pull back, hands upraised and mouth closed. "I think I'll pass."

The old woman's smile doesn't break, and she presses harder. "It's only a little grape juice." She raises the goblet toward me. "We all had a sip, and you complete the chain."

I take the shimmering goblet. On the cup's surface, the sun is etched onto one side while the moon is on the other. The juice smells like cardamom, burnt cinnamon, and fresh honey.

Gertrude waits and nods, expecting the inevitable. I take a small sip. Then, I grimace, gag, and come close to spitting it up. The juice tastes like they dumped in a carton of Pixy Stix. Olivia grabs the cup before I dump it onto the floor.

Once I recover, the women undo the metal clasps at their necks, letting their cloaks fall to the ground in unison. Underneath, they wear dark corsets and billowy white skirts.

They hold hands and form an unbroken ring around me. It's silent except for the wind gusting against the house. An eerie energy fills the room as if we're being observed by the ghosts of restless souls.

Stifling a yelp, I jolt as Gertrude breaks the silence with a low-pitched hum. I swear that I've heard the tune before, but I can't recall from where. After a minute, Alice hums as well, adding resonance and depth to the melody. One by one the other women join, and the sound grows louder and higher in pitch. The song is so familiar. At some point, Gertrude's hum transforms into the lyrics of a folk song. Her voice is beautiful—deep and soulful. I don't recognize the foreign words, but I sense sadness and wistfulness.

On an unspoken cue, the other women sing as well. Together, their voices are like a choir of angels, harmonies rising in pitch and volume. All the while, their wide-eyed stares drive deep into me.

I know this song.

The melody changes. As they take up the same sustained note, the room vibrates with power. My breath catches and heart matches the beat as the song invades my body.

The rough qualities of their voices strip away. What emerges is a flawless sound. It's at a pitch outside the range of human hearing, but it's there, and it's beautiful.

The note continues for minutes, and the hypnotic sound mesmerizes me. My feet may as well be bolted to the floor. The neurons in my mind explode like an infinite chain of firecrackers.

My hands and feet tingle with the same feeling of the aftermath of an intense massage.

The sensation spreads up my arms. It invades my chest, gushes into my stomach, fills my lungs, surrounds my heart, and floods between my legs. Finally, it enters my mind, and everything melts to liquid bliss as if I'm floating in a vat of gelatin. Gone is my fear—no more worry or anxiety. I connect to a level of oneness with the universe that I've never felt before. Far away as a whisper, I still hear the priestesses, but a dense haze obscures my vision. The faces of the priestess are phantom images; one moment there and another moment gone.

I force my eyes wide, challenging myself to gaze through the fog. When my vision focuses, a sudden spike of surprise shoots through me.

Like shaky images on a slow moving film reel, the faces of the women change. One moment, Alice has black hair and flushed skin. But if I glance out the corner of my eye, she transforms. Her skin smooths out to polished stone. The wig disappears as her burgundy hair streams down, and her profile converts to a flawless, beautiful bust. All the women metamorphose into gorgeous, youthful versions of themselves. They radiate a golden aura which pulses like a beating heart. Gertrude transforms as well—her back straightens, her wrinkles iron away, her gray hair darkens to a rich earthy brown.

The note changes again; it rises like a mirage. The sound vibrates through my entire body, and it lifts me off my feet. Am I hovering? How is this possible?

Then things get really weird. The women disappear in the fog, and a flame appears like a lit match. I focus on the light, and colors, images, and movement whirl together. I don't know how long I stare into the flame before I'm aware of the meaning of the images. All sense of time has been lost. I'm existing in a different realm of consciousness, and my mind deciphers pieces of the chaotic jumble. The colors and images form into objects, things, and people. It's a movie in my head, and I'm watching snippets of scenes.

A woman appears with a sharp angular face, a fit frame, and black hair. She wears khaki shorts and a tight olive green shirt. The woman squats among dark-skinned men in a circle, surrounded by jungle. She speaks Swahili, and to my surprise, I understand what she's saying. But more than this, I know things about her. I know her thoughts, emotions, and even her deepest secrets. How do I know her?

Before I can find the answer, the flame splits in two.

In the second flame is a small bald man—skin tinted the color of dark honey. His eyes sparkle with love and empathy. He's lean and skinny as a flower stem, and he wears a white robe wrapped around slender shoulders. Like the African woman, I know things about him. I know his passions and everything he sought, desired and fought for in his life.

Who are these people? Two flames split into four. The images fly by faster. More people, more lives. All somewhat familiar, yet I'm sure I've never met any of them. They come from every culture and country in the world; they come from different eras and times in history.

The flames light the horizon and extend far into the distance

—destroying the fog. Hundreds, thousands, maybe millions of flames as far as I can see. I can't keep track of all the people and their stories as they bombard my senses like a meteor shower, drowning me.

One of the flames blazes up greater than the others.

In the fire, I discover a night blacker than ebony. Overhead the stars spread out like a billion white Christmas lights.

The next moment, I'm there, in the flame experiencing the moment. I'm naked and exposed to the chill of the air, wild hair dangling down my back. It's my body, yet it is also not. I stand in the center of a grassy field staring into the infinity of space. From the sky, among the stars, an inferno grows in size. It's a speeding comet heading straight toward me. It devours the darkness and consumes all. A fiery ball of power heading straight at me. I don't turn or run. I reach toward the light.

Closer.

Heat radiates from it. I desire this sphere like I yearn for a lover; it will burn away the bad in me. The purifying light will set me free.

Closer.

I stretch out my fingers. All I view is the light, and I must touch it. It is my destiny and fate. Once I touch the light, all will become one, all will be right. Almost there. Another second more.

Closer.

Right when my fingertips are about to brush the fiery light, right when I am about to connect and be one with it, an explosion knocks me back.

The light retreats like a fleeing army. The warmth and glow disappear, leaving an icy chill that freezes my skin. I hurtle backward. Tumbling away from all the familiar images and people. They retreat as well—hiding and running away from whence they came.

A moment later, I am back in the Witch House. I'm dizzy and

disoriented. The priestesses still encircle me, but the chanting has changed. It is no longer many voices combined as one. The sound is neither beautiful nor angelic; it is one voice. One person. One woman who is screaming. A horrible, frightening, bloodcurdling scream.

The room is colder than the morgue, and fear rides through my legs. I'm still in the middle of the pentagram, not having moved an inch.

The priestesses stare at someone behind me, and white terror floods their eyes.

Groggy and confused, I turn to find the source of the screams. It is Alice. She's no longer a flawless priestess; instead, she's Jasmine again. In her arms, she cradles the body of Gertrude. Blood pours from a huge open wound on her chest, creating a pool around them. The old woman's lifeless eyes are forever locked on mine. A second later, another explosion booms. Glass breaks.

Alice's head explodes like a red supernova.

CHAPTER SIX
Slaughterhouse

This can't be real. It's a nightmare. It has to be. But my eyes lurch down to my shoes, and fresh horror makes my stomach sick. Small pieces of gray and red matter stain my Converse. My gaze shoots up; blood oozes from the death wound on Alice's cracked head.

This is no dream.

The priestesses scatter like animals from a barn fire. They run for the exits and dive for cover behind furniture. The windows shatter inwards, and glass shards shower the room. The black curtains dance and shred into pieces, while red beams of death streak through the room. A beam lands on a woman cowering in the corner. In an instant, she's knocked back as if punched. Her mouth opens in pain as a red star blossoms on her bosom. She collapses forward, white hands clenched tight into small balls.

I cover my mouth to suppress a scream swelling up inside me. I'm frozen with shock, unable to do anything to stop the mayhem unfolding. The women topple to the ground and crash into the walls—struck down by the red beams. Their corpses create a crossword puzzle of death on the room's floor. My mind spins.

In just seconds, I'm the only one left alive. Fear crawls up my spine and courses through my veins. I know I have to move, but I can't. Raw dread petrifies me in place.

A red pinprick of light appears on the other side of the room. The beam creeps over the worn floorboards, searching for life to destroy. Six feet away from me, it traces the pale profile of one of the murdered priestesses. Three feet away, the beam disappears into a pool of dark liquid. It re-emerges on my right foot. The beam climbs up my leg, pauses for a second over my stomach, continues its march across my chest, and finally flashes across my eye. I take my last breath. Gone is the brilliant light, the strange yet familiar people, and the faraway lives. I will never behold them again. I want my last thoughts to be something happy, but fear strangles and blocks every thought.

There is a cry. A window shatters, cutting through the black curtain. A force crashes into me, hurling me to the ground. A puff of air passes where my head was a quarter-second ago, and a chunk of wood explodes on the opposite side of the room. I slam into the floor, and pain streaks through my chest. A heavy mass squishes me down like roadkill; the pain reawakens my other senses. The smells of blood, gastric acid, and death flood my nostrils. I dry-heave, and it takes all my effort not to empty my stomach. The volume shoots from zero to earsplitting.

"Mattie!" someone screams.

I look around and find the guy with the whale tattoo flattening me. His face is numb and blank—except for his eyes, which are like storms of distraught. He rolls off of me, and I take a deep breath.

A second later, I translate the bursts of noise from his mouth into words. "We got to get out of here!"

"W-w-what's going on?" I stutter, head spinning.

He glances toward the broken windows. We're behind a heavy oak table, flipped on its side. "Stay close and follow me.

Do you understand?"

I nod, but hell if I understand.

The table convulses as if someone is punching the other side. Sharp impacts push the table toward us. It occurs to me at that moment: those are bullets. My adrenaline launches through the roof, and my heart slams so fast I fear it's going to pop out of my chest.

The guy crouches like a sprinter on a starting mark.

When the gunshots stop, he charges a side door with his head down and shoulders rolled.

But instead of crashing through the door, he slams into it and comes to a full stop. Stunned, he staggers back and shakes his head. Regaining some balance, he turns the doorknob and opens the door. The cold night air rushes into the steamy, hot room. The guy disappears into the night, leaving me alone with the dead. I wrap my arms around myself and curl up into a ball. I want this to be a terrible dream; I want my life back.

"We're clear. This way!" he shouts from the doorway.

But I can't move. My legs refuse to operate. The thought of the red beams and the sight of the dead women lining the walls chain me in place.

The guy runs back and slides for cover behind the table. He grabs my arm and yanks me toward the exit, and my feet follow as if they were remote-controlled. We escape from the house into the night. My skin bristles with goose bumps, while my breath makes clouds of vapor. He drags me along. No sooner are we outside than shouts break the evening silence. An explosion of gunfire shatters whatever calm remains. Bullets sing after us, slamming into neighboring houses, and kicking up clumps of dirt inches from my feet. The guy jerks me down a cobblestone path, his hand maintaining a handcuff grip. The gunfire continues as we arrive at an open garden with empty rose trellises and barren beds of flowers standing forlornly in the foggy evening. We race through the garden and arrive at a broad street with old colonial houses lining its sides. Fluorescent lamps cast the street in a spectral blue glow.

He leads me to a rusted Pontiac Caprice from the eighties with missing hub caps and a bent antenna. He releases his tight grip and throws open the driver side door, then makes a jagged cry. "Get in!"

As I run around to the passenger side door, I hear the screech of tires. I swing my head around. A black SUV—with high beams blazing—barrels down the road toward us.

The guy turns the ignition, and the Pontiac's engine growls. Gunshots explode from the SUV when I open up the passenger side door. The bullets ricochet around my feet, kicking up pieces of brick and asphalt. Screaming, I dive head first into the Pontiac. Before I have time to close the door, he guns the car in reverse. We smash into a Prius behind us, and its bumper collapses with a sickening crunch. He swings the steering wheel and throws the car into drive. The Pontiac screeches as it makes a U-turn. The passenger door slams shut, coming close to taking off two of my fingers.

Gunshots blast from the SUV, and the back window of the Pontiac shatters.

The man's face is icy and calm despite the hellfire erupting behind us. He slams down on the gas pedal, and we shoot forward. My eyes are as wide as the moon.

I risk a glance behind us. The SUV is twenty feet away and closing fast. A man leans out the passenger window and aims an automatic weapon. "They're going to shoot—"

The driver swings the steering wheel and makes a hard right turn.

I'm thrown against the guy as the entire car leans to the left. I think for sure that we will flip, but the screeching tires find traction.

Afterward, I fasten my seat belt.

Out the side mirror, the SUV makes the tight turn, and its engine roars. A second later, it slams into the back of our car. The sound of crunching metal jangles my frayed nerves. The Pontiac races down a narrow street, gaining a few precious feet. We turn onto a flat stretch of road. Old brick buildings, closed store-fronts, and leafless trees whip by. We soar through a red light without even a tap on the brakes. Somewhere in the distance, police sirens sing. The SUV is right behind us. The occasional burst of automatic fire stitches the back of our car.

"Why are they shooting at us?"

The man ignores me and says, "Hold on. I'm going to try something."

"What?" I reply, breath seizing.

He turns the car down what I'm quite sure is a pedestrian-on-ly walkway. The car barely fits between the metal guardrails and bounces hard down the cobblestone street.

"Are you crazy?" I scream.

The SUV follows us.

"Wait for it," says the guy to himself. "Almost there." He takes a breath and glances out the rear view mirror.

"Watch out!" I yell.

He turns the wheel at the last second to avoid crashing into a fire hydrant. "Shit," he says.

The gunfire blasts in my ears. My eyes jump from the road to the side view mirror. After each shot, I see the gunmen realign his aim. I scrunch down farther into the seat.

"Now!" The guy says. He makes a tight turn down an alley-way. The car glides on only two wheels. We hang in the air for what feels like an eternity before slamming back to earth.

The SUV tries to make the same turn. It leans precariously to one side. But then—epic fail. The vehicle careens to the left, somersaults, and smashes into an oak tree. Airbags deploy, and steam arises from the wrecked SUV.

The man exhales. "I think we're going to be OK," he says, his voice like a robot, lacking feeling. He loosens my white clenched-knuckles from his arm.

"Where did you learn to drive like that?" I ask, my voice wavering.

"Massachusetts, obviously," he replies. The road bends around a curve, and the smoking SUV disappears from sight.

We exit the alleyway and turn onto the main road.

My mind swirls from relief to excitement before settling back to fear. I risk a glance at the skinny, good-looking man that I initially pegged as a competitive gamer. Who the hell is this guy?

The Pontiac sails through a packed residential neighborhood. On our right, we pass the dark bay and the old three-masted ship. My brow furrows. It was near here that the madness of the evening began. Where Tear Drop attacked and Gertrude convinced me to follow her.

My thoughts are cut short by a shadow leaping from a side street. The shadow materializes into another black SUV gunning straight toward the left side of our car. The next moment, the SUV t-bones us.

I'm thrown against the window as the Pontiac spins across the street like a Matchbox car. My head slams into the back of the seat, and stars shoot across my eyes. We careen out of control until the car comes to a stop on the sidewalk. Hot oil, burning plastic, and exhaust sting my nostrils. I touch the back of my head and cringe.

My driver is unconscious—his head lolls to the side, eyes closed, and a trickle of blood runs out of his nose.

Out of the cracked front windshield, the black and ruined SUV smokes. The front half is collapsed and the headlights are shattered.

But the driver-side door swings open. A man emerges, and he runs his hand through jet black hair gelled into a tight widow's peak. His trimmed goatee and mustache do not hide his sallow hungry cheeks and sharp teeth. He glides out of his wrecked vehicle as if he didn't T-bone us. He dusts off his black business suit with one hand while his other hand carries an automatic rifle.

Prickles of fear crawl up my skin, and my arm hair stands on end like needles. The fear is not from the gun; it's the man's head. He's morphed into a demon: a bull with blood-stained white horns, giant flaring nostrils, and a black foaming snout. A murderous grin emerges on the bull's face.

I scramble for the door handle, but it refuses to twist. The crash must have broken the door. I roll down my window halfway, and my fingers fumble at my seat belt.

The bull man walks with a casual air up to the front of the Pontiac. He stops and stares at me. The malice in his beaming cobalt eyes freezes me to the core. He raises the gun to his shoulder; the barrel aims right at me.

This is it. I throw up my arms in a desperate attempt to stave off my own destruction. The rifle fires, but we shoot backward down a side street. Bullets smash into the empty pavement where the Pontiac had been.

My driver leans over the steering wheel, and pain creases his face. His heavy, rattling breaths send worry through me. "Are you OK?" I ask.

The man bristles, shakes his head and keeps his eyes focused on the road. "It's nothing. Just hang on."

He whips the Pontiac around in a half circle and aims it down a side street. Our car makes the sound of a dying animal but still accelerates forward. Twenty seconds later, the broken SUV emerges behind us.

The houses shrink, and the ocean peeks through on the right. We pass a sign that reads: "Winter Island."

We race down a thin road and across an isthmus. Passing an empty campground, we enter a large vacant parking lot. Boats sit on stilts covered in white tarps and an airplane hangar looms off to the far side. Out on the water, a handful of boats bob in a heavy fog.

The man turns the wheel hard and grunts from the effort. We swing a one-eighty and now face the way we entered.

A cold chill passes down my back, and my hands clamp down on the safety handle. "We're trapped. Aren't we?"

The guy doesn't reply. He watches the parking lot entrance, mouth tightening to a thin red line.

The SUV emerges from the entrance with a growling engine and destroyed front-end. The Pontiac and the SUV face-off. The man revs the Pontiac's engine, and it clamors with a broken rattle. The SUV responds by revving its engine.

I shoot a worried look toward him. "You can't possibly be thinking what I think you're thinking?"

The man keeps his eyes fixed on the SUV ahead and says, "Trust me."

I don't have a chance to respond. The SUV's wheels squeal, and it peels out straight toward us. The man jams down on the Pontiac's accelerator aiming for the SUV.

We drive right to each other. At fifty feet, I scream.

At thirty feet, I see the hell-bent insanity in the SUV driver's eyes.

At twenty feet, I know I'm going to die.

The Pontiac swerves to the left ten feet away from crashing into the SUV.

We sail down a long wooden dock while the thudding of the uneven boards rattles through me. My eyes go wide when I realize there is only open water awaiting us. A second later, we crash through a wooden guardrail, and the Pontiac sails through the air. I rise in my seat, and then we splash into the water.

I fly forward, but the seat belt yanks me backward.

We float for a few brief moments before the water gushes in through the open windows. The rushing torrent of water quickly fills the inside of the car, and the coldness shocks my system, turning my body into a near-cadaver.

The air in the car disappears, and right as we are about to go under, I take a deep breath.

Under the murky water, I struggle with my seat belt. I fight with the metal contraption for several precious seconds, before remembering that it's stuck. All the while, the Pontiac sinks deeper.

The biting temperature wants me to stop trying; it wants me to sink to an icy tomb, but with a twist of my hips and a back bend, I get enough slack and free myself. I scramble out the half-open window, but my hopes plummet when I can only stick my head out. In the blackness, I grapple with the window crank, but it stubbornly refuses to budge.

All the while, the pressure on my lungs becomes excruciating. I resist the urge to heave and swallow the water as if it is air. An array of white lights flashes across my vision as I realize that I'm trapped. There is no escape.

Right as I'm about to convulse, gag and chug brine, I bite down on my tongue and suppress a scream. The pain sears through my numb mind, and in that moment of pure hurt, I remember the shattered rear window.

I pull myself over the backseat and with urgent, desperate strokes, and I swim up through the broken passage. Halfway up, my gag reflex kicks in, and I inhale the ocean.

When I break the surface, I unleash a fit of coughing. After a few seconds, I breathe normally, but the glacial water makes my body shiver while my heart pounds like a stampede of elephants. I look around for the man, but I don't see him.

A horrible realization dawns on me.

I don't want to dive back down, yet without a moment of hesitation, I take a huge breath and dive under. I see the silhouette of the Pontiac after a few strokes. It is settled on the muddy bottom twelve feet below.

I swim down and once near, I find the man struggling inside the car. He's trying to open the door, but it's not budging. He sees me and pounds on the window.

I place my feet on the side of the car and tug upwards on the door handle.

Nothing happens. I pull harder and a stream of precious bubbles slip out of me. Again, I feel the familiar pressure at this depth, and my lungs begin their fast burn.

The man's efforts grow weaker; his eyes waver, lose focus and close half-lidded. A second later, he's floating limply inside.

I yank again. Pain shoots through my arms, and I let out a scream of bubbles.

The door doesn't open.

I feel the last of my air leaving me. Either I go up for another breath or I join the man.

Teeth clenched, I commit myself; I'm not leaving him. I've never experienced such pain. My lungs want to explode, and stars streak through my vision.

As I'm about to open my mouth and breathe in the water, the door opens with disheartening slowness. With frantic movements, I grab the man and pull him to the surface. I don't know how long I hold my breath. I kick my legs with my last ounce of strength.

We surface, and I suck back the sweet air of life, swallowing gulps of it, promising I will never take it for granted again.

I hear the man gasp, look over, and see his eyes bulge. We tread for a few seconds more until he gets his breath. "Come on. This way," he instructs weakly. He swims for one of the moored boats.

Before following, I spin back to the marina. Far away, the driver of the SUV stands outside his vehicle. He's staring at me with those cobalt dead eyes. A new shiver streaks down my spine, and it's not from the water. The man with the bull head is smirking.

CHAPTER SEVEN
Ship of Souls

We swim to a moored fishing boat; the short distance may as well be ten miles. I lose my sneakers, but by some minor miracle, I keep my glasses. My toes freeze to miniature popsicles. The only way I muster the strength to continue on is from the adrenaline pumping through my veins.

The guy arrives at the boat first and climbs up a ladder at the stern. I get there a minute later and tread water, my body's life energy slipping out of me. I fumble with frozen fingers at the ladder until he helps haul me onboard.

Out of breath, I fall flat on the deck. Around me, stacked lobster traps tower upwards and release the stink of low tide. I wrap my arms around myself to keep warm.

The guy, who has recovered from almost drowning, retrieves a key hidden in a slide compartment. He shoots me an urgent expression. "You need to get out of those clothes now," he nods to the hatch down to the boat's cabin. "There is a spare set down below."

The cold sucks the life out of me. Wiping my face of salty water, I pick a piece of seaweed out of my hair. "OK-K-K," I say, tongue numb.

Standing up with wobbling legs, I glance back at the dock. Fog rolls in like waves from a tsunami, and our attacker is gone.

My body worsens from shivers to violent, teeth-chattering shakes. "Come on," he insists, guiding me with a hand on my shoulder. "You're going to get hypothermia if you stay up here."

I stumble down into the cabin, a bachelor pad with dirty clothes on the floor and posters of supermodels pinned to the walls. But the space heater literally saves my life. I turn it to high and stick my face in front of it, savoring the thaw. A duffel bag lies on top of a yellow foam mattress, posing as a bed. Inside is a towel, a pair of worn jeans, a brown long-sleeve shirt that's two sizes too large, and a bulky wool sweater decorated with a smiling moose. Beat-up Nike pump sneakers, straight from 1992, complete my ensemble. In a hand mirror tacked up to the wall, I catch a glimpse of myself: a shocked white face and hair matted to one side as if pressed in a waffle maker. I'm as weak as a 90-year-old as adrenaline clocks out and exhaustion takes over the night shift.

The boat's engine growls to life; exhaust fumes mix with the dead fish aroma. The boat accelerates forward, and I rock from side-to-side as we plow through small waves.

When I re-emerge, the man has changed into rough-worn beige pants and a maroon fleece vest. He is arched over the steering wheel. His body shakes, and I hear a soft trembling sob.

I knock into one of the lobster traps by accident; he wipes his hand across his face.

When he turns to me, his eyes—wide and bloodshot—give me the faintest of glances. He looks small at the helm of the boat.

He pilots the boat out to sea, and we disappear into the fog. Even though he can't see a thing, he steers the boat as if it is as bright as day.

"Did you learn to drive a boat in Massachusetts as well?" I ask.

The guy doesn't turn to me, but says, "My dad was a fisherman. This is his buddy's boat."

When he doesn't say anything else, I sit down on an empty lobster trap, hugging myself to fend off the cold. The man steers the boat in silence. He doesn't acknowledge me. Once we're out of the bay, he speeds up.

"Hey, what's your name?" I ask.

He says something inaudible. After a minute of being ignored, my patience breaks. "Hello!" I yell over the loud motor. "Where are we going?"

The guy doesn't even respond, so I get up, walk over, and grab his shoulder.

He spins toward me, blue eyes heavy, and he brushes a tear from his cheek, and then throttles down the motor a hair. "What?"

"Is everything OK?"

He clears his throat. "Everything's fine," he replies too brusquely. Then, as an afterthought, he adds, "Thank you."

I'm completely flustered. "For what?"

"You saved my life. I would have drowned if it weren't for you."

"You're welcome?" I reply, having no idea how to respond. I stare at him, noticing for the first time his youthful face and tangled brown hair. A shiver runs through me, and it's not from the cold. "I asked you your name."

"Sorry, it's Jared. Jared Stone," he says, awkwardly extending his hand. His fingers are cold to my touch. Jared looks away and says, "I have to concentrate. The harbor is full of rocks."

I rub the back of my neck, trying to ignore the swirling mix of confusion and exhaustion humming through my body. "What happened back there?"

Jared shakes his head. "I don't know."

"You don't know? They were shooting at us."

"Yeah," he replies.

"That shouldn't be happening. People don't shoot at you."

"I agree."

"We have to call the police," I insist.

"They won't do anything."

Is this guy for real? "They will arrest them."

"I doubt that will happen."

"What are you talking about?"

"I understand you're in shock right now, but you're not thinking clearly. If you were, you would know the truth."

"What exactly is the truth?"

He exhales and explains, "For men with that type of firepower, the police are the least of their worries."

I want to say he's wrong, that he's crazy, but a part of me realizes he's right. It's as if a trapdoor opens up beneath my reality. This free-falling feeling isn't helped when I notice a clock on the boat's dashboard: it reads two in the morning. "It was early evening when I arrived at the Witch House."

"Yeah, the ceremony lasted several hours. The Ascension is exhausting. You should really rest."

The Ascension—suddenly, I remember everything. The memories cascade down: the ceremony, the visions, the murdered women. My stomach lurches, and a wretched sickness crawls over my body. I thrust out a hand to steady myself while a thousand questions bombard my mind like pop-up ads from a computer virus. "Oh my god. Did they really die?"

Jared's spine becomes as a straight as a steel beam. His eyes widen, and his mouth drops open.

"They killed those women—" I falter and suppress a sob, a tear splattering onto my sleeve.

"Stop talking about them," he says, his voice harsh.

"What?"

"Just stop. I don't want to talk about them."

"Why?"

"If I start thinking about them, I—I won't be able to stop."

"But why did they die?"

Jared turns slowly, tiredness ringing his eyes. "They died because of you."

I rock back on my heels, stunned by his words; guilt erupts inside of me. "Well, thanks for making me feel better."

"I didn't mean it that way."

"No, please. Place the guilt of ten murdered women on *my* shoulders. That's what I really need right now." I turn away on the edge of more tears, not wanting him to see me cry.

He waits a minute before saying, "I'm sorry. It isn't your fault they died. I mean—I meant—what I'm trying to say is that they died for a greater purpose—you living."

"Stop!" I yell. "You're making me feel worse." I wipe my eyes and clear my throat. "What did they do to me?"

Jared's mouth tightens. "It was your Ascension."

"Gertrude promised that I would remember my dreams. Nothing about me has changed."

At the mention of her name, his whole body slumps, and his face goes slack. After a moment, he replies in a flat, monotone voice. "That's because you're still a Descended." I look at him as if he is speaking Russian. "It means you're a goddess who can't recall her past lives. The only way you can unlock your memories is by undergoing the Ascension ceremony, which destroys the mental barrier that separates your current life from your past lives. If the ceremony was successful, then you would have become an Ascended goddess." He says this as if he's reciting some memorized verse.

"It wasn't successful?"

Jareds shakes his head. "The ceremony was interrupted before it could be completed."

"So, you're serious, you think I'm a god?"

With a hesitant glance, Jared says, "You aren't literally a god, but because of all the knowledge you have accumulated through your lifetimes, humans have labeled you a god."

"None of this makes sense."

"I couldn't agree more," he says under his breath.

"What?"

"Listen, I know it sounds crazy. But think of it this way—the human body is a ship." He gestures to the lobster boat. "It carries the soul through life. A ship of souls. When the body dies, it's like the ship is sinking. But the soul doesn't die. It doesn't go away. It finds a new ship, a new body, and starts a new life."

"Yeah, that's reincarnation."

"Exactly," he says. "But gods, like you, are special. For the majority of people, memories of past lives are inaccessible. For me, there's no way to tap into those memories. But *you* can remember all your past lives."

"Ok," I say, slowly. "This is nuts, and I don't want any part of it."

"Trust me. I wish there was an alternative explanation."

I back away. "Why didn't anyone tell me that this ceremony was some drugged-out hallucination?"

Jared bites his lower lip. It's as if some pressure is pushing in on him. "No one drugged you, and I'm sorry there wasn't enough time to explain everything to you. The ceremony can only happen during a certain time of the month."

"Let me a guess: a full moon?"

He nods. "Also, honestly, would you have undergone the ceremony if you had known what you were getting into?"

"You tricked me."

"No, they were trying to protect you. They knew there were others searching for you as well."

"You knew about those guys in the SUVs?"

"Yes," Jared says. "But they were willing to take the risk of conducting the ceremony in the hope that your Ascension would be completed."

I groan, and my head falls into my hands. "This can't be happening." I turn toward him. "If you knew that those killers were going to be there, why didn't you call the police?"

"In your world, there are different rules. The police aren't always there to help you."

A burst of light-headedness sends me wobbling; this supposed new reality is still too much to process. "Who are they?"

"I think they serve another god."

"You mean there are other—what was it you called me—Ascended?"

"Yes, but this Ascended god wants you dead."

At that moment, it's as if I have ten-pound weights hanging from eyelids. If I had a magic lamp, I'd use all three wishes to be back home, fall asleep, and forget everything. It's not fair that I'm at the center of it all. "Listen Jared, thanks for helping me, but can you just bring me home? I'm done with all of this."

"What are you talking about?"

I point over to the distant shore. "Just pull over and drop me off."

"You want us to sink?" His eyebrows raise with the rhetorical question, and I have an urge to slap the confused expression off his face. "The shore is too rocky here. We have to get to a port."

"Fine, we get to the port, and I'm out of here."

"I'm sorry, but I can't leave you," Jared says, holding back his frustration.

"Listen, this isn't some video game, and I'm no damsel in distress. I don't want to be part of this."

"Do you not think I realize how fucked up this all is?"

"I don't know, do you?" I list off the offenses on my fingers. "In the last hour, we were shot at, in a high-speed chase, almost drowned and nearly died of hypothermia."

"Yeah, it wasn't fun for me either."

"I'm serious. I'm done."

"I can't leave you."

"You're not listening to me." I feel my face grow flush, and I'm at the point of screaming. "I'm not going anywhere with you."

"I can't bring you back," Jared says. "They'll kill you."

I clench my hands into fists. "They don't know who I am."

"They will." His gaze returns to the sea. "Whether you like it or not, I'm staying with you."

I swivel toward the far away shore. I expect the man with the bull-head to be watching me. Instead, the fog blankets the ocean's surface.

"You don't need to worry about him. We lost him."

"Who was that guy? And why did he have a head like a bull?" I ask, disconcerted that Jared can somehow read my thoughts.

Jared spins and stares, mouth agape. "Are you sure you saw a bull's head on him?"

"Yeah, how strong was the stuff you put in that juice?"

"Crap," he says under his breath.

"What?"

"It's nothing," he says, casting his attention on the front of the boat. I want to challenge him to explain further, but I'm suddenly too tired to continue the conversation.

The fog disperses, and a town appears in the distance. As we round a jetty, bright lights illuminate buildings and a long dock. On a warehouse, I read 'Gloucester Fish Processing'. Jared cuts the engine; as we glide next to the wooden floats, he jumps out with a line in hand and ties it to the cleat.

As soon as we're secure, I jump off the boat and walk fast down the dock and away from him. Jared races up and grabs my arm.

"What's the deal? Leave me alone," I say, wrenching my arm free.

"I can't let you go. You're not safe."

"I already told you." I glare back at him. "I don't want any part of this."

"What's your problem?"

"What's *my* problem?" At that moment, the dam breaks, and I seize the collar of his vest and shove him away. "You expect me to do whatever you want? 'Come with me, Mattie. Run, Mattie. Swim, Mattie. Don't get killed, Mattie!'" I take a defiant step forward. "I'm done!"

Jared's eyes are wide, and he backs off. "I'm sorry. I'm under a lot of pressure right now, and I'm trying everything in my power not to think about what happened at the Witch House." He sighs, hanging his head. "You're confused, scared, and exhausted. I get that. But we don't have much time. The men chasing you are very powerful. They're going to track you down. We need to leave right away, but I'll make you a deal." He steps close to me; his eyes are earnest and his voice sincere as he says, "Let me drive you home."

I eye him with no shortage of skepticism and ask myself why he had the sudden change of heart. Yet, I consider his proposition. On one hand, I don't want anything to do with him; on the other, I have no idea how to get home. It's the middle of the night, and I left my wallet and phone back in Salem. After a long moment of deliberation, I ask, "You promise to drop me off?"

"I promise I won't bother you ever again." He sticks out his hand. "Deal?"

I pause, wondering if I can actually trust him. At this hour, a ride home sounds too tempting to deny. "Fine," I finally concede and shake his hand. "Where's your car?"

"Come on," he waves and guides me down the pier.

I nod toward the boat. "Are you just going to leave it here?"

"I'll tell my dad's friend where it is."

We walk toward the parking lot and arrive at an old Toyota Camry missing all four hubcaps and duct tape over one of the back windows. "You really have great taste in cars."

Jared ignores my brilliant wit and opens the door for me.

He gets into the driver's seat, finds the keys behind the visor, turns up the heat to max, and speeds out of the lot. After five minutes, we pull into a gas station.

"Why are we stopping?"

He points to the 24-hour Dunkin' Donuts inside the station."I'm starving." He jumps out and runs in.

A few minutes later he re-emerges with a bag and two steaming cups.

Once he's back in the car, he pulls a bagel from the bag and takes a sip from the cup. "Here," he says already chewing on the bagel.

My stomach rumbles, and with a reluctant shrug, I take a poppy seed bagel. The cup smells like hot chocolate, and the food makes my mouth water. But I don't touch a thing. "I swear, if you drug me again, I'm going to kick your ass," I warn.

Jared shakes his head, ignores me and takes another bite of bagel. Finally, I dive into the bagel and chug the hot chocolate, burning my tongue in the process.

He puts on the radio to a classical music station and pulls away into the street.

After eating, I stretch and yawn. "Why were you even at the Ascension ceremony? Doesn't your Y-chromosome disqualify you or something?"

Jared stares straight ahead at the road. "I'm your protector."

"Protector?" I snort with a laugh.

He nods his head. "Yeah, I'm not a priest. I'm someone who protects the priestesses and goddesses." Jared pauses and shoots me a small smile. "But you're the first goddess I've ever protected."

"Really?" I eye his thin frame. "You're my bodyguard?"

"Who were you expecting? James Bond?" He levels his eyes at me. "There isn't a long list of dudes who sign up for the job of protecting goddesses."

"Will you please stop calling me that? My name is Mattie."

"OK, Mattie. My job is to protect you. Until you are fully Ascended, I'm responsible for you."

"Great. Well, consider your job done after you drop me off in Cambridge."

"You bet."

The car is warm and cozy; fatigue has caught up with me. The food makes me full and comfortable. Covering my mouth to suppress a yawn, my mind slows as Jared drives fast down dark, country roads.

I close my eyes for a second but force them open again. A part of me knows that staying awake is the most important thing, but the world recedes fast, and my fight to ward off sleep weakens to a war of attrition that I have no hope of winning.

CHAPTER EIGHT
Hidden Opportunities

The jail cell's cold floor sends chills through my bare feet. Moonbeams filter through a small rectangular window at foot-level, but even with this light, the darkness is so complete I can barely spot my own hands. I bend down, and my knees scrape against the rough stone. Grasping the rusted bars of the window, I pull with all my strength. I pray that my previous attempts have loosened their foundation. My muscles are on the point of splitting, sweat drenches my brow, and my fingers cry out in pain. But the bars don't budge.

A terrified scream echoes through the stone tower. I whip my head toward the cell door; I don't have much time. They will come for me next.

When the Christians raided the village, they killed the men, children, and old. Then they raped the women, and afterward, murdered them as well. I knew about the crusaders, as they called themselves, from my cousin. He had said that their invasion of our land would only result in their defeat. But I'd received false news that their path of destruction and death was sweeping away from us.

I wasn't even supposed to be in the village. Trading sheepskins on behalf of Papa—who had been away for months dealing with the Fatimids—if the villagers hadn't offered such a good price, I wouldn't have left the safety of Damascus.

Although my family follows the teachings of Allah, Papa says that in business, as well as in life, one must always be resourceful and search for hidden opportunities. That is why we trade with the Christians, Muslims, and even the Jews—if they offer a good price.

After pillaging the village, the crusaders took the three prettiest of the women as captives. A girl named Esther sprained her ankle on the long hike through the desert. They put her down like a dog and left her to the vultures. The screams in the tower come from Diana, who is Christian, but that doesn't appear to mean anything to the Franks.

A flame lights up the black prison hallway, and I hear the fat jailer stumble toward my cell. I back into the corner, my muscles tightening. I'm determined to fight if it's my turn, even if it means my death. I will not be treated like an animal.

At the barred door, he pauses. He carries a tallow candle, which illuminates his toothless hyena sneer and bearded, rough face. "You are next, my dark beauty," he says in a vulgar form of Latin that I can barely understand. I smell the wine on his breath all the way from the other side of the cell. He tosses a meat bone in front of me, and it lands on the floor with a dull thud. "Our King says you need strength for what's to come. He doesn't want you dying like the others." My response is a malevolent stare, despite the fear charging through my veins, but his hearty laugh darkens my silence. He turns and disappears down the hallway.

I stare at the meat bone, which is likely pork. Despite my rumbling stomach, I refuse to touch it.

I'm locked in a tower of the old fort in Acre. The irony is that I spent much of my youth in the city. If I can get out of the cell, I can unite with Papa's business partners, and they can smuggle me out of the city. Escape from this accursed prison is all that matters. My cell is at roof level of the surrounding buildings, which offer a means of escape if I can get through the metal bars. I can push my head through the window, but it's too narrow for the rest of my body. I check the door again. But it's solid iron and oak, and it's locked from the outside.

Papa says you need to be resourceful; always search for the hidden opportunity.

That's when I realize it. That foolish jailer left his candle hanging on a ledge outside the cell. It shines enough light that I can now see and explore my prison. I've already been in here for a day and a half and have fumbled in the darkness with my hands, but maybe I missed something. I check every square cubit.

Diana's hoarse screams raise the hairs on my arms like the thorns of cactus fruit. I have to escape; there is no other option.

That's when I notice the marks on the wall that were hidden in the darkness. I go over to inspect them and find deep gouges have been worked away at the mortar between the bricks on the exterior wall. My finger runs along the smooth crevices as if my own hand created the marks; my breath catches when I realize why they exist.

Past prisoners have thought the same as me, and they tried to claw their way to freedom. How many women have worked at these grooves? How many failed?

I will not let their last moments of life be in vain. I will live for them.

My nails scratch away at the old mortar. To my surprise, it crumbles to the floor. As I work, Diana's cries weaken to faint wails. I don't know how long I work at it, but finally, my fingers find a gap in the mortar—an air pocket left behind because of shoddy workmanship. With a hooked finger, I claw out the remaining mortar along one side.

Hope soars.

I put my fingers inside the gap and pull. It doesn't budge, but I attempt a new tactic. I rock the stone from side to side. The brick wiggles a little—back and forth. Over and over again. Little by little, the brick comes free from the remaining mortar. With a suddenness that surprises me, the brick slips down and crashes to the floor. My heart thumps wildly from the success. I did it!

I rush over to the opening to make my escape, but right away, my hopes plummet. There is no open air on the other side; there is only another stone wall.

At that moment, Diana's screams peak with pain, and then cut short, as if her throat was torn out. In another part of the tower, I hear men curse one another. "Why did you kill her? I hadn't had my turn." My blood freezes as I realize that Diana is dead, and I am next. Time is up.

Should I give up, lie down and cry? I put everything into removing that brick, and I failed. But from within me, I remember Papa's words.

No, I can't.

Think. Think. Think. Fear drowns out all other thoughts.

What can I use to my advantage? What is different?

The sound of the dripping candle sparks an idea as I rush to the cell door. The candle is out of reach but its drippings have made a puddle in front of the door. I reach out, picking up some of the warm tallow on my finger.

A thought blossoms in my mind.

Will it work? Could it work? Do I have any other choice?

I smell the tallow. It's pork fat. The Prophet would disapprove of what I'm about to do, but then again, does not the Koran say, 'He who saves a life will be as if he had saved the lives of all humankind?' I assume this also means for one's own life.

"Get the dark-haired one!" one of the Franks yells. "I still have energy for one more." This is followed by a round of cheers from the other soldiers. My body freezes.

If it is my only chance, I must do it now. Although it's improper, I pull off my bulky outer robes. I unbutton my dress and take that off as well. I hesitate, bite my lower lip, and remove my undergarments until I am as naked as a newborn. Papa would disapprove. But then again, Papa would prefer to have me live.

I glance down the hallway. Please, Allah, do not let the guard come.

After I make this plea, I hear the cursing of the Frankish jailer as he lumbers up the stairs toward my cell.

I reach out and scoop up two palm-fulls of the warm tallow and spread it down the length of my torso, rubbing the warm fat all over my shoulders and hips until it glistens off my skin. Naked and greased with the fat of unclean animals, I rush over to the small window and fall to my knees. I push my head through the bars. This I know I can do. But my shoulders stop me from going further.

From behind me, a light brightens the hallway. The jailer is here. I've run out of time, but despite this, I keep pushing.

Come on. I push harder and the pain sears through my body. I can't do this.

But I remember poor Diana. No, I have no other choice. Despite the pain, I push harder, and the pain sears my shoulders.

I think for sure that the guard will be coming in at any moment, but then, I hear a stream of liquid hitting stone, followed by a relieved sigh.

Harder. My bones crack and muscles rip.

Please.

One of my greased shoulders squeezes through an inch. Hope flares up inside of me like rays of sun after an infinite night.

That instant, the sound of piss ends. I have less than a minute before he discovers me.

I push harder, encouraged by my small gain.

One shoulder slips through, and a moment later, my other shoulder follows.

The midwives said I was cursed with thin hips. My pregnancies will all be painful, they said. Yet that curse has now delivered me my greatest blessing.

The rest of my body slides through like a snake through grass. I smile, triumph ringing through me, as I reach back into the cell and gather up my clothes.

I leap onto a surrounding building and race off as the full moon shimmers off my skin.

As I disappear into the night, I hear the guard let out a futile cry of alarm.

I wake up—chest heaving. My eyes snap open, a cascade of chills runs down my spine.

When is it? Where am I? *Who am I?* I'm shocked to be asking the question, but in truth, I don't know.

My hands leap to my sore shoulders. I expect pork fat smeared over them. Instead, I find a bulky sweatshirt adorned with a smiling moose. It takes me a moment to realize that I'm not in Acre, and there are no crusaders coming to kill me.

What the hell was that? I felt everything that girl felt; it was like I was her. A creeping realization burrows its way into my mind. I know what that vision was.

It was one of my lost dreams, the dreams that haunted my childhood, adolescence, and adulthood. Dreams I never remembered—until now.

But that was nothing like what people described as normal dreams.

The dream of the imprisoned Muslim girl was too vivid and too real. Warm grease still tingles my skin, and Diana's screams echo in my ears. My shoulders actually hurt; adrenaline pumps through me. My head spins, searching for any type of rational explanation, but I come up with nothing. A new realization hits me: I have no idea where I am.

In front of me, three blurry televisions wobble, and the ceiling and walls undulate. I don't remember chugging a pint of vodka and going on a merry-go-round. One thing I know for sure—I'm not at my apartment in Cambridge.

The room stops spinning; I sit in an armchair with peeling fake black leather. I pick at a piece, and it flakes to a battered industrial gray carpet. The three televisions merge into one like a magician's trick. The rundown room—reeking of garlic and ginger—has water stains sneaking in from the ceiling's corners.

Why is my head spinning? It could be that I remember my dreams, but I have a sense it's for a different reason. The next moment, the front door opens, and Jared Stone enters carrying a plastic bag. "You're awake," he observes.

I stare at him through vision that seesaws. "You drugged me?" I accuse, slurring my words. I tighten my grip on the chair's armrests to keep the world from spinning apart. "Again?"

Jared shakes his head. "They didn't drug you for your Ascension."

"Bullshit."

He swallows hard, and his expression is pained. "I'm really sorry. I know this was the last thing you wanted, but I couldn't let you run off. You're in serious danger. Your life is at risk." His head droops and his gaze avoids my eyes. He places the plastic bag on a table, and weakly adds, "I got you some Ramen in case you get hungry. There's soda in the fridge."

"What am I doing here?"

"I had to bring you somewhere safe." He walks over and checks the locks on the barred windows. "You don't need to worry. The stuff will wear off in an hour. It was just a few sleeping pills After, you'll be fine."

"Fine as sunshine, right as rain." I think I'm going to throw-up.

Jared avoids looking me in the eyes. "Listen, I'm truly sorry, but for the time being, you're going to have to stay here."

"Is that the game we're playing now?" I stand up to challenge him, but it's like walking on a trampoline. I lose my balance and fall back into the seat. "Am I officially kidnapped?"

"You don't realize how much danger you're in," Jared says. "I'm protecting you."

"Sure, sure. The police will definitely buy that as an alibi."

He opens his mouth, maybe to defend his actions, but sighs and decides against it. "I'll be back soon. You have food and drink. Watch TV if you get bored." He turns to leave.

"Wait, where am I?"

Jared stops with his hand on the doorknob. "Where else?" He

points to the window. "The City of Gods." He opens the door and leaves; I hear him click the lock from the outside.

I stand up—a dizzying array of colors flash in front of my eyes—and stumble toward the door, hitting the wall instead. I yank hard on the door handle and nearly topple over. It takes me a few seconds to realize it's locked from the outside, and I need a key to open it from the inside.

"Asshole!" I yell.

With the balance of a two-year-old, I stumble over to the window. I'm able to unlock it, but the window only goes up an inch, and metal bars crisscross the inside. The outside window displays a skyline I recognize in an instant. The morning sun glints off the polished glass skyscrapers of Midtown.

I'm in New York City.

Five stories down, I find a chaotic side street filled with fruit and vegetable vendors and honking trucks stuck in traffic. Police sirens fill the air.

I put my mouth to the one-inch crack and scream, "Help!" For five minutes, I yell at the top my lungs. Not a single person below even tilts their head up. Next, I scream at the walls of the apartment, hoping one of the neighbors will hear my cries. I have to stop when my head gets light.

Exhausted, I slump back into the armchair; my head spins faster. If I don't rest, I will pass out. I close my eyes and go through a series of deep breathing exercises I learned from YouTube yoga classes. Twenty minutes go by, and I feel better.

I run my fingers along the concrete walls. There must be at least a foot of rock separating me from my neighbors.

"OK, Mattie, think," I say out loud. I stand up, slower this time, and am pleased that my knees don't give out from under me. I need a plan to get out of here, wherever here is.

The apartment is tiny. It takes me all of thirty seconds to find the one bedroom with a yellow, sheet-less mattress on the floor. A steam heater hisses from a decrepit moldy bathroom, and the smell of old Chinese food comes from a narrow hallway kitchen. I go over to the door and pull on it with all my strength, but it's one of those New York City siege doors that require a police battering ram to break down.

Next, I try a more aggressive approach: I wind up and hurl a teakettle at the window. It ricochets off the metal bars and slams into the television, cracking the screen. I groan.

I check off all the possibilities: door locked, window barred, and no one can hear me. I don't know how long Jared will be away, but I know that I have to be gone by the time he gets back.

"Damn it!" I shout. "How do I get out of here?"

Be resourceful. That's what Papa says.

The Muslim girl. I remember her fear and desire to be free. She did it. Why can't I? But, another part of me says that I'm crazy. It was only a dream.

In the kitchen, I pour myself a glass of water which sputters out rust colored. I contemplate how screwed I am as I lean against the wall.

That's when I hear a voice: "Come on down! You're the next contestant on *The Price is Right.*" A voice floats through the wall.

I drop the glass. It shatters into pieces in the sink, but I don't care.

I turn toward the wall and yell. "Hello, anyone there? Please help me!" I wait for a reply. But none comes. "Come on! Please!" No reply. "HELP!" For ten minutes, I throw all my energy in contacting the person in the next room. No one responds. Finally, I slam the wall with my fists, pounding out my frustration.

"Bob Barker reminding you: help control the pet population. Have your pet spayed or neutered."

I break down into tears and collapse, defeated, onto the floor with my back to the wall. Someone is there; I know it. Why can't they hear me?

Search for hidden opportunities.

Damn that dream! There are no hidden opportunities. It kills me that I'm so close to getting out, yet this damn wall blocks me from my freedom. I'm going to be a drugged-up slave to Jared for the rest of my life; anger floods into me. I can't give up, and I don't have any other choice. I stand up, determined to make contact. I turn, but my fist freezes in the air. My jaw drops. I can't believe it.

There's a crack in the wall.

I didn't realize it until now, but the wall isn't concrete like the rest of the apartment. It's drywall. A new idea dawns upon me. I throw open the cupboards in the kitchen; there must be one here.

Seconds later, my legs wobble, and I release a shaky laugh when I find the orange-rusted cast-iron pan. Picking up the pan, I take a step back, raise it over my head, and take aim.

I lunge forward and slam the pan into the wall. There's a satisfying crunch as the pan sinks into the drywall. "Argh!" I scream, pulling it out and slamming it again.

Over and over, I smash the pan through until the crack widens. When the hole is two feet in diameter, I drop the pan and yank out the remaining pieces of drywall to reveal a patchwork of wooden beams, wiring, and rat droppings.

But on the other side, there's another sheet of drywall. "Here I come!"

I lift the pan and bash it through the neighbor's wall. The pan goes through, and when I pull it back, I discover light on the other side.

Peering through, I find another dilapidated kitchen. I pound through the wall, and after thirty minutes, I create a passageway large enough for me to slip through. When I step into the neighboring kitchen, the smell of cat urine stings my nose. Stacks of dirty dishes lean with a precarious Jenga-like balance in the sink. Mold and water also stain this apartment's surfaces. I leave the kitchen and turn into a living room adorned with floral prints that usually decorate the bathrooms of Thai restaurants.

It takes me a moment to notice the old woman, bundled up in about ten sweaters, sitting in a rocking chair, sipping on a box of grape juice. Her eyes, magnified through glasses that have one-inch lenses, watch VHS re-runs of *The Price is Right* at max volume.

When I come into the room, she squints up at me with cataract eyes, and in a frail voice says, "You're not my grandson."

I drop the pan, and it crashes onto the peeling linoleum floor. I release a satisfied sigh and reply, "Hell no, I ain't."

CHAPTER NINE
City of Gods

I emerge from the tenement building into the heavy heat of Chinatown. The streets crawl with droves of people shopping among the produce vendors, and the smell of rotting fish flips my stomach upside down.

Gagging, I stumble within reach of a man lying on the street, bundled up in a dirty sleeping bag. His fingers graze my leg. I leap back, and by accident, I kick over his half-full bottle of King Cobra. He unleashes a loud groan, and I dash to the busy street choked with cars.

In the center of an intersection, I locate my savior—an NYC police officer directing traffic. I wave my hand to get her attention, but a thought hits me broadside: should I tell her what's happened?

The impulse to confess, like a criminal, is strong. I want everything to be how it was before. The way to do that is to get help, yet, why the doubt?

Dizziness hits and I bite back a surge of nausea. What hallucinogens float in my system? Will she believe me? I don't even believe the things that have happened to me in the past twenty-four hours. The police officer might arrest me for drug use. Does an unemployed teacher need a strike on her record?

As the officer is about to notice my upraised hand and pleading expression, I turn away and disappear into the crowds.

But all is not lost; I have a backup plan. Patrick Lynde, my best friend, lives in the city, and I have a vague idea of where to find his West Village apartment.

I've still got a problem. In the chaos of last night, I lost my bag with my cash, credit card, and phone. New York City does not tolerate such handicaps.

I arrive at the corner of Canal and Essex. Playing a near-deadly game of Frogger, I weave through the traffic; inspecting a subway map, I release a huge sigh when I find that I'm within walking distance of the West Village.

The ant-line of tourists carries me off in what I think is the right direction. The diesel trucks spewing exhaust and the heavy humid air renew a fresh bout of queasiness. I need to get to Patrick's.

After a minute, I strain to focus on the couple a few feet in front of me. Something is different about them. They march at a leisurely pace with locked arms and matched steps.

The man wears a gray tweed suit, ironed and starched, and he balances on an ivory cane. The woman, her hair tied up in a tight bun, sports a yellow cardigan and fuchsia-colored stretch pants.

Their meandering pace halts at a Chinese herbal medicine shop. They lean over to inspect a barrel filled with unidentifiable, desiccated sea creatures. I follow the progression of walkers that curves around them. Something about the man's face isn't right. My fingers freeze, eyes riveted on his cheeks as they shift in front of me.

It's as if someone photoshopped his face—twisting the expression, painting alien colors and airbrushing foreign texture. Is he wearing a mask? No, that isn't a mask.

I gasp. Heart slamming, I take a step back. The fear mounts inside of me like sand filling an hourglass, but I can't pry my eyes away. My mind can barely process what I see.

Streaks of yellow, brown, and orange cross his face in parallel lines. Razor-sharp teeth, glistening white, descend from his jaws. Black whiskers sprout from a snout, while his pointed ears quiver as if sensing prey. Clamping my hands over my mouth, I choke back a scream.

The man has a face of a tiger.

The strangest part is that everything else about the man is normal. He's still dressed in a prim tweed suit with a blue carnation pinned to his lapel. He wears black polished shoes, and one of his human hands grasps his cane while the other holds the hand of his normal, petite wife.

Is this a mirage from the heat haze radiating off the asphalt?

The tiger man turns and stares at me. My pulse pounding, I see a crimson red aura hanging around his head like fog. The tiger's nostrils flare, and from his throat rolls a deep snarl.

Leaping backward into the street and hitting a parked taxi, I can't blink or turn away. My lips tremble, and my stomach does backflips.

For a half-second, the tiger's amber eyes and mine connect. Something ignites in his feral face, but before the meaning presents itself, I climb from the taxi, tear myself away, and get lost within the flow of pedestrians.

Within seconds, the man's eyes bore into the back of my head. I spin around, despite my chest rattling with fear.

The man's face has transformed; it's no longer that of a tiger. He's an old man with deep-set wrinkles, round glasses, and shallow cheeks.

But he still stares at me—as if expecting me to do or say something. I stifle a cry and race away, feeling the tiger man's eyes tracing me. After another block, I look back, but he is gone.

Questions rain down like hail. What was wrong with his face? Why did he stare at me as if he recognized me? Why did he remind me of the bull-headed killer?

Running my hands through my hair while sweat pours down my back, I can't think about this now; I have to get to Patrick's to figure out what's going on. That's all that matters. Patrick's home is a sanctuary.

As I push my way through, the crowds thicken like gelatin. The panic from the tiger man slowly subsides like the tide. The man couldn't have a tiger's head; it was a hallucination—the same as the ceremony in Salem.

Despite it being autumn, I'm overheating in the moose sweater and lightheaded as the sun blazes. I have to get out of Chinatown. Something doesn't feel right here.

As if answering my fears, the crowds part, and I stare down at a woman—wretched with dirt-encrusted fingernails, chapped skin stretched over a thin bony frame, and pitiful dark eyes—sitting on the ground. An old winter coat drapes across her shoulders and a brown dusty blanket lies on her lap. Her only adornment is a necklace of large, round polished stones.

In black Sharpie on a piece of ripped cardboard, she's scrawled "Pleese help. Im Hungry."

I can smell her from a few feet away, and the other pedestrians avoid her. I should ignore the woman and her outstretched hand.

But again, something about the woman strikes me as not right. Maybe it's her unnatural black face—like all light disappears into it. My feet stick to the ground like lead boots.

The woman's thick hair hangs around her in wild tangles. Her eyes—two pebbles of white jade embedded in coal—angle up at me, while cupped hands extend outwards.

A long, blood red serpent's tongue licks the air. Her mouth opens into a maniacal, silent cackle. My jaw drops, and a scream builds up inside of me when I spot the woman's necklace. Those aren't stones around her neck.

They're miniature human heads.

Screaming, I fly backward. I fall into a group of tourists, clutching Hello Kitty handbags. They scream because of me.

Panic everywhere.

I glance back at the woman, but her face has undergone a metamorphosis. Her features are normal. No more snake tongue, human heads nor infinite black face.

That's it. I can't take any more of this. Shoving people aside, I run. I have to get away. People stare at me as if I'm crazy. Am I? My mind races, searching for an explanation. Why are people different? First the tiger man and now the woman with the necklace of skulls. These aren't hallucinations. They're real. I know for sure.

What happened in Salem? What did those women do to me?

At the first possible turn, I run off Canal Street and slow to a fast walk. Casting a quick glance behind me, I check to make sure no one is there. The heat must be making me hallucinate. My throat cries out for water, and it's like I'm carrying a fifty-pound bag on my back. The quiet side street has fewer people on it. Eyes darting from face to face, my mind teeters.

As I pass other people, nothing appears strange about them. I walk north, and the crazed energy of Chinatown grows distant. There's nothing wrong with me, I assure myself. Everything is fine, and soon I will be at Patrick's.

I take a few deep breaths. My heartbeats slow, while my feet drag and eyelids sag. My mind must be playing tricks on me; that's why those people appeared different. After a few minutes, I breathe easier and cold sweat no longer drips down my neck.

I arrive at a large, verdant park, packed with people. I've been here before. It's Washington Square Park, and Patrick's apartment is close. Sun shining down, it's one of those beautiful autumn days when everyone enjoys the lingering heat of summer. Groups of musicians belt out songs from the sixties, while old men play chess and Scrabble. Some NYU students shoot a film, and children splash around in the water fountain.

Despite the apparent normalcy of the scene, my head spins, and my heartbeats race out-of-control again. Everything isn't normal, and I don't think my sanity can take it.

For every fifteen normal people, there's one person whose face is transformed into something else. I spot at least five people with animal heads. My head jerks from a wolf here to an eagle there. A dog man walking a pug. A Buddha slacklines between two trees. My breathing bursts in and out as I spy a troll-faced man selling hot dogs. A businessman, in an expensive suit, has horns and a devil-red face. I release an uncontrolled whimper. Misty multicolored auras surround all of their heads.

I dry-heave, and my arms shake. I have to get out of here now. I'm running, but to where, I have no idea.

As I run, without any sense of time, desperation drowns me. I need things to be normal. Why can't the world be how it was? This isn't a dream. Something is wrong with me. These visions are real and getting worse. Who are these people? Why do they regard me as if expecting something?

I don't know how, but I find Patrick's apartment building. A five-story brownstone deep in the West Village. I run up the stone steps and jam down on the buzzer.

No one answers.

I can't take it anymore. I curl up on the stoop, cover my head with my hands, and rock back and forth. My reality cracks like thin ice. One wrong move and I may plunge through, never to re-surface.

CHAPTER TEN
My Savior

"Mattie?" A falsetto voice pipes behind me. It draws me from my cocoon of fear. "What are you doing here?"

Relief, like a warm quilt, wraps around me when I hear Patrick's voice. "Thank god, you're—" When I turn toward him, I know I've gone mad.

He's dressed in a flowing, red sequin dress. A bleached blond wig crowns his head while four-inch stiletto heels support his long legs in pantyhose. Thick foundation powders his face—lips the color of Lolita cherry red.

My mouth hangs open. Is it really him?

"Are you OK?" he asks, rushing up to me while clutching a Louis Vuitton bag by his hip. "You look like you've seen a ghost."

He grabs my hand, concern in his eyes. The touch awakens my other senses. I take a hesitant breath. "Patrick?" I whisper, holding back the tears.

He nods and gives me his best smile. My face collapses, and I cry.

"Oh dear . . ." Patrick says as I fall into his arms. A moment later, he draws back and adds, "Oooh, Mattie, you stink!" I sniffle and smile despite everything. He pats my head.

Two businessmen in sharp suits with folded, moussed hair, walk by, and they don't even glance in our direction. A drag queen comforting a woman in a moose sweater at eleven in the morning would be strange anywhere except in New York City.

"Come on up. We'll get you sorted out," he pauses and sticks his nose into the air, "and showered."

While I wipe the tears from my eyes, Patrick leads me up the spiral staircase to his third-floor apartment. Once inside, he sits me down on a plush, neon blue coffin couch. "You rest here while Pattie gets out of his work clothes," he says with a wink.

Pattie was the nickname I gave him when we were at college together. Pattie and Mattie, the "Inseparable Duo." He disappears down the hallway into his bedroom, and my crying tapers off to sniffling.

His apartment is huge for city standards. A rainbow collection of boas hangs from the walls along with framed photos of famous drag queens. Vintage eighties furniture dots the living room, and bright swaths of silk cover the walls. An army of white pillows spreads across the pink and red shag rug like marshmallow islands.

The apartment belongs to Chantel, a famous drag queen who had been featured on the RuPaul Show. Patrick is his part-time lover and full-time confidante.

He returns to the living room, still bewigged, and made-up, but the stilettos have been replaced with furry bunny slippers. He carries a baggy t-shirt and sweatpants under his arm.

"Is Chantel home?" I ask.

Patrick shakes his head. "No, he's out in LA—doing some shows. He'll be back next week." He hands me the pajamas. "Why didn't you call and tell me you were coming?"

"I—I—" I don't even know where to begin.

Noticing my consternation, he cuts in. "There, there. Don't worry about it now." He turns around. "You mind unzipping me?"

"Sure," I unzip his dress, revealing Patrick's pale white shoulders and a brazier that holds two ripe, Ruby Red grapefruits.

"Ooohhh . . ." Patrick sighs. He wiggles out of the dress and stretches his back. "It's so good to be out of my work clothes."

One of my eyebrows raises. Is this the skinny boy with whom I shared all my secrets? "I didn't know you were … uh … performing."

Patrick winks and bites his lower lip. "A girl's gotta make a living, right?" He takes out the grapefruits and puts them in a fruit bowl on the breakfast bar. "Chantel got me the job. It pays well. I'm still auditioning for shows, but in the meantime, I need cash." After college, Patrick had packed up and moved to NYC to make it as a Broadway actor. He'd gotten some Off-Broadway chorus parts but was still waiting for his big break.

"I hear you."

Patrick crosses his arms, a mother-like authority in his face. "Before I hear about the latest debacle in the Life of Mattie, why don't you take a shower, and I'll fix us something to eat."

"Sounds amazing," I say.

In the bathroom, I stare at a stranger in the mirror. Deep shadows underline my eyes, and my hair is as disheveled as a plate of spaghetti. Patrick's right. The smell that I thought was the sewer is me.

Thank god for the building's scalding high-pressure shower. The hot water scours my skin, washing away the accumulated grime, sweat, and salt water. Afterward, I'm almost human again. I re-emerge pajama-ed and more relaxed than I can ever remember.

Patrick, without a wig or makeup, wearing a Care Bears-imprinted pajamas, sits on the couch. On the coffee table in front of him is a tray with sliced cheese, sourdough bread, green grapes, and a French press of fresh coffee. My stomach growls.

He opens his hands wide and declares, "Let's feast!"

"Patrick, you're a saint."

He blushes and waves his hand as if it were nothing. I join him on the couch and devour a piece of cheese and bread. I drink half a mug of coffee despite it scalding my tongue, still raw from the hot chocolate. Patrick watches me eat with round eyes. "Slow down, you might choke," he pops a grape in his mouth and reclines.

"Seriously, you are my savior today," I say while stuffing my face with an embarrassing amount of food.

"Oh, honey. You know you're always welcome here." Patrick reaches behind the couch and takes out a three-foot bong. "Do you want a hit?" he asks.

"Given the events of the past day, I think it would be best if I passed."

"I can't wait to hear this story," he says. Patrick lights the bong, which fills with a yellowish-gray smoke. With a well-prac-ticed deep breath, he inhales the entire contents, holds it for a few seconds, and exhales a plume of smoke. A skunky, pungent smell fills the room.

"OK," he says, putting down the bong, taking my hand and giving it a light squeeze. "So, what's the story? I haven't heard a thing from you since you wrote about losing your job, and then, out of the blue, you appear on my doorstep dressed like Oliver Twist and as shaky as an addict on Methadone day. It's all very un-Mattie Fisher." He takes a sip of coffee and he leans toward me, "Needless to say, you've piqued my interest."

"I . . ." Where to begin? I ask myself.

Patrick squeezes my hand again and senses my enveloping shock. "Relax and start from the beginning. We'll figure it out together. I'm here for you."

I exhale, slouch into the couch, and stare across the room with a blank expression. I tell him everything.

When I'm done, I think for sure that Patrick will suggest I check myself into a mental clinic. Instead, he shakes his head and says, "I apologize, honey. You don't need coffee. You need a stiff drink and a hit of this." He gestures to the bong.

I stare at him as if he was the crazy one. "You believe me?" I ask, "because, I don't even think I believe myself."

"Mattie," he confides, "if there is one thing I know for certain, you don't lie. You're incapable of fibbin'," he says, letting his Southern accent slip and staring me in the eyes. "Of course I believe you." He hesitates. "That being said, I'm wondering what that woman slipped into your drink cause I kinda want to try it."

A grin appears from the gloom on my face. Patrick will always be Patrick. "Do you think I went through some type of—transformation?"

"You're asking whether you're a goddess?"

I give an embarrassed nod. I can't believe I'm asking the question. But after the tiger man, the woman with the human head necklace, and the freak show in the park, I'm not sure what to think anymore.

Patrick's face shifts to all business. "Girl, you've always been a goddess in my mind." I feel my face blush. He continues, "No really. With or without some trippy ceremony. I ain't exactly ecstatic about the whole religion thing—given what most holy books say about my life choices. But what you're saying isn't religious. It's like anyone can be a god. It doesn't matter what you believe in. Gods are only people. Gods make mistakes. They do good and they do bad. They're drunks and they get PhDs. Heck, maybe I'm even a god, and I don't know it."

"So you don't think I'm crazy?"

"No," says Patrick with a soothing voice. "But I think those women slipped you one mean roofie, and it messed with your head bad."

"OK, that's what I thought." I finish off my coffee, turn away, my worries already traveling to all-too-familiar lands. My head drops. "This business in Salem feels like a new low in my life. I just don't know what to do anymore. Ever since I got let go from my job, it's felt like I've been drowning."

"What do you mean?" he asks.

"For the past few months, I've barely left the house. I've binge-watched more episodes of Dr. Who than I care to admit. I mean, what's the point? I don't have a job. No big plans. I've never even had a real boyfriend. It feels like I'm nothing."

Patrick makes a tsk-tsk sound. "Girl, you are smart, funny, and damn sexy." He pinches my butt.

I push away his hand. "I don't feel that way."

"Fine, if that's the case, then you need to go out there and have some fun."

"I've been trying." I shake my head. "But now that we are out of college, it's just hard to meet anyone."

"There was that one guy from Tinder."

"Patrick, he was as boring as an Ikea instruction booklet, and he never called me back."

He shrugs. "Well, I personally like the sound of this cute Jared guy. "

"The guy kidnapped me," I reply, mouth agape.

Patrick's eyes flutters. "Some of us like giving up control. I don't mind being tied down from time to time."

"The *goddess* willing," I say mockingly, "I'll never see him again."

"Too bad. I think he's the type of guy that would be good for you."

"What are you talking about?"

"You want to know?"

"Yeah."

"OK, no more kid gloves." His chin rises and he gives me a no-nonsense stare. "Mattie, for some reason you've always fallen into relationships with guys that don't respect you. I mean, most of them were losers. You deserve someone awesome. You deserve someone who is going to save you from an imagined sniper attack."

"What part of 'he drugged me' did you miss?"

"Sounds like you were really out of it, and he was trying to protect you, not hurt you."

I close my eyes and let my head fall back against the couch. I may not agree with him about Jared, but I do agree with him about my past relationships. "I don't know who I want to be, and it feels like everyone around me has their life together."

"You have to disconnect from Facebook. That shit is putting you down."

"Is it? Look at the people we went to college with. They all have jobs. They're all in relationships. They're traveling and having adventures. What am I doing with my life?"

"Well, in the past twenty-four hours you've connected with your past lives, gotten shot at, almost drowned, and escaped from an old woman's tenement prison."

My eyes roll. "Yeah, like I'm going to update my Facebook feed with pictures of me tripping. Potential employers are going to love that."

Patrick shakes his head. "You're missing the point. All you need to know is that everyone's lives are as screwed up as your own. No one has their shit together. Doesn't matter what they post to the world. Look at me, I might seem like Miss Perfect, but I'm just as fucked up as everyone else. Same is true for everyone."

"Yeah, maybe you're right," I say, in an Eeyore-esque tone. "But I still don't know what I'm going to do. I just want to be happy."

Patrick flashes a broad smile and pulls me close to him. "Then I have the perfect solution," he replies with a beaming face. "You're moving to New York City."

I eye him as if he has sprouted a second head. "Patrick, I can't move here. I have almost no cash."

"Nonsense. For the time being, mi casa es tu casa! It's what I've been saying for years. New York is where you belong."

"It's not possible," I reply. "What about Chantel?"

"Oh, he travels so much he's almost never here."

"But where do I work?" I can't believe I'm actually considering this.

"You were a waitress in college. I'm sure I can get you a job at the club. You'll make plenty of tips."

"Being a waitress is not my idea of a successful life."

"Mattie." His hand takes mine. "I want to give you a break from your reality. I want you to have some fun. Life ain't a straight road or an exam where you check off all the boxes. Sometimes you have to take a detour to get back on the path."

I smile and wonder how Patrick always knows how to say the right thing. "Really? You would let me stay here with you?" A flame of excitement lights up inside of me.

"Rent free for the time being. Have I sold you yet?"

Tears well up in my eyes. "I'll think about it."

"If that's not a 'yes' from Mattie Fisher, then I don't know what is."

"Thanks, Patrick. It means a lot to me."

"It's what friends are for."

He pulls me up and drags me toward his bedroom. "Now, I think we both need a good rest. You're exhausted, and I guarantee you'll feel great after some sleep."

I suppress a yawn with the back of my hand. "Now, there is a good life plan."

Dim light comes through the gossamer curtains when I wake up. It's dusk. A horn honks in the street. A drunk yells, and the city hums. Patrick is in a deep sleep, cuddled up in a ball, hogging most of the comforter. A ribbon of drool puddles on his pillow.

I prop myself up on one elbow. I'm calm and relaxed. Not like before, when my nerves felt like broken glass. I get out of bed, and Patrick continues to snore.

I enter the third bedroom of the apartment—Chantel's and Patrick's personal dressing room. The closets and dressers are full of extravagant clothing.

Fortunately, Patrick and I are about the same size. I find his dresser and borrow a pair of tight jeans and a lacy black top. In the closet, hundreds of shoes await on shelves going up to the ceiling. I ignore the leather high-heel boots and opt for simple blue flats. Having a drag queen for a best friend does have its perks.

As I walk down the hallway, a loud creak moans beneath me on the parquet floor. I freeze, hoping I didn't wake up Patrick. I peer down the hallway into his bedroom and find him still asleep.

I borrow his laptop, grab the spare set of keys and a few dollars from a fish bowl full of spare change, and head for the door. I don't leave a note. Once Patrick discovers his laptop missing, he will know that I'm at the closest coffee shop with Wi-Fi. Chantel has a fear that wireless devices cause cancer.

I open the door and am about to leave when my eyes land on the beat-up moose sweater. I take it because it might get cold. The sweater still smells like the ocean. My chest tightens as I remember Jared.

Outside, the air is cool. Dusk transforms into night. The City of Gods. That's what Jared called New York City. I push the thought away and turn down the street. A group of fashionable women with bodies like models walks past me. Not far behind, a pack of men follows with hungry stares.

The city is gearing up for its Saturday night Dionysian festival. No doubt, Patrick will convince me that the best medicine for my troubles is a long night of dancing.

I turn the corner and find a coffee shop. It's a typical yuppie

West Village cafe with paintings by local artists lining the walls. I order a chai tea, a five-dollar cupcake, and find a comfortable reclining chair.

I open the laptop and go to Google. I'm not crazy, and the best way to prove that is finding confirmation on the Internet. Did those women really die last night? A search of "Salem, Priestesses, Massacre" yields only costume pictures of Halloween night. There's no story in any local newspaper. It's as I thought. None of it was real.

Emails swamp my inbox as usual. I've always lived by the philosophy that it's better to keep than delete. Maybe this means I'm a future hoarder.

My eyes narrow on a new email. A charter school, with locations in Boston, New York and DC, has requested an interview with me. I can't believe it. I'd been searching for a new job for two months and hadn't even received a nibble of interest. The school says they want to interview me ASAP as the position has to be filled fast.

I smile and remember that sometimes bad things happen in order to allow good things to occur. I close the laptop and stand up fast. I need to talk with Patrick now. Together we can figure out what I should do next.

I rush out of the coffee shop. The temperature has dropped, and I put on the moose sweater. It is nighttime when I climb the steps to Patrick's brownstone. My fingers tingle, and a strange strength fills my bones. It's new energy. My life is about to change for the better, and I'm ready for it.

I bound up the steps, jumping up two at a time, my spirits raising the entire way. But when I arrive at Patrick's apartment, a sour taste floods my mouth and I can't breathe. My excitement drizzles out of me like oil from an old clunker.

The door to Patrick's apartment is ajar, and I hear voices inside.

CHAPTER ELEVEN
Popping Balloons

My feet are concrete blocks. The laptop in my arms weighs as much as a dumbbell. Why is the door open? Who's inside?

I should turn, run down the stairs, and never return. I should call the police. I should scream.

Instead, I place my hand on the cold metal doorknob and push the door open. It eases wide without a squeak. Inside the spectral apartment, a light comes from Patrick's room down the long hallway.

Despite my hammering heart, I enter, careful to avoid the patch of parquet floor that always creaks. I gulp and find my mouth as dry as gravel. One slow step after another, I inch toward Patrick's room.

The apartment gets quieter the farther I walk. My breath makes clouds in the sharp air. Halfway to Patrick's room, a shadow passes in front of the light, and I freeze.

I open my mouth and form Patrick's name on my lips, but before I utter a noise, a sharp cry cuts from the room. The sound turns my blood to ice. It's Patrick, and he's moaning in pain.

My free hand clamps down on my mouth. I grip the laptop close to my chest as if it's a talisman. I breathe faster, chest heaving. But my feet, as if directed by a puppeteer, continue their march toward the room.

Through the crack in the door, the sight drains me of any courage I might have had. Like a broken garden hose, fear gushes out in a bulging, wild torrent.

Silent shock forms in my widening eyes. Patrick lies in the center of the room on the white carpet, now stained red. His face is a Hawaiian sunset—a mélange of reds, oranges, yellows, and purples. A shut swollen eye. A split lip. A deep, fresh gash running across his cheek. I've only found him like this once before.

During our senior year, a group of lacrosse players jumped him while he was walking home from a bar. He came home broken and bruised, and worse, emotionally deflated. The attackers only got suspended because the sports community rallied behind them. Those assholes deserved jail time.

Now, desperation and dread fills Patrick's broken face. Duct tape binds his ankles and wrists. A bundled up tube sock blocks his mouth. I take a step toward the room to help him, but invisible lines of terror pull me back.

A person crosses the room. He's a troll of a man with hulking shoulders and a brown leather jacket. His military-style buzz cut frames shoe polish eyebrows and a square German profile. He looks like one of the men who chased me in Salem or one of the lacrosse players, all grown up.

A new voice chimes from the room. It's a woman's voice, and to my surprise, I recognize it. "Hold him up," she says. She wears a stylish suede jacket. A plaid schoolgirl's skirt brushes the top of her knees, revealing fishnet stocking and high black boots. She has jet black hair with a ribbon of silver through it. I can't catch a glimpse of her face, though.

The troll kneels and props up Patrick. Blood trickles from his nose, soiling his pajamas.

"Now sweetheart. Tell me," coos the woman. "Where did your little friend go?" She plucks the tube sock from his mouth.

A moan escapes his lips. Patrick shakes his head, staring down at the ground. "I don't know. I swear." His broken voice pleads, and tears roll down his cheeks.

The woman squats and faces him. "Oh, don't cry, honey. You don't need to feel any more pain. You tell me where your friend went and we'll let you be."

Patrick takes a trembling breath. "I really don't know."

The woman nods, as if understanding, and then she slaps him hard across the face. The sound makes me wince.

Patrick's head whips backward, and his face collapses into heavy sobs.

The woman turns away and at that moment, I recognize her. She was one of the women at the Witch House. One of the priestesses. What is her name? The young one with attitude. Tina? Tonya?

Tatiana. That's it. How is she here? I thought all the women died at the Witch House. Why is she torturing Patrick?

Irritation grows on Tatiana's face. She grabs Patrick's jaw and twists it toward her. "Listen, queer. We know she was here. You're lying to us and if you keep lying, we won't have any more use for you. Where is she?"

Patrick whimpers, and his head rolls away from the face of his inquisitor. His one good eye finds mine stuck in the hallway. Silently, it screams at me: *Run!*

I don't need any more encouragement. I'm getting the police. These psychos are going to pay.

I'm mid-turn when the parquet floor behind me creaks. The spot on the floor that always creaks when someone steps on it. The realization hits me a millisecond later. Someone is behind me.

I'm trapped.

On instinct, I leap into the dark dressing room. I slip into the enormous shoe closet without making a sound and close the door until there is only a crack open.

The front door closes and locks. Heavy footsteps trot down the hallway, and another man, as large and as intimidating as the other, walks by and enters Patrick's room.

"Well?" Tatiana asks with an expectant voice.

"Nothing," responds the second man, "I checked the two floors above and the basement. She's not here."

There's a brief silence. "She's probably out," Tatiana concludes. "In which case, we'll get her when she returns."

The first man speaks, "Or this fucking sissy will cooperate," a muffled cry comes from Patrick. "Then we can be done."

"Does she know other people in the city?" the second man asks.

"The teams are investigating," Tatiana replies tersely. "The girl doesn't have many friends."

"What about the job offer? Has she replied?"

"No, but that's a fallback plan. The boy all but confessed she was here. Malachi, you wait by the door. Brutus, you stay here." Malachi's bulky frame trundles down the hallway.

My mind spins. How did they know so much about me? They were the ones who sent me the job offer. How did they find out about Patrick?

"These fucking fairies," exclaims Brutus. "He's wasting our time."

"They aren't all bad," Tatiana interjects. "They have an excellent sense of style. I'm looking forward to shoe shopping in his closet."

A surprised gasp escapes from me, and I have to restrain myself from doubling over. I have to get out of here.

I force myself to calm down. The apartment is quiet except for Patrick's hoarse breathing. Tatiana and her men are taking their time and will wait for me.

I pick my brain for a plan. I place Patrick's laptop on a shelf filled with running shoes. Maybe there's a phone in the room. When I peek my head out, I hear Brutus. "Why is this girl so important?"

"It doesn't concern you," replies Tatiana. "All you need to know is that it's important to your Lord."

Brutus snorts. "You mean, Gurzil. Jesus! Couldn't Diamante choose a better name? It's fucking ridiculous."

Tatiana's voice cuts like a scalpel through the banter. "Show respect, or you'll be punished."

He ignores her threat. "You actually believe this god crap?"

"You mean, do I believe he's a god?"

"Yeah."

"Of course I do, and the sooner you start praising him as one, the quicker you will understand."

"Bull-fucking-shit," Brutus replies. "Let me tell you something, you leathery bitch. I've been rolling with Oscar Diamante since he was a punk-ass kid in Miami. We were selling blow and smuggling shit from Mexico while you were still in grade school."

"How dare you slander his name!" she cries.

"I'll give him credit for one thing. He's a deranged lunatic. I've seen him butcher enemies and still have the energy to do in their families. The things I've seen him do to a traitor would make you piss your panties. But hey, I'd rather be with him than against him."

"This is your last warning. Apologize, and he may have mercy on you."

Brutus barks a laugh. "If that sick son of a bitch is a god, then I'm Elvis fucking Presley."

"Your lack of faith has been noted," Tatiana replies coolly. "When the Purging comes, you will be punished."

"Ha! That's right. The 'Purging.' That's why we're searching for a big scary middle school teacher. The only force on earth capable of killing Diamante. Bullshit."

"If you disagree with him," she replies. "Why don't you say so to your Lord's face? I'm sure he will take your comments to heart."

The thug's tone turns serious. "I'm not stupid. What I might mention is that our time may be put to better uses. We could be bringing in heroin or cooking meth. We could be shaking down businesses or getting girls to work the streets. Instead, we're looking for a teacher who is, let me paraphrase our great leader, 'The only true threat to his existence.'"

"You're blasphemous," Tatiana replies.

The man marches out of the room and turns. "You want blasphemy." He raises both hands and extends his middle fingers. "Sit and spin, sweetheart. How's that for blasphemy?" He continues down the hallway toward Malachi.

Silence again fills the room, and the tension drowns me. I have to get out of here. Tatiana could come into the dressing room at any moment. I can't go down the hallway. They're waiting for me. I'm screwed, and I don't know what to do.

Then I hear the tapping.

It's soft and faint, like a bird's beak against a glass. For a second, I write it off to a branch scraping against the window, but it's too rhythmic to ignore.

Peering around the dark room, I realize the sound is coming from the closed window. I stick my head out of the closet. At first, I don't see anything. My eyes adjust to the dark, and I make out a face.

Jared Stone.

Despite the loathing I felt for him earlier, my muscles go weak. He wears a calm expression, but his eyes remain focused and serious. He waves me to the window.

I don't think twice. It's Jared or death.

Opening the door, I edge out of the closet. Halfway through the door, I hear Brutus. "We should take care of the fairy now."

I freeze from the implication in his voice; I can't let them hurt

Patrick.

At that moment, my eyes land on a regional Emmy that Chantel won, and I grab the heavy shiny metal award from the shelf.

"If he's not going to give us information, I don't feel like dealing with him later when we get the girl."

Maybe if I rush in, I can surprise them, but my feet refuse to move.

"Fine," replies Tatiana as if the task bores her. "You handle it. I'm going to check out the shoes."

My heart shoots up to my throat. I take two silent steps and I'm across the room, pressed against the wall next to the door, holding the Emmy to my shoulder.

A second later, Tatiana's shadow fills the door frame. She takes a step into the room, the sketch of her profile less than a foot away. Now is the moment. I should bash her with the Emmy, but I just can't do it.

"How do you want me to do it?" Brutus asks.

Tatiana inches into the room. "I don't know. Be creative." Her head jerks and she pauses. I think for sure she's discovered me, but she swivels around and returns to Patrick's room. "But keep it clean. I don't feel like dealing with a mess," she says like a shrill housewife.

I hear her high-heel boots clicking closer to the dressing room. I can't decide what to do: try to save Patrick or save myself. A second later, her body returns to the door. I raise the Emmy above my head, but still I don't strike. I don't have the will to hurt her.

"He looks like he has something to say," Brutus says, saving me as Tatiana is halfway through the door.

She spins around and goes back into Patrick's room. I whip my head back to Jared. He waves me toward the window. The realization hits me, and my chest seizes. I can't help Patrick.

I'm not brave enough.

I'm at the window a second later. Hands fumbling at the lock, I undo it and lift up the window. With a small creak, it goes up two inches and jams.

I release a frustrated whimper and push until my muscles hurt, but the window refuses to budge. I open my mouth to a silent scream—my nerves jagged. Why isn't it opening?

On the other side of the window, Jared, with anxious gestures, points, and whispers something. But I can't understand him.

"He's wasting our time." I hear Tatiana say from the other room. "Finish him."

"With pleasure, your majesty." There's a short silence and then the sound of three small balloons popping. My face melts as I realize what happened.

They murdered Patrick.

I couldn't stop them. I couldn't save him. Why am I such a coward?

"Well done. Now make sure not to get any more blood on the carpet. I'll be in the shoe closet." I hear Tatiana coming into the room. I'm out of time.

I push at the window, but it refuses to move. It's hopeless. Finally, I notice Jared's mouth, and the sounds crystallize into words: "Child lock."

My eyes flash to the window frame. Sure enough, two plastic pegs prevent the window from sliding up. I push them in and pull up. The window eases open without a sound.

I toss myself out the window, and the cold air hits my face. Jared grabs me and pushes my head down, and we both lie belly-down on the metal fire escape.

A second later, I hear Tatiana enter the room. "Hey!" she calls out. "Did you leave the window open?"

An interminable, fragile silence follows the words. The slightest suspicion will mean our discovery.

"I think it was open when we arrived," Brutus replies.

I let out a desperate sigh, but the next moment, Tatiana's

hands appear on the windowsill. She's over us, staring at the lit street. All she would have to do is lower her head, and she would find us.

"Don't touch me!" screams a voice.

My eyes turn, and I spy two figures down the street. A woman shoves back a man. "I don't want you coming up, so fuck off!"

The man says something, and the woman screams, "Screw you!"

Instead of glancing down, Tatiana is focused on the action.

"Good for you, girl," Tatiana whispers.

The figures fight for what feels like an eternity. All the while, Tatiana watches them. Lying flat on our stomachs. I'm so close to her that I can smell her peonies-scented perfume.

Finally, she exhales, grows bored, and shoves down the window with a loud oomph.

The next instant, Jared crawls away from the window and gestures me to follow. We crawl to the fire escape's ladder and descend. He helps me down to the ground.

Jared grabs my hand and yanks me away. I run as fast as I can. The sound of those three balloons popping echoes over and over again.

CHAPTER TWELVE
Book of Gods

We run to 14th street—crammed with traffic and bustling people. Jared rushes me down into the subway. We wait on the
platform for the next train. I don't care that Tatiana and her men
could arrive at any moment. I don't care how close they came to
finding me. I'm catatonic.

They murdered Patrick. Nothing makes sense.

The train arrives with screeching brakes and ear-blasting cer-
titude. Jared pulls me inside and sits me down on an empty
bench.

All I can think about is Patrick. I lost him. My best friend.
Dead. I slump down. None of the other passengers make eye
contact or notice my grief.

A man, dressed in soiled jeans, a ripped warm-up jacket, and
military boots, comes onto the train and makes a speech about
being a veteran. Jared gives him a ten-dollar bill. The soldier
pats him on the back and moves onto the next car.

The train jolts to a stop. A voice crackles from the speakers
and announces that there will be delays because of track work.

A collective moan slips from the other passengers.

Jared sighs, and his tension ratchets up. He runs his hand through his brown hair and pushes it away from his eyes. He scans the subway car with U-boat-like vigilance.

"How did you find me?" I ask, my voice heavy with exhaustion.

Jared's upturned lip is a reply unto itself. "The same way *they* found you." I don't need him to explain that "they" are Patrick's murderers. He reaches into his pocket and retrieves an iPhone. He plugs in a code and shows me my Facebook page.

"You Facebook-stalked me?"

Jared shrugs. "You should be careful what you put on the internet. It was an easy assumption you would go to him."

My face crumbles from the realization. It breaks me to think that the message I sent to Patrick about getting fired was the reason for his death. "Why did they kill him?" I whisper. "He had nothing to do with them."

Jared tries to gaze at me without emotion, but a flicker of sympathy crosses his face. He realizes now what type of state I'm in. He sits down beside me and leans close. "They want you, and they'll kill anyone that stands in the way."

My hands clench into white-knuckle fists. In the reflection of the subway's windows, I catch a glimpse of a foreign, smoldering anger in my green eyes. "We need to call the police."

He shakes his head. "That will lead them to you."

"Stop being a paranoid fuck!" I say, louder than I intended. Nearby passengers shoot me raised eyebrows. I lower my voice. "They murdered my best friend. They're going to pay."

To my surprise, Jared takes my hand and squeezes it. Empathy fills his blue eyes. The hard edge in his voice disappears. "Don't let his death be in vain," he says. "Stay alive. That's the most important thing."

I take a deep breath. His words help to quell the storm inside me. I let some of my anger drip out, but not all of it. "No. The most important thing is getting justice. Who is she?"

"Her name is Tatiana Williams. She was one of the priestesses in Salem."

"Yeah, I figured that out," I say, my eyes narrowing. I pull my hand from his grasp. "Your cult really recruited some winners."

Jared winces and he rubs the heel of his palm against his chest. "Obviously, they would have never revealed the secrets of the priestesses to Tatiana if they knew her true nature. She was a spy, and I know for a fact that none of the priestesses ever suspected her."

"There was no attack," I reply. "I checked online. There was no mention of a massacre."

"Don't you realize now how powerful your enemies are?" Jared asks, his shoulders quaking and chin trembling. "They can hide the cold-blooded murder of a dozen women, and you're surprised that they found you in New York?"

His words send new shivers through me. "Why is Tatiana after me?"

"She's working for the god who is trying to kill you."

I sigh and pinch the bridge of my nose. "Stop bringing up this delusional crap." A few of the nearby passengers get up from their seats and move to the opposite side of the car. I don't care. "You can live in your fantasy world all you want, but I don't want any part of it. So cut the god crap."

He shrugs and stares ahead with tired eyes. "Whatever you want."

"Where are we going?"

"Somewhere safe." He doesn't elaborate or turn in my direction.

I glare at him. "Tell me where we are going."

He sighs and replies, "We're going to the Prophet."

"The who?"

"An Ascended god like you. He will know where we can find another coven of priestesses."

"Wait, hold up," I say. "You're saying we have to go talk to some crazy person, who will tell me how to find more crazy women."

Jared shakes his head. "They weren't crazy, and yes, we need to talk with the Prophet."

I smile at the idiocy of his statements and how he expects me to follow him without question. "Why exactly?"

"You need to complete your Ascension. The ceremony was interrupted."

"Ha!"

"What's funny?"

"I'm not going through that psychedelic head trip again. I'm a teacher. I don't eat acid like it's Pez candy."

"What's your point?"

I stare at him as if he's from Jupiter. How can one man be so thick? "There's no way I'm going through that ceremony again."

He rotates and regards me with fierce eyes. "Do you want to die like your friend?" His question makes my blood run cold and lips tremble. "You have to trust me. These people are out for your head, and I'm the only one who can help you." He rounds on me, and a fire lights up in his eyes. A passion and anger that I didn't know existed. "If you had stayed where I put you, none of this would have happened."

My shoulders and neck tighten. "You think you're going to gain my trust by imprisoning me?"

"No, I've already proven myself after I saved you the second time."

The truth in his words cuts deeper than I thought. Before Patrick was murdered, I could write everything off to a hallucination, but it's hard denying the truth after his death. In short, my very understanding of reality is slipping through my fingers. After what happened to Patrick, my faith in the old rules of the world is broken.

I stare at him for a long time. "Fine, we'll go see your Prophet friend. But I'm not drinking anything you give me, and I have questions of my own."

Jared turns away. My declaration is nothing more than he expected.

The subway starts up again, and we get off in the East Village. The night energy builds like a tsunami. Hoards of hipsters and uptown socialites gather for a night of debauchery. Jared guides me down the dark and trash-laden avenues of Alphabet City. Domestic squabbles erupt from bodegas.

We arrive at a brownstone with a tall gate blocking it off from the street. Lights brighten all five floors of the building. The immaculate structure stands in contrast to its neighbors, which are one health inspector violation away from demolition.

Jared pushes the button on the intercom. "It's me. I've brought her."

The gate buzzes, and the door swings open. Inside the foyer, it smells of sandalwood incense. An elevator at the end of a bamboo-paneled hallway opens automatically. Buddhist chanting hums from hidden speakers as we get off on the top floor. A frail Asian man dressed in layered white robes greets us with a silent, meditative face and a bow. He has to be at least 100-years-old. The man gestures for us to follow him, and he deposits us in a library with books lining its shelves.

"I will notify him that you've arrived," says the man before disappearing.

I sit down in a chair in front of a long table. Jared searches the bookshelf, running his fingers down the spines of the ancient volumes. Finally, he removes an oversized leather-bound book. It's about the size of a Webster dictionary and appears as if it was handmade centuries ago. He slams it down on the table releasing a cloud of dust.

The cover's title reads *The Ascended Gods.*

I groan, turning away from the book. "Not this again."

"Yes," Jared replies, and he grabs my shoulder with an iron

grip, twisting me to face the book. He points down to the page. "It's time you understand a few things."

My spine calcifies to a steel rod. He might not look like it, but the guy is strong. He flips through the pages. He points down to a colorful picture.

The title reads: Gaia

It's a picture of a woman wearing a white dress with blond hair spilling over her body. Rich brown earth anchors her bare feet. "You need to accept that this is your reality."

"I'm not a blonde, and I'm not a god," I say, through gritted teeth. "When are you going to get this through your stubborn thick skull?"

Jared's eyebrows raise. "You're telling me that things haven't been different? I remember what you told me on the boat. The guy in the SUV—you saw him differently." I remember the man with the bull-head and the blood red aura, and my stomach twists into pretzel knots. "Gertrude—" His voice catches and his lower lip trembles for a split second before he continues, "I mean, the priestesses didn't complete your Ascension, but they got through a lot of it. Some part of you has reawakened. Some part of you has Ascended. Haven't you seen anything strange today?"

How could he know about the tiger man and the woman with the human head necklace? But I can't acknowledge those things. A part of me won't allow it. "No!" I reply. "Everything has been the same."

"You're lying," Jared replies, seeing through me.

"You drugged me with something, and I've been hallucinating!" I shove the book off the table, and it hits the floor. "I'm sick of you and sick of your lies. I'm calling the police. I should have never come here." I stand up to leave, but as I take my first step for the door, I glance down at the book.

The picture staring back at me makes my stomach cramp even more. The image is too familiar. It's a goddess with skin as black as a moonless night. Tangled wild hair and a red serpent's tongue. I stop, lean down, and inspect it closer. The goddess wears a necklace of human heads. My pulse drums with every heavy heartbeat.

The name at the top of page reads *Kali*.

Jared notices my expression. His eyes jump from the picture and to me. "You've seen her, haven't you?"

Without answering, I reach down and pick up the book. I read the title description.

Kali—the Indian goddess of time, change, and destruction.

"How is it possible?" I ask in a whisper, "I saw her on the street. I don't understand how."

Jared shrugs. "New York City is the City of Gods. Some of the most ancient deities walk the streets without even an inkling that they are older than time itself." He points down at the book, "There are hundreds of thousands throughout the world."

A tingling intuition flutters in my chest. My fingers possess a life of their own as I flip through more pages. Until I reach one that explodes like a bombshell in my mind. My jaw drops; it can't be true.

The page reads *Gurzil*.

A picture of a bull-headed man accompanies the name. A god of war from Berber mythology. It's the same image of the man who chased us in Salem.

I remember Tatiana's conversation. "Gurzil. That's the name of the man who is after me." I turn to Jared. "Do you know him?"

He winces and curls up his lip. "I've heard of him."

"What have you heard?"

"Not good things." He pushes the book to the side.

I spin away, a massive weight pressing down on me. My knees feel weak. "This guy, Gurzil, he isn't going to stop looking for me?"

"He will keep on searching no matter what. His mission is to kill you, and he's not a guy. He's a god, like you."

"Why does he want me dead?"

Jared shakes his head. "He fears you."

But why does he fear me? I take back the book and flip through its pages. Hundreds of gods flash before my eyes. Why doesn't Gurzil fear any of them? A word jumps up from one of the pages, and I remember something. "Tatiana mentioned that I was needed for some type of Purging. Do you know what that means?"

Jared suddenly turns away and slams the book shut, sending a fresh cloud of dust into the air. Before I can question him further, the robed man returns.

He stares at me with expressionless, drooping eyes. "He's ready for you. Come this way."

CHAPTER THIRTEEN
The Prophet

The old man leads us up a stairway to the roof. He pushes open a thick door inscribed with a foreign language. The outside air has a chill bite to it, and the remnants of the warm day fade with the onslaught of the cloudy night sky.

I gape, wide-eyed, at the structure before us. It's a Roman temple. It's not huge, but still, it's impressive in contrast to the surrounding brownstones of the East Village. It's new—not like the ruins you'd find at archaeological sites. Two rows of polished marble colonnades run parallel, and hold up an arched roof of heavy wooden beams. In between the pillars, fires dance in massive bronze basins. Violin music drifts toward us; Jared and I exchange a baffled look. He appears as astounded as I that this place exists.

Our escort leads us through a metal gate, which he closes behind us. I notice an eight-foot mesh fence topped with razor wire that surrounds the perimeter of the temple and courtyard.

The man abruptly stops and raises his walking staff toward the glowing interior of the temple, where shadows scamper.

We proceed across a wide-open marble-tiled courtyard. Along the facade of the temple, I notice inscribed more of the same strange language. We walk into the temple and pass the burning basins. On the far side of the temple, we hear the source of the violin and discern an outline of a figure. When we get close, we find a tiny man with his back to us reclining on a psychiatrist couch. The man wears a pristine white robe, draped over his shoulders and folded around his body with precise skill. He plays the violin as if it's his last day to live. The song is passionate and wild, while at the same time, controlled and precise. At first, it has qualities of something classical, but every tenth note or so, it reminds me of something I would hear from a Top 40 station.

When we are within a few feet, the song screeches to halt. The man puts down the violin, and he turns toward us. My breath seizes as if it's sucked from my body.

A radiant blue aura shrouds two rugged faces. Each face stares in the opposite direction but each connects to the same head, which blossoms with gray curls. His wrinkled, grooved faces speak of experience and time. But what really grabs my attention are his four golden eyes. They are as deep as quarries.

"So it's true. You've returned," intone the faces in one voice.

The voice doesn't match the body. The image of the two faces flickers, and after a second, flutters and fades. I gasp when I peer upon the true person lurking under the illusion. "You're a child," I say.

It's a young boy, no older than ten years. He has a bowl cut of brown hair. He's small, and my first thought is that he could use a milkshake every day to fatten up. The only thing that remains the same are the curious eyes, which stare at me unyielding. The little boy pouts as if I took away his iPad. "I am no child," he says with petulance. "And I'm not accustomed to petitioners insulting me in my own temple. I should have my priest toss you back onto the street."

Beside me, the old man grins, and I wonder how the priest would be able to toss us out without cracking a hip.

Jared leans to my ear. "Mattie, bow!"

I stare at him as if *he* has two faces. "Why?" I ask. "He's not even in middle school. The kid needs a time out," I shoot my best teacher eyes at the little brat.

"We need him." There is a pleading urgency in Jared's voice. "He was the only god I could contact who was willing to see you. If you insult him, he will not help us."

I remember Tatiana and her thugs, and my fists clench. I want her to pay for Patrick's sake. If that means sucking up to a little prince playing Roman dress-up, then I can swallow my pride.

Sighing, I turn back to the boy, curtsy, and declare, "My deepest apologies, oh, Prophet."

The boy analyzes me with Preying Mantis eyes. "You have no idea who I am?"

"The Prophet?" I answer, but this doesn't satisfy his demanding face, so I add, "Some god?"

His eyes thin to serpent slits, and his voice deepens. "You can know me by the only name your tiny mind would recognize."

"Which is?"

His voice rises like a chorus from a Greek tragedy. "The Guardian of the past and future. The Portender of War and Peace. The fortune teller. The future reader. The god of a thousand cultures and older than time itself. I am Janus!" he declares with booming self-importance.

I can't help but snort with laughter. The boy's face bunches up with annoyance.

Jared elbows me in the side and hisses, "Janus, the Roman God."

"Wow, isn't he special?" I reply and turn back to the little god. "My deepest apologies, oh great Janus. I was surprised by your appearance."

Janus reclines, staring at me with his metallic eyes. "I'm new to this body and this life. Why are you surprised to be address-ing a god of any age? The Ascension can occur at any age. You, above all, know this as truth."

Why would I know this better? But something else begs my attention. "Wait. You went through the ceremony with the witches, the trippy hallucinations, and the chanting?"

"You mean the Ascension?" Janus responds, incredulity lin-gering in his tone. Then, a realization crystallizes his expression. "You are still Descended. Interesting," he says, surprised.

"So, when did you Ascend?"

"A new vessel was chosen prior to my last death."

"By vessel, you mean a baby?"

"Of course. When I died in my last life, my priests performed the Ascension, and I was reborn into this body."

I shake my head, not believing any of this. "First of all, how could they do that to a baby? I mean, that's child abuse."

"A newborn baby is a blank canvass, and although my body is a child's, my mind is thousands of years old. This is the way that it has always been done."

"Why?" I ask.

"You—who are not even fully Ascended—want to under-stand why?" Janus dismisses me with fluttering eyes, filled with impatience. "Do not waste my time with such profound ques-tions when you don't even know the simplest of truths. Now ask me the real questions for which you seek answers."

"How many questions do I get?"

"Do you think I'm a Jinn?" he questions. "You can ask as many as you want."

"Where can we find a new group of priestesses?" Jared asks.

The boy's eyes blaze with anger. "Silence, mortal! I only speak to gods."

Jared withdraws, head bowed. I can't believe this kid just put him in his place. "This is too weird," I mutter to myself. The boy taps his foot, but I already know my first question. "Why do certain people look weird? For example, you looked different from when I first saw you."

Janus examines his fingernails. "You have the ability to see other gods."

"What does that mean?"

He swings his legs off the couch. "You're seeing their deistic form—the eternal image that identifies them. This is one of the gifts that we, the Ascended, have. We can identify each other. You are seeing other gods and goddesses like you. Some are Ascended, while others are Descended."

"The majority of gods are Descended," I say, remembering Jared's words.

"True," Janus confirms. "Only a small fraction are aware of their true nature."

"Why can't every god Ascend?"

"Each god is unique, and each requires a different ceremony to conduct the Ascension. Also, only the priestesses and priests can control the Ascension so that a god can reincarnate into a specific body. Sometimes, through history, the details of the ceremonies are lost. The gods are killed or die unexpectedly. Every time a god's body dies, the god is brought back into life as a new person. But we all begin in a Descended state. Only after the Ascension do we become aware of our true selves."

"How is this possible? The whole idea of gods and goddesses doesn't make any sense. In terms of science, how does reincarnation occur?"

Janus scoffs. "Once you complete your Ascension, you will realize that there is much more mystery and magic in the world than there is science to explain it. I remember when it was a fact that the earth was flat, when the stars in the sky were our dead ancestors, when fire was prized over gold. All truths are eventually overturned. Everything will become clearer once you fully Ascend."

I gulp because he hit upon a concern that has been creeping

up on me like a bad cold. "What will actually happen when I Ascend?"

"You will remember your past lives. All of them. Down to incredible detail."

"During the ceremony, I saw things. Were those my—my past lives?" I ask.

"Exactly. The Ascension ceremony unlocks those memories."

"But I can't remember any past lives now."

"It appears as though your Ascension ceremony was interrupted. You're stuck in what is called a limbo state. It's very rare, but it has been known to occur. You can't tap into the knowledge of your past lives. It lies beneath the surface of your psyche. This explains why you can see the true forms of gods but can't remember your own lives. Have you had any dreams?"

I take a sharp breath and nod, remembering the dream of the Muslim girl trapped in the prison.

"Those dreams are memories and experiences from your past lives," Janus says, "when you fully Ascend, your past lives will merge with your current identity."

"What do you mean they will merge?"

"You will become a new person."

"You mean, I will stop being me?" It's like a troupe of dancers launch a series of high kicks in my stomach.

"In a way, yes, but in a way, no. Because you did not Ascend at birth, your current life will be the dominant one. But you will transform into a new person. You will certainly speak dozens, if not hundreds, of languages. You will have skills and knowledge that were before inaccessible. For example, if you were a doctor in a past life, you will have all the knowledge of healing."

"But who will I become when I Ascend?"

"Like me, you've been known by many names, but perhaps Gaia is the best."

"That's what the priestesses in Salem called me."

His voice detaches from emotion. "You are the Earth goddess.

The goddess of motherhood. The giver of life. You have been a mother to humankind since humans were still living out of caves. You were the first to help mankind evolve. You have lived more lives than even me. You're one of the oldest goddesses."

My brain might as well have been dropped into a pinball machine. I don't know what to think. "If I'm so great, why is someone out to kill me? They've already killed my best friend." The thought of Patrick brings me close to tears, but I suppress the rising emotion.

For the first time, a spark of empathy enters his eyes. "When you complete your Ascension, you will learn that, like mortals, some gods and goddesses are petty and evil. Some view their immortality as a justification for cruelty. They live forever; therefore, they should dominate all. You already know who is trying to kill you?"

"Gurzil," I whisper, the name sending the hairs on my neck on end.

"You know what he stands for and what he is capable of."

"But why me? Why do I need to die?"

"Some things you are ready to hear. Others take time to understand."

"And what is the Purging? I heard them mention it," I ask, my voice hesitant. "Is that why they're after me?"

Janus shakes his head and twists away. "I know your future already. I was the one who prophesied your fate."

"What prophecy?"

"That the Goddess will die and be reborn in the City of Peace on the day the dead arise."

I try to remember the words that Alice recited to me. Somehow it's connected. But I can't recall any of the specifics. "So, Salem on Halloween?" I turn to Jared. "But how did you know that I was going to be in Salem? I didn't even know I was going to be there. It was a spur of the moment, random decision."

"*Salem* derives from *Shalom* in Hebrew, meaning peace," replies Jared. "But perhaps what you think was an impulse was actually fate."

"The conclusion of the last parts of the prophecy are near," says Janus. "You must first complete your Ascension to understand the greater truths and understand what is at stake."

He's keeping something from me. First Jared and now Janus. Why am I so important? I need to somehow force them to tell me the truth.

"What if I don't want any of this? Is there any way to reverse the Ascension and go back to the person I once was? To forget everything and become a teacher again. Can I do that?"

"You can't change who you are." His eyes light up with ferocity. "Pandora's box has been opened, and you must accept the truth. There is no greater power than the truth. Know thyself, and you will know all."

As if to emphasize this point, a high-pitched alarm tears through the night. The sound deafens, and I spiral around, confused. That's when I notice Janus's eyes are wide with fear. "You must go now. You are in great danger," he warns. He turns to his servant and commands, "Escort them away."

"Hold up!" I say. "Where do we go?" I turn around, and the old man stands behind us. Grabbing my hand with a force greater than I thought possible, he pulls me toward the exit. The alarm screams, causing my head to spin. Jared's face crinkles with concern as his eyes shoot to the exit. "Wait!" I yell to Janus who follows behind us. "What do we do now?"

After I ask the question, raw surprise ignites his face. I turn to follow his gaze, and terror shutters through me.

A bull-head and blood red aura emerge from the stairwell. Gurzil steps onto the roof, and hatred burns in his expression. Followed behind him are Tatiana, Brutus, and Malachi.

Jared pulls me back from the exit to the temple, and the old man stands firm in the gateway he just opened.

"I told you that she would seek out the Prophet," Tatiana says with a smile.

"You may not enter here if you intend harm to the goddess," Janus declares. I turn around and find the ten-year-old ready to throw a temper tantrum.

"Silence, Prophet," Gurzil cries. "You have sworn an oath not to take sides in the Purging. Yet you give sanctuary to our greatest enemy?"

"As per the oath, all who seek their future can come here without fear and be safe while they are in the temple."

"Technicalities that will soon be forgotten. I don't have time for this foolishness."

"Careful, young god," Janus warns. "Do not dare break promises which were made before you existed."

Gurzil dismisses him with a wave of his hand. He turns to Brutus and Malachi. "Get me the goddess."

They rush forward, but the old man doesn't flinch. He's about to get crushed by the twin linebackers barreling toward him.

Just as Brutus is about to crash into him, the old man steps to the side. Brutus trips over the man's walking stick and flies headfirst into the gate. He crashes into it and crumples into a dazed pile.

Malachi comes next and throws a punch at the old man, who again sidesteps the blow. He swings his walking stick, and it cracks with a painful snap on Malachi's kneecap. The man collapses to the ground, howling. The priest raises his stick and smashes it down on Malachi's head. The old man hasn't even broken a sweat. He stands relaxed in the gateway.

"This is ridiculous," Gurzil roars. He reaches into his jacket, retrieves a handgun, and aims it at the man.

Tatiana pulls down on his arm. "Don't hurt the priest. You will be punished," she warns.

With a rough swipe, Gurzil pushes her away. "Do not tell a god what he can do." He levels the gun at the old man and shoots him. Blood spews out from the priest's chest. I cry out. The man stumbles backward, his face still a mask of calm bliss. As he falls back into the fenced-in area, he hits a hidden button, and the gate slams shut and locks.

Gurzil screams, and the next moment, Jared grabs my hand and pulls me behind one of the marble columns. Gunshots blast, and pieces of stone splinter into the air.

Janus cowers behind his couch, and Jared and I remain exposed on the rooftop. We're stuck. Jared scans the top of the building, searching for any way to escape. Despite the flying bullets, his expression is calm.

"What do we do?"

"Fire escape. Now."

Before I have a chance to respond, he drags me to the other side of the roof—across the exposed expanse of the temple's interior. I think for sure we're going to get hit. Gurzil reloads his gun. Brutus steadies himself against the fence. Tatiana assists Malachi from the ground.

As soon as we get behind the column, a bullet ricochets near my head. The temple's wall provides cover for Jared. He leans over the side of the building, but the next moment, he spins around frustrated. He curses. "They removed the fire escape."

My heart sinks, and fresh fear floods into me. I hear a new sound—like metal clashing. I peek around the column, and Brutus kicks at the gateway. It's only a matter of time before it falls.

I pull my head back as another gun blast blows off a piece of marble. To shield my eyes from the mist of rock, I spin around. That's when I notice that something's changed.

"Jared, look." I point to the psychiatrist couch. "Janus is gone. Where did he go?"

He smiles. "There must be another way off the roof."

The gun blasts once, twice. On the third blast, Jared sprints off with me in tow. As we cross the open space, I glance over to the gateway. Gurzil slams a fresh clip into his gun and raises his hand toward us. Brutus and Malachi kick away at the weakened and bent metal gate.

We throw ourselves behind the psychiatrist couch. Jared flips the couch on its side. As it lands, a fresh rain of bullets collides against it.

We discover the trapdoor on the ground. Jared leans over and pulls up hard, but the door remains shut. "Come on. Open up!" The veins on his neck bulge, and his face reddens, but the door doesn't budge.

I pound on the door with my fists. "Janus, let us down. Please!"

But instead of a response, all I hear is a distant noise—like a chained animal fighting for freedom.

Jared's face twists with exertion. He slams his fists on the door, cursing at the top of his lungs.

A splintering crack draws my attention back to Gurzil. The metal gateway hangs limp and broken from its hinges. One more kick and they will be through.

My pulse hammers as a clawing desperation tears at my insides. The trapdoor—our only chance to escape—isn't going to open.

The tightness in my chest hurts so much I can barely breathe. We're out of options.

That's when I hear the sound of air being beaten into submission. It's a distant noise, but getting closer. It's like a hurricane. I stare out from behind the couch, but winds buffer me back. I hug the couch expecting to be blown away.

The wind diminishes, and a helicopter descends into the courtyard, blocking Gurzil from us.

It touches down. A woman with fiery red hair sits in the cockpit, staring at me. Over an intercom, her voice booms. "Get in!"

I hesitate and turn to Jared. "Can we trust her?"

"We don't have a choice," he says, nodding toward Gurzil.

We sprint to the awaiting helicopter. The force of the rotors sends my hair into a wild swirl.

After climbing into the back, I hear Gurzil's gunshots ping off the side. Malachi and Brutus kick down the gate and rush toward us. But the chopper has already begun its ascent.

"Keep your head down," Jared warns.

But instead, I rush up to the cockpit where I find the woman with radiant hair and skin paler than a vampire's.

"Who are you?" I ask.

"My name is Caroline, and I am here to escort you to my employer," she replies as if she is a New York City cabdriver.

"How can we trust you?"

The pilot rolls up her sleeve and on her inner arm is a tattoo. It's the same jagged crescent moon which is on the side of my face. "I'm here to serve the Mother Goddesses." She returns her gaze to the front and yells, "Hold on! This is going to get rough."

The helicopter lifts up, banks sharply to the right, and curves away from the temple. Gurzil—furious and fuming—aims his gun at us. His bullets ricochet off the hard plastic front window. Malachi and Brutus stand where the helicopter was only moments ago, fists raised.

We're flying, but no sooner are we a hundred yards away that smoke billows into the helicopter.

"Are we going to be OK?" I ask Caroline.

"He hit some part of the engine, and we're losing pressure fast, but I think we should be able to get to the jet."

"Jet? Wait, where are we going?"

The next moment, a loud beeping comes from the control panel. A red light blinks angryily. "Get into a seat and buckle up. We may need to make an early landing," Caroline says.

Jared takes my hand and leads me away. "Mattie, we can't go back," he says, reading my thoughts.

I spin around. The dirty brown smoke of the engine clouds the city. He's right. There is no going back.

CHAPTER FOURTEEN
Le Marquis

The first time we made love was in the back of the linen closet. I'd gone to fetch clean sheets for the guest suites, and he had surprised me. There was no fumbling excuse, no "Pardon Mademoiselle," no hesitation. He advanced with brown eyes blazing and a parted, hungry mouth.

The Marquis pinned me against the towel shelves. His lips pressed against mine, and his hands undid the clasps of my dress and corset with suspicious skill. I tried pushing him away.

He held my thigh tight and raised my knee. His tongue tickled at my earlobe, and eager but gentle hands touched my bare skin. My defenses melted, as washcloths cascaded down around me like falling leaves.

We were probably heard halfway across the Château. The truth was simple: I was more afraid of him stopping than of being found out. I didn't know how much I needed him—wanted him—until he made the move that I'd desired for months.

His wife and children were away visiting her parents in Nice. She had taken most of the servants with her. Although we were not discov-

ered that first time, later on, a part of me wished we had been.

I had had lovers in the past. Not many, but enough to be no foolish maiden. None were like this affair. Every encounter was like drinking from a glass of sweet wine—one sip encouraged another.

We became intoxicated off one another, and our lovemaking was feverish. Even when I was asleep, my dreams relived our meetings. Each touch, each mumbled word, each caress was examined, categorized, and remembered.

I had heard rumors that I was not the first servant that he had seduced, but I held onto a feeble hope that I was the first to whom he confessed love.

The intensity of that one week atoned for a lifetime of passionless pursuits. I felt more alive than I'd ever thought possible. My senses found details that before had remained hidden: his flush lips, the scratch of his evening beard, his voice growling deep, the way that our smells intermingled along with our bodies—creating a maddening bouquet.

The last time we made love was in his marriage bed. With tears mounting in my eyes like an overrun spring dam, I told him that it couldn't continue. Despite his petitions, his promises, his confessions, I was firm in my resolve.

Now, through his mask, he stares at me with burning eyes. The same expression he had in the linen closet.

I give a faint but decisive shake of my head—as if to push an itch away. This can't happen again. Especially not here, not now.

Distracted by the intensity of his gaze, I stumble into someone. A wine glass slips from a hand, and its contents splatter on my white apron.

I don't immediately recognize the woman leading the entourage because of her elaborate mask. But a second later, horror floods through me, as I notice the billowing crimson gown embroidered with gold flowers, the pearls as fat as quail eggs, and the frilled white blouse.

"Watch where you're going, you stupid girl," scolds the wife of the Marquis. "I nearly spilled wine on myself."

I touch the purple blossom stain on my front. "My apologies, my lady," I reply, keeping my stare fixed at the ground.

Her venomous expression is not hidden by her gold and silver mask. "You waddle like a duck," she spits. One of her friends titters at the comment. Encouraged by the reaction, she adds, "And you have the hooves of a mule."

"As you say."

"Farm girls," she says with a dismissive glance to her friend. "I would give my left hand for a properly trained Parisian maid."

She flips out a fan and waves it on herself with an aggressive flutter. "Your pay will be docked if your apron needs replacing," she continues, before turning away from me. "The dessert table needs replenishing. Get a new apron before going out. You look disgusting."

I curtsy and fight the urge to say that cows have better manners than she. "Oui, my lady." I spin around and rush back to the frenzy of the kitchen.

As I pile Bonbons onto my tray, my friend Emma comes up beside me. She sticks out her tongue, and says, "I heard her out there. She's a bitch in heat." I flash a tiny smile. Emma, too, has gotten the ill-attention of the Marquis's wife. She lowers her voice and confides, "Tonight after the masquerade, we are gathering in Francois's room. He has stolen a bottle of Cognac."

"I will try to make it if I'm not tired."

"Good, because I think Francois has eyes for you," she teases.

I shrug and fight back tears. Why does she get to be his wife? She, who is so undeserving and selfish. It's not fair. I turn to go, but Emma catches my arm, "Don't forget your mask," she adds. I slip on the paper mask adorned with stars and swirls.

At the dessert table, the Marquis intercepts me. He pulls me behind an ice sculpture of a swan imported all the way from the Alps.

"Why do you ignore me?" he accuses, voice hurt.

"I told you. We cannot continue this. Forget me."

He grabs my arm. "I will do no such thing."

"It is for the best."

"I don't care what is for the best!" His outburst draws the attention of two whispering ladies.

I raise the tray of Bonbons to appease his anger. *"Why won't you leave me be?"* I whisper through gritted teeth.

"I have something to tell you."

My eyes dart away. The aristocrat women have turned their attention to a young man spilling more Champagne on his shirt than in his mouth. Each bottle equal to one month of my wages. The aristocrats waste wine like the peasant children of my village waste their youths. *"Not here."*

A sensibility returns to his crazed eyes as he realizes that we are in the center of the entire room. *"Meet me in the garden of Eros,"* he declares before disappearing into the crowd.

I survey and spy his wife on the other side of the room—being entertained by the dancers. The piece is the newest by Mozart. No one will notice my absence if I'm quick. I take my tray of desserts and pretend to offer them to guests. They are too full of wine to care.

Outside, the summer heat has cooled. It's a moonless night, and the stars spread out like crystals into the horizon. Checking behind me, I place the tray onto the ground and hurry off.

As I navigate around the hedges, I hear more than one bush rustle from the presence of hushed love making. A groan here. A flash of white flesh. As the burning lights of the Château dim in the shades of the garden, so do inhibitions.

When I get to the clearing, all I find is a winged cupid statue balancing on one foot in a fountain of still water. The calm of the garden is in contrast to my wildly beating heart.

The Marquis surprises me, and I let out a yelp that I fear will attract attention. He lifts me off my feet and carries me to a secluded corner of the grove under a hanging trellis of flowers. His lips advance on my neck, and I melt at his touch.

Despite the burning inside of me, I push him away with soft strikes to his chest. *"We can not continue this. You are married. You have children,"* I insist, tears of anger forming in my eyes.

"We can. We will. You mean everything to me."

"Lies," I say, turning away. "You're from a different world."

"Then let us escape to a new world."

I don't understand his expression. "What do you mean?"

"We can sail for New Orleans. I own property there. We can establish a new life for ourselves."

"What about your wife? And children?"

"She cares more for the newest fashions than for a man. My children call my wife's father 'papa' instead of me. I will only be happy when I am away from them."

"You can't be serious." He says this all too simply.

"They don't know true passion. They will never know what we have."

I cannot let him seduce me. He will ruin me, but his hand runs along my side. His mouth finds my ear and again, my resistance fades. As he unbuttons my blouse, I realize I've thrown my lot with him. For this one moment—this instant—I will believe him.

The jet banks hard, and my ears pop from the sudden altitude change. I bolt up, adrenaline rushing, and release a heavy breath. A layer of warm sweat sticks to my clothes. My whole body is as hot as freshly baked bread.

Now *that* was a dream.

I close my eyes to recall the lingering passion. I wouldn't mind having that dream every night, but my wry smile fades. If I'm to believe Jared, then that was no dream. It was a past life.

I search my memory for more details of the woman—grappling for any clue of who she was. But all my memories are constrained to that one moment in her life. I run my hands down the side of my body, remembering the touch of the Marquis. Despite myself, I groan.

"Are you OK?" Jared asks.

My face turns the color of tomato juice. I sink low into the plush, beige seat. More embarrassed than I can ever imagine, I stare at the curved ceiling of the private jet, avoiding his eyes. I dip a bar napkin into a cup of water and press it against my neck. The coolness against my skin calms me down. "Yep, everything's fine." I muster the courage to gaze at him.

Jared is apparently having a heart attack. He grips the armrests with white knuckles, while his face is purple. His clenched teeth make him appear as though he's enduring a Civil War amputation.

"What's wrong?"

Jared takes a ragged breath. "I'm not a fan of air travel."

"You're afraid of flying?" I can't believe it. This guy was as cool as a Klondike Bar when people were shooting at him.

He shrugs and stares forward with an intensity that could burn a hole in the seat back.

"Is there anything I can do to make you feel better?"

The plane bucks from a bout of turbulence. "M-m-maybe keep talking." He trembles. "It helps distract me."

"OK," I rack my brain. After a few seconds, I smile. "How about I tell you a joke?"

"Sure. Anything."

"What's a bagel that can fly?"

His head shakes and he shrugs.

"Give up? A plain bagel."

"That was stupid," he says, but his grip on the armrests has loosened.

"Hey! My usual audience is 12-year-olds, and they think it's hilarious."

Jared sucks back when the plane bucks again. "What did you teach?" he asks fast.

"English."

"I always liked English class."

"Oh yeah, what was your favorite book?"

He eyes me with wariness as if he's confiding a deep secret. *"Where the Red Fern Grows."*

"And I bet you wanted a dog for every Christmas afterward."

"And I never got one." He smirks, and his face starts to assume a normal color. "What about you? What's your favorite book to teach?"

"Oh, I'm a sucker for the classics. *To Kill a Mockingbird*. Hands down."

"You teach that in middle school? I didn't read it until high school."

"The sooner you read it, the better the person you'll be for the rest of your life. Seventh grade is the perfect time to read it. Loss of innocence, compassion for others, class struggle, and the role of gender. Heck, it should be mandatory reading for adults."

"Yeah," Jared agrees. "But don't forget to include Vonnegut, Faulkner, and Atwood."

I recoil as if Jared just admitted that he enjoys knitting. "Wait, you read Margaret Atwood?"

He nods. "Of course, she's incredible. Why? Are you surprised?"

"Well, I just assumed you would rather play Call of Duty."

"Ah, what is it they say?" A sly grin emerges on his lips. One that I've never seen before. "Don't judge a book by its cover."

"Touché."

"I do like gaming," he acknowledge, "but I also like reading."

"What do you do for work?"

"Up until a few days ago, I was a web developer," he says.

"So you spent most of the day on the computer."

"Pretty much."

"You're kidding me." He appears confused. "How do you explain all your action hero antics? People were shooting at us during a high-speed chase. You barely broke a sweat."

His chest puffs a bit with what I suspect is pride. "I guess you can thank my father. When I was growing up, he taught me a lot of stuff—survival training and such. At the time, I hated every moment of it. I just wanted to be a normal kid."

"From computer guy to my Protector. What a change, right?"

"I try not to think about my life before this all started, and it's hard to believe how everything can be different in a couple of days."

Amen to that. I don't know what to believe anymore. Ascended, Descended, war gods, Prophets. The idea of the Ascension scares me to the core. It sounds like I'll lose my mind. "Did you always believe all of this goddess stuff?"

He winces and stares down at his lap. "You want to know the truth? No, I didn't believe any of it, but then I saw what happened at the Witch House, and it's the only thing that makes sense. I should have always believed."

"So you really think I'm the goddess Gaia?"

"Now I do."

"OK, as the goddess, I demand you tell me about the prophecy Janus mentioned."

The warmth in his face evaporates, and his voice crystallizes to a metallic resonance. "Truthfully, I don't know."

Before I can call him out on the lie, Caroline bounds in from the cockpit interrupting us. In the light of day, her blazing red hair contrasts even more with her pale white skin. She's wearing skinny black jeans, a Palatinate-colored kimono sleeve blouse, and lacy heeled Jimmy Choos. "We're landing soon," she announces with a surprising cheeriness. An accent spices her English. "Strap yourself in."

Out the porthole window, the ground comes up fast from below. The next moment, the plane's wheels touch down. Jared releases a long sigh.

After we taxi off the runway, I ask, "Where are we?"

"Amsterdam," Jared replies, pointing out the window to the terminal. "Schiphol's the international airport."

"Very good," Caroline says, "I love men who notice details."

"Why couldn't you tell us last night we were coming here?" I ask.

Caroline stands up and stretches her arms over her head. "My employer travels so often that I don't even know where he's going to be." She tosses her hair over her shoulder in a way that I thought was only possible in movies.

"And you travel often for your employer?" Jared asks.

"When he wishes me to do so," she says, shooting him a wink.

The jet comes to a stop, and Caroline throws her shoulder against the door, which swings open. "Come. The limo awaits." She disappears out the door.

True to her word, there's a limo waiting for us at the bottom of the stairway. Inside, we find a table set with a full breakfast of fresh coffee, crepes with jelly, and fruit salad. My stomach rumbles. Caroline pats me on the shoulder. "No shame. I know you Americans love a big breakfast."

Good thing I agree with her; otherwise, I might have taken offense.

We eat as the limo leaves the airport. The food is delicious, and the coffee is doing wonders for my mental outlook. Caroline eats like a bird, pecking and nibbling at the items on her plate, while Jared devours foods with the same efficiency one finds in professional eating competitions.

After we're done, I ask, "So who exactly is your employer?"

Caroline grins, "We're going to meet him now."

"Why does he want to meet me?"

"Who wouldn't want to meet you?" she replies with a dash of sass.

My smile wanes to a grimace. "You're not answering any of my questions."

"Nor do I think I have to," Caroline says with a sudden sharpness.

"Mattie," Jared interrupts, "her employer is either a god or works for a god. She has the same tattoo as the birthmark on your face. You didn't know this, but all the priestesses in Salem also had this mark."

"Do you have it?"

His ears turn red, and he rubs the back of his neck. "Yeah," he says, rolling up the sleeve of his left arm. Sure enough, there is a tattoo of a jagged crescent moon.

"A whale and the moon," I say, remembering the tattoo on his other arm. "The whale is for your dad? A fisherman?"

He nods.

"And the moon?"

Jared looks away, and Caroline places her hand on his knee. He gives her an uncertain glance. "It means that we fight for the Mother Goddesses," she says.

"Mother Goddesses?"

She stares at Jared and shakes her head. "She really doesn't know anything."

"As I mentioned in the message," he says, his tone defensive, "her Ascension was interrupted."

"Wait, you guys know each other?" I ask.

"Not exactly," Caroline says, her hand moving up Jared's knee.

I force myself to ignore this. "How did you know we were with the Prophet?"

"Mattie," Jared says. He finally grabs Caroline's roaming hand and pushes it away. She doesn't take offense. Instead, she smiles as if it's a game. "The priestesses had given me instructions on who to contact if something bad happened. While we were in New York, I sent out distress messages to several gods, but I received no response."

"But I saw dozens of gods in New York."

"They were all Descended. We needed the help of an Ascended god. Also, as you've seen with Gurzil, there are many gods out there who want you dead."

"We received your message," Caroline interjects, "but we did not respond right away. It is much too dangerous. We had to research and make sure your claims were true."

"Either way, when I didn't receive a response, the only god I knew was the Prophet."

"Janus loves to be the center of attention," Caroline confides.

"I knew there was a risk in visiting him, but it was a risk I was willing to take."

"Aha," Caroline exclaims, "you didn't realize that Janus is barred from providing support to either side?"

"No, I didn't," Jared affirms, "but it was the only option I had."

"Lucky for you, my employer predicted your actions. Otherwise, well, you wouldn't be here."

We enter the city of Amsterdam. The streets are lined with beautiful old buildings with gabled facades. Swarms of people on bikes crowd the streets, and we pass over picturesque bridges. In the canals below, long house boats bob in the water.

The limo comes to a stop, and Jared gets out first. As we're leaving, Caroline pulls me to the side. "Are you and Jared seeing each other?" she asks.

The question catches me off guard. "What?"

"Oh, I thought you were a couple."

"Really?"

"Maybe I was mistaken. But you guys aren't a thing?"

"No, of course not."

Caroline smiles and pulls away. "OK, good to know. He's very cute." She flashes her perfect smile. "Come. My employer is waiting."

My ears burn red, and a twinge of distress sparks like a burnt out light bulb. For some reason, I remember the Marquis and his wife.

CHAPTER FIFTEEN
Caishen

We exit the limo, and neither Caroline nor Jared takes notice of the city's salad bar of entertainments. Coffee shop packed with travelers and *Amsterdammers* exude thick plumes of hashish smoke. Suburban couples, with tentative steps, enter theaters advertising sex shows. Gangs of drunken British footballers haggle with lacy lingerie-clad women who sell themselves out of pink-lit shop fronts. This place makes me feel dirty all over.

We proceed down a detritus-laden alley between a brothel and an abandoned bank. At an unmarked metal door, Caroline knocks, and an eye viewer slides away like a 1920s speakeasy. She flashes a smile, and immediately the door unlocks revealing a hulking man with a shaved head and vigilant eyes. He steps to the side, and Caroline gives me a quick, playful wink before taking my hand and pulling me inside. The hard, pounding beat of electronic music greets us.

Black lights illuminate neon green strips, and they form a path down a dark corridor. We pass a coat check manned by women wearing silver wigs, orange suspenders, and near-transparent white t-shirts. They need bras—badly.

I shoot a 'can-you-believe-this' look to Jared but see his eyes lingering over the women. My muscles clench, and I look away quickly.

A quick turn brings us to the main room—a dance floor flooded with flashing lights, dense fog, and throngs of dancers. They grind their bodies to the fast, computer-generated song. Most of the men don't wear shirts, and to call the clothing of the women "dresses" would be an overstatement.

Caroline, unfazed by the scene, snakes through the middle of the dance floor. High above on a balcony, the DJ wears a donkey mask, and his hands pump toward the ceiling.

After enduring a half-dozen cigarette burns, we arrive at a spiral staircase guarded by another huge bouncer. He swings to the side as we approach and allows us to enter the VIP section. I'm not much of a club girl, to put it mildly. The one time I went 'clubbing' in Boston, I was relieved to go home at the end of the night.

The VIP section has a private bar and the same waitresses dressed like girls from the *Fifth Element*. But it's the other guests that make my eyes widen and breath catch.

They are an incongruous pair of gods, and they stare at me as surprised as I stare at them. One of them is a Viking with a long beard, burning crown, and tangled gray hair, while the other is a beautiful woman with brown skin and flowing black locks. They stand by the bar with their auras beaming.

As I stare back, their auras fade, and I'm even more shocked because I recognize both of them. The now-blonde woman is a famous actress. Her name escapes me. The Viking is a well-dressed man with alert eyes. I'm pretty certain he's the president of France.

Caroline tugs at my sleeve. "Come. He's waiting for you."

I tear my eyes away from the politician and actress. We arrive at a booth where another god greets me. His aura is bright orange, and an image greets me of a jolly-faced Asian man with a long white wispy beard, bulging chipmunk cheeks, and a funny little square black hat on top of his head. He stands and towers over me.

A second later, the image and aura fade, and it's replaced by a giant man with ebony skin and a shaved head. The behemoth has limbs the size of tree trunks. A massive Rolex shines on his wrist, and numerous gem-encrusted rings twinkle on his sausage-sized fingers. Glittering gold teeth fill his mouth, and the whites of his eyes glow.

He extends his hand, which fully encompasses my hand like a bear paw. He says something, which I can't hear over the music. "What?" I reply.

His expression bristles with irritation. He pulls away and claps his hands. "Silence!" he shouts. The music screeches to a halt, and all the dancers freeze. It's like he pressed pause on a DVD. "Leave us. I desire privacy." Within a minute, the entire club empties, except for us and the two gods at the bar, who stare at me with amused expressions.

"Ah, that is better," he growls. "The music seems to get louder and louder every century." His voice is aristocratic and colonial. It reminds me of the Marquis. "As I was saying before, it's good to see you, my little killer."

"Do you require anything else?" Caroline asks, a little bit of annoyance in her voice.

"No, thank you for bringing her." He waves away Jared and Caroline as if they are mosquitoes. "I wish to talk to the goddess alone."

Caroline nods and pulls Jared away. But he resists. "I'm not leaving her."

"Mortal, do not irritate me. I've already saved you once. Don't make me reconsider my generosity." When Jared stands firm, he adds, "If I had wished her harm, she would already be dead."

After a few more seconds, Jared's glare softens. "Fine," he

says, and Caroline leads him away to the bar.

I gulp, but the inside of my throat is parched. I turn back to the giant with my best poker face. "If you're done trying to impress me, you can tell me who you are."

He throws back his head and roars with laughter. "After two thousand years, you're still a stubborn hard-nosed woman."

"I don't even know you."

"Caroline informed me of your condition. I can't even remember meeting a god stuck in a limbo state. It's too bad. If you were fully Ascended, it would make things simpler."

I notice the thousands of dollars worth of jewelry he wears. "Who are you?" I repeat.

"Call me Caishen. I'm a god of wealth," he replies, waggling his diamond-studded fingers.

"What are you, African, Chinese?"

"A little of both. I'm from many times and places. Caishen is a god in Chinese mythology. But I've held positions of power and importance many times through mankind's history. It's a shame you don't remember any of this, my little killer."

"Why do you keep on calling me 'little killer'? Was that, like, my nickname in a past life?" I ask with a sarcastic tone.

One of his eyebrows raises. "Oh, so you haven't heard?"

"Haven't heard what?" The dread in my voice is all too apparent.

"You will love this," he says with a grin. He snaps his fingers, and one of the orange suspender waitresses rushes over with a jewel-encased iPad. He flips it open.

I drop my eyes and find my teacher picture. No one had told me it was picture day, and I had come to school wearing a pink knitted sweater that was well past its expiration date. My hair was not cooperating that day, and being a new teacher, I have a stressed, shell-shocked expression. The overall effect is that my picture is more like a mug shot for a woman who has way too many cats and hoards copies of *Soap Opera Digest*. The picture is the first image that appears on *The New York Times* website.

I snatch the iPad away and click through to the article. Sickness, like a lizard, creeps over me. The article says that a warrant is out for my arrest. I read on and wish there was a hole to crawl into and never come out.

The article says that I'm the prime suspect in connection with Patrick's death. My belongings and fingerprints were found at the scene of his brutal murder.

Supposedly, I left behind a note confessing to the crime as well as detailing my loathing for homosexuals. Reading through, I find that the article makes it sound like I've committed the hate crime of the century.

My brain somersaults, and chills run through my body. This can't be happening. "I'm being framed," I say, letting my shoulders slump. "How is this even possible?"

I raise my hand to slap the all-knowing smile off Caishen's face, but restrain myself. "They are trying to flush you out like a rat in a sinking ship."

I shudder as if someone dumped ice cubes down my underwear. "This can't be happening," I say, shaking my head.

"I wouldn't be surprised if they cleared out your bank accounts and maxed out your credit cards." He gestures toward the iPad. "You should check. Don't worry. The connection is secure. They will not be able to track you here."

My throat constricts. It's like the day in college when I lost my wallet on a public bus. With frantic fingers, I type in my login information for my bank and credit accounts.

Sure enough, I'm wiped clean. Every cent that was in my name—which wasn't a lot to begin with—has vanished. Weird foreign charges max out my credit cards. I check out one of them, which reads: Kiddi69funXXX.net.

"What the hell is this?" But it becomes too apparent when the first picture appears on the website, making my stomach knot. *Child porn*. Only a cold shower and a flesh scouring could remove the disgust covering my skin.

I pass the iPad back to Caishen, and he places his hand on my shoulder to comfort me. "You should know that they are only doing this because they can't find you. This is good news."

I laugh on the edge of tears. "Good news? I'm wanted for the murder of my best friend. I'm penniless, and according to my credit card charges, I'm addicted to kiddie porn. There is no good news. I'm screwed. My life as a normal person is over."

"Well, you should take comfort in knowing that you were never a normal person." Caishen sits down in the booth and offers me a glass of champagne. "Sit, we have business to discuss."

I decline the champagne but take the seat. I stare at the huge man with the trepidation of a mouse eyeing a snake. "Who are you really?"

"I am a god like you. A god of riches," he flashes his rings again.

"So what? That's your thing. You're rich?"

"When you live forever, it's foolish not to invest wisely."

I point a thumb toward the actress and politician who still stare at me with awe. "Are they who I think they are?"

Caishen peers over and shrugs. "Don't be surprised. They have had lifetimes to become masters of their craft. The Ascended have always been influential. They have shaped mankind and its progress throughout history."

"Why don't the history books say anything about them?"

"Who do you think writes and publishes the history books? The Ascended are in the positions of power throughout the world. They are the CEOs of the largest corporations. They are presidents and leaders of nations. They are famous actors and influential scientists. They are the generals in the armies and the admirals at sea. They have been kings and queens. They have been prophets and the creators of religions. You shouldn't be surprised that I am the richest man in the world."

"You? You're richer than Bill Gates?"

"Please," he derides. "Little Billie doesn't have a fraction of my wealth. The Ascended are far richer than any mortal you know of."

My head spins, and the fact that I'm wanted for murder drums through every thought. "This is all too much."

"Understandable. If you were Ascended, it would all make sense."

"So," I begin, fear pulsing through me. "Are you going to do this Ascension thing for me?"

Caishen recoils with surprise. "Me?" He shakes his head. "Impossible. I could never conduct your Ascension nor would I ever dare to. There are gods much more powerful and dangerous than I who want you dead. I saved you because I owed you, and I always pay back my debts." His eyes narrow to slits. "There is no way that I'm getting into the trouble you are in. The way I've survived for thousands of years is avoiding such dangerous entanglements. My philosophy is to stay out of the fight. Let the others bicker and kill one another. I will be content with my fortune." He shoots me a serious stare. "The quicker you Ascend, the sooner you will realize the true danger you are in."

Fear balloons inside of me. "What do you mean?"

"The Shadow God wants you dead."

"You mean Gurzil?"

He snorts. "No, no," Caishen replies as if I said something stupid. "Gurzil is a young god. He's been assigned the job of hunting you down. No, I'm talking about one of the ancients. A god that is the same status as you. One of the first gods that emerged as mankind evolved."

"So you're saying an even more powerful god is hunting me as well?"

Caishen nods, and my heart sinks.

"What the hell am I going to do? I have no money, no passport, a warrant for my arrest, a bull-headed psychopath hunting me down—"

"Calm yourself, goddess!" he declares, "The Gaia I knew would not succumb to hysterics. You are one of the oldest among us. Live up to your legacy."

I point my finger at him as if it is a knife. "Excuse me, Mr. Money God. But I don't know what this legacy is. I don't remember any past life. I'm a middle school teacher. That's all I know. So excuse me if I'm freaking out."

The giant man bares a smirk. "You're not so different from the goddess I knew. Let me be of assistance."

"How?" I ask, remembering the old adage: Beware the snake oil salesman.

"I will put you in touch with an old friend of yours. He will complete your Ascension. All funding and documentation will be taken care of. In short, you will not be found by your hunters."

I hate that he uses that word. Because that means I am the prey. "Why are you really helping me?"

Caishen downs a glass of champagne in one gulp. "I owe you a debt, and I always repay my debts."

"What did I do for you?"

Caishen reviews me with dead seriousness. "You saved my life."

"Saved your life? But you're Ascended. You never die."

"No, to Descend and be ignorant of your past lives is death. You Ascended me. You kept my Ascended soul alive."

"How did I do that?"

"I would need many hours to tell that tale. Time is something you don't have. No, you will know all once you Ascend."

I'm not going to take that excuse again. "What is the Purging? Janus mentioned there was a prophecy about me. What is it?"

Caishen releases a deep roar of amusement. "Oh, I will not be the one that tells you those secrets. Your old friend can explain the real trouble you're in." He raises his hands and claps.

The music in the club restarts as if someone has pushed the play button. The dancers re-emerge.

I turn back to Caishen, and he's fondling one of the waitresses, guzzling another glass of champagne. Without glancing at me, he adds, "Consider my debt repaid, goddess. Never ask for my help again."

CHAPTER SIXTEEN
Bahut Bahut Dhanyavad

In front of me, the sea rises—blue, calm, infinite. Behind me is a river of people—stretching back two miles. We cross the subcontinent and flow outwards. We are a river purifying the country and all who dwell here.

They are my people: Women and men. Brahmin and untouchable. Hindu and Muslim. Together we march and sing with one voice and many. Our voices Ascend to a greater Dharma that will transform us all.

The ocean air tickles my nose, and my weary feet press on. Two hundred and forty miles separate us from the beginning. The potential energy of the people is ready to explode.

Along the way, we speak in villages similar to the thousands that sprinkle the land like pebbles on a beach. Hours upon hours of re- search, strategy, and calculation; all culminating in this one moment. Gulls screech, and grains of sand grind in between my dusty toes.

A street child grasps my hand, and he clutches a bamboo flute in his other. The boy is a Harijan, a child of god. In this moment, he is my son—the son of a soon-to-be-born nation. His face is pure jubilation.

They have tried everything to stop this moment. They have silenced, beat, and killed, but I have not lifted a finger. I take their blows. In fact, I accept them with delight. For when my enemy strikes, I will love them greater, and in my love, their violence will be violence upon their souls.

I climb up the final dune, and my feet sink deep into the hot sand. Hundreds of feet follow. We traverse the great sea flats, and beside me, the child of the new country smiles. The ocean surf breaks on a deserted beach.

A budding, white lump of salt sprouts from the sand. After food and water, what else is more important than salt?

Salt will be the weapon to erase centuries of discrimination and division. Salt will overthrow an empire.

I reach down, pick up the lump, and break the law.

A shudder runs through my body. For the first time, I realize that my arm is not my own. It is dark brown, slender, and frail. My hand extends upwards until it blocks out the sun as the fiery light burns away the image.

The dream melts away, and the glaring sun screams through the half-closed blinds.

Unlike the previous times I'd awoken from dreams—where it had felt like I had jumper cables clipped to my toes—I awake from this dream refreshed and relaxed. The remnants of the dream fizz in my mind. I swear that I can still smell the ocean.

Who was that? Who had I been? I stop suddenly, and the hairs on my arms stand on end as I realize that a part of me believes that these dreams are past lives.

The air conditioner whirls—pumping frigid air into the stale room of the guesthouse. A chorus of exhaust-belching cars and muddled voices drift up from the street.

A soreness lingers in my body—likely the result of too much sitting on airplanes. We arrived into Mumbai late in the night. Despite Jared's fears, we didn't have problems with immigration. The bleary-eyed Indian official inspected my fake passport from Caishen for less than a second.

Muscles aching, I pull myself up from the bed. I check the adjoining bedroom, but Jared isn't there. My body is heavy like a sack of flour. I find a folded pile of clothes, a cash-filled envelope, and a note from him on the bureau.

He's out meeting Caishen's contact to find the Ascended god who will conduct my Ascension. He warns me not to leave the guesthouse.

The embroidered dress on the bureau is a pinkish hue that screams the eighties. The accompanying baggie pants would put MC Hammer's to shame. I wonder if Jared's joking.

But, to my surprise, the dress fits perfectly, and the pants are the most comfortable I've ever worn. In the mirror, I look like I'm straight out of a Bollywood film.

I leave the room and am greeted by a bulging woman, wearing dozens of gold chains and bracelets. She sits me down at a dining table and serves me a gigantic crepe filled with a chili and potato, which she calls a *dosa*. It's so spicy I think I'm going to explode. But I'm starving and it's delicious, so I eat it all, breaking only to indulge coughing fits and chug several bottles of water.

Staring out a window, I watch a foreign kaleidoscope scene. A cow lingers across the road and creates a traffic jam of yellow and black taxis. Most of the cars appear as though they were built in someone's backyard. Palm trees cast long shadows, and half-naked little boys sleep on the sidewalk.

But at that moment, the world freezes. Across the street, I notice a bright orange aura. My heart leaps and jaw drops. It's—it's —I refuse to say it, but it slips out as a whisper, "*A god.*"

I understand that I shouldn't leave, but I don't like Jared dictating my every decision. I'm tired of feeling out of control. I want to take back my life and one way to do that, is to figure out this new world by myself.

Throwing down some cash, I head for the door. The difference between the air-conditioned interior and the dry sauna outside shocks my system. The sounds, sights, and people suck me up. Honking horns and shouting. Dust billows up from the street, coating my face with a fine sheen of foundation.

I find a gap in the traffic and navigate between zooming rickshaws. The god has an image of a holy man with a white loincloth and bare feet, but the thing that sends my stomach lurching are his heads.

Yeah. Plural. Heads. The guy has four heads. Each with the same face: an old man—wrinkled and wizened—with a white beard trailing to his feet. Each head is capped with a golden-coned crown.

The guy takes a quick turn down a street filled with spice shops releasing pungent odors of cardamom and turmeric. Food stalls offer fried food, watermelon juice, and sugary sweets. It's a symphony of senses bordering on cacophony. This city is too familiar, and I can't deny it. I've been here before; more than that, I've lived here. The dream about the ocean and salt flats flashes back.

The aura around the four-headed god fizzles and fades. His human form emerges as a young man with a thin mustache, worn khakis, wiry black hair, and a singular head. Who is he? Why is he here? Is he Ascended or Descended?

I trail ten feet behind and follow him down a side street. Two blocks later, we round another corner, and I know where he's headed.

A gigantic temple with a steep, domed roof, and tall walls looms in front of us. Etched into the stone exterior are depictions of gods, each one painted in bright colors. One in particular stands out. The demon has huge unblinking eyes and a spiked tail ready to strike like a scorpion. His monstrous mouth poses, about to bite with jagged teeth.

Despite the terrifying image, dozens of people mumbling

prayers wait to enter the temple. Along each side of the street, merchants sell incense, candles, and religious tchotchkes.

The four-headed god takes a place at the end of the line, but then turns and stares at me. His lingering eyes take me aback, but I figure it's the novelty of finding a foreigner. A minute later, he turns back around, thus confirming my suspicions that he is Descended.

The line is long but moves fast, and as we get closer, the prayers grow louder. The temple towers over me. Far from a place of peace, it sends shivers across my skin and fills my mouth with a rancid taste.

Something irks me about the temple. I'm ready to turn and leave when the hairs on the back of my neck spring to attention. The people bristle like falling dominoes. Angry shouts erupt ahead of me; crowds fan out and form a circle.

It's like the moment before a fight in the cafeteria. I take a step back. The less attention I draw the better. I'm walking away when a sustained high note tears through the air like shattering glass. A liquid shot of fear runs up my spine.

It's a child's scream.

I spin around and push past the frozen, enthralled people until I'm at the edge of a clearing. When I break through, I'm sick and mad all over.

On the ground is a girl—not even seven years old—curled up in a ball. Scrapes and sores cover her body. Tears stream from her eyes down onto her dirty sari. Her hands protect her head and face from the blows raining down on her.

Her assailant is quadruple her size, a potbellied guard in an olive green uniform. He sports a bushy, black mustache, and a round, bulbous nose. Exertion and glee edge his pudgy face while he whips the girl with a thin bamboo switch—raising it over his head and striking without mercy.

"Disgusting dog!" the guard screams in between blows. The sound of the switch striking her makes me wince.

My muscles quiver and teeth grind, my fists clenching into tight balls. Why isn't anyone stopping him?

"You dare to enter Rava's temple?" the guard asks, the switch cutting through the girl's shirt, leaving a sharp, red welt on her back.

She screams louder. The crowd stands silent and still.

"I will teach you to respect the gods!" yells the guard, a sadistic glimmer in his dark eyes. He strikes again, and the girl releases a muffled cry.

At that moment, the whole world spins like a tornado. My eyelids flutter fast and my skin tingles like a thousand pins are softly pressing into it. Deep in my chest, it's like a geyser exploding as some unknown, elemental, and ancient force comes surging to the surface.

What's happening to me?

The girl's hands slip from her head, exposing her face. "When I'm done, you'll know your place!" the guard cries, his mouth twisting with cruelty. He raises the switch, aiming for the girl's eyes in order to blind her. His arm flashes down.

But the switch freezes in mid-air.

I don't know which one of us is more surprised—the guard or me. Because I realize that it's my hand holding the guard's forearm in place. The man's face morphs from surprise to disdain before settling on rage.

He tries to wrench his arm free, but my grip is as tight as a vise. I don't know how I have so much strength. The cop reaches back with his free hand to strike me, but while he's off balance, I push him backward with a light touch.

The man stumbles. His arms pinwheel, and he topples over. He lands with a loud grunt on his backside. The guard's mouth drops to a grimace, while his ears and cheeks burn red. He tries scrambling to his feet, but I put my foot on his shoulder and pin him to the ground.

Fresh anger flashes in his eyes, and a verbal assault mounts on his lips, but before he can utter a syllable, a calm and forceful voice shoots from me like a cannon blast. "Shameful little man," I proclaim, pointing my finger at him. "You, a citizen of this land, should be protecting this girl, not punishing her."

This is beyond strange. Because it's my voice, but in a way, it isn't. It's as if someone else is now in the driver's seat of my mind. Someone else is speaking and pulling all the levers, and I'm a backseat driver to my own consciousness.

His eyes blink as if he's clearing dust from them. "Th-th-this girl. She's an-an-an untouchable," the guard stutters. His eyes search the surrounding bystanders for confirmation, but only baffled expressions meet him.

"No," I answer, my voice growing with a life of its own. "She's a child of god." The guard cocks his head to one side, and I continue, "You are an Indian. She is an Indian. We are all Indians. We are all the same. We are all children of god."

"You can't interfere," the guard says. "This is not your business."

I tower over him, my foot pressing him to the dirt like a worm. "I object to violence when it appears to do good. The good is only temporary. The evil it does is permanent." I stare down at the battered girl. "You should love her like you would love your own child. Because love will release you from hate. Until you can release your own hate, you will be a slave to it."

When I finish, I remove my foot, but my words have deflated the man. He remains on the ground, staring up wide-eyed. I kneel and scoop the girl up into my arms. She's as light as a touch. "Are you alright?" I ask.

The timid girl sniffles, nods, and says, "My back hurts. I want to go home."

"Let me take you," I reply.

I walk away from the temple and through the dazed crowd. As if on cue, the crowd separates, creating a path. As I pass, one of them reaches up, touches my shirt, and mumbles a prayer.

I don't turn back. The child nuzzles her head into my chest. Her crying stops, and she holds me tight as I carry her all the way back to the guesthouse. When I finally let her down, the trance breaks.

My eyes flutter, and I'm beyond dizzy. I reach out to steady myself. The world spins, like before at the temple. The same force that possessed me now disappears from whence it came. When the dizzy spell abates, all my senses are dull and weary. But I'm again in control of my body. What the hell just happened?

The girl refuses to free my hand. She smiles up at me—quiet with bright, glossy eyes.

I clear my throat. "Are you good?"

The girl's face wrinkles, and she shakes her head. "Goood?"

"Are you good?" I repeat.

The girl shrugs, and her head wobbles. My cheeks redden. Of course the girl wouldn't understand English. I smile, reach into my pocket, and give the girl the envelope of money from Jared. "Stay safe, OK?"

Her mouth drops. The girl stares down at the envelope of money. *"Bahut Bahut Dhanyavad."* She finally whispers and then turns to run down the street.

"Mattie, what are you doing outside?" I turn and see Jared— mouth slightly parted—stalking toward me. "It's not safe out here."

"I was just . . ." I turn back to the girl and catch a fleeting glance of her as she disappears into the crowds.

"Damn it, Mattie," Jared says, ushering me away. "You can't wander around."

At that moment, I realize something that makes me break out into a cold sweat. All my fears pale in comparison. The girl understood me earlier but not later. Everyone understood what I had been saying. The crowd, the girl, even the guard. There is only one way this was possible.

I was speaking another language.

"You need to be more careful," Jared chides while pulling me inside the guesthouse.

Before the door closes, I catch a glimpse of an aura. A sudden flash of red draws my attention back to the chaotic street. The door slams shut before I can make out the god. All that remains is my pounding headache and a crippling terror that someone had hijacked my mind.

CHAPTER SEVENTEEN
Sushi

The next morning, we take a train to Trivandrum, in the south of the country. Halfway there, a strike of railroad workers forces us to stop in the city of Goa for the night. We search for a hotel with two open rooms, but the only one we can find is an expensive hotel on the beach where a wedding is taking place.

Once we check in, Jared, in his usual paranoid style, refuses to leave the room. But he gets hungry, and I argue with him that no one can possibly find us in a random hotel in India. Eventually, his hunger overcomes his reason, and we go down to the bar for a bite to eat.

As we are finishing our fish curry, a slightly tipsy elderly couple from the beach-side wedding sidle up next to us and invite us to join the party outside. Jared initially refuses, but after some persuading on my part, he reluctantly heads outside.

A full moon lights up the night like a magnificent disco orb, while music blares from huge speakers. The beach-side dance floor is packed with hundreds of guests decked out in gowns and tuxedos. The couple drags us onto the dance floor.

The old man, dressed in formal wear and red suspenders, gy-rates his hips like a pop star. I can barely keep up.

Jared's dance partner, an aged Auntie in a neon green gown, sways her large behind to the Bollywood beat. Jared dances as if he's having muscle spasms. He's probably the worst dancer I've ever seen.

The song ends, and despite the pleading from our respective dance partners, we retreat back to our seats at the outdoor bar, where I find my glass of Cabernet Sauvignon still half-full.

"Are you having fun?" I ask, taking a bar napkin and wiping my brow.

Jared's lips break into a smile. "I haven't been to a wedding in ages."

"You're quite the dancer."

"Is that sarcasm I detect?"

"Oh no, I love your energy."

"That sounds like the kind of back-handed compliment you would give a student."

"I've just never seen moves like that before."

Jared leans in close, and I detect the not-unpleasant smell of sweat off his skin. "I'll tell you a secret," he pauses and looks over his shoulder. "I took dance lessons for years."

"Fat good they did you."

"Don't be mean. I could never get down the timing of the steps."

"Wait," I say, holding back a laugh. "You're serious?"

Jared takes a quick sip of beer, his arm brushing against mine. "Yeah, my mom made me take lessons."

"I would think that you'd have at least a sense of rhythm."

"Don't be so critical. You're no twinkle toes."

"Yeah, but I dance from the heart," I say, finishing off my wine.

He glances back at the dance floor. "At least our dance part-ners are having a good time."

"Too good of a time, if you ask me." The old couple is now nearly dancing on top of each other.

"What about you?" he asks. "You have any secrets from childhood?"

I consider all the possibilities and decide on the most harmless. "Up until the fifth grade, the only food I ate was sushi."

"Wait, like, only sushi?"

"Yep, nothing but sushi. My mom had to go to the fish store three times a week, and she always had a pot of rice on the stove."

Jared crackles with laughter. "Wow, that's kind of pretentious."

"Hey! Be glad that I finally discovered PB&J."

"I'm sorry, but the image of your mom slaving over sushi rolls leaves an impression."

"Still, at least I can dance, Jared."

He continues to snicker. "Your poor mom."

"Yeah . . ." My voice drops and fades. I reach over and grab an untouched glass of wine that a wedding guest left behind, and take a big gulp.

"What happened to her?" he asks.

"She ran off with some guy," I say, pushing down the lump in my throat. "They live in Wyoming."

"That doesn't sound bad."

My eyes narrow, and I glare at him.

"I take it you were close with her."

"Yeah, I was." I pause, but then add, "I mean, I still am, but it's different now. I'm lucky if I get a phone call once a week from her." I finish the third glass of wine in two gulps. "On the other hand, I realize that she was really lonely while raising me. She's happy now. I guess I'm selfish because I want her to myself. It's hard when people who were close to you grow distant."

"It is difficult."

"Part of it was also my choice, she's always said that I'm welcome to go out there and live with them. But, that's not where I want my life to be, and I got the hint that it was time for me to live my own life."

"What is she like?" he asks.

I shrug and let out a ragged breath, cough, and avoid his eyes. "She was always there for me. After my dad left, it was me and her. She is loving, kind, strong and really fun."

"Yeah, how so?"

Smiling to myself, I say, "We used to have creative kitchen day." Jared gives me a confused look, and I explain, "Before a big shopping day, we would open all the cabinets, take out whatever food we had left and made a weird meal. Then, we would set the table with a fancy table cloth, nice china, candlesticks and eat whatever we made."

"She sounds nice."

I look away, telling myself not to feel anything or think about her. Farther down the beach, on the outskirts of the wedding, a group of local fisherman pulls their wooden boats into the breaking surf to try their luck in the full moon. I commandeer another glass of wine for medicinal purposes.

A few seconds of awkward silence tick by. "So, I've told you my secrets. Time for you to fess up. How did you get involved with the Ascended?"

The warmth of Jared's face becomes cold, and he shakes his head. "I really don't want to talk about it."

"Are you kidding? We wouldn't be here right now if it weren't for this uninteresting story."

"True," he replies but doesn't add anything else.

"So? Come on, what's the big deal?"

Jared sighs, rubs the back of his neck, and takes a long pull from his beer. "The Ascended has always been a part of my life," he begins, a sliver of bitterness in his voice. "But it's something that I never took seriously until it was too late."

"It's OK," I interject, sensing I may be broaching a subject like entering an antique shop governed by a "you break it, you buy it" policy. "You don't have to tell me if you don't feel comfortable." I take a small sip of wine—telling myself to slow down.

Jared stares with heavy eyes at the dancers, before saying, "No. It's fine. You have a right to know." He leans in close. "Gertrude was my mother."

I nearly fall off my seat. A sudden coldness strikes me at my core. I remember his tears on the boat leaving Salem. He'd seen his mother murdered. "I'm so sorry. I didn't know."

His face darkens. "Don't be sorry. There was no way you could have known." He stops and stares out at the sea. "She had me late in life. I grew up with the idea of the Ascended. It was like a religion. When you're young, you just accept whatever you're told. But as I grew older, I thought it was all bullshit." He pauses. "What would you think if every Friday night, you lit a bunch of candles and chanted weird songs with women in robes?"

"No stranger than some other religions."

Jared looks away. "True, but maybe if I took it more seriously, maybe if I listened and wasn't so skeptical, then they wouldn't all be dead. Those women in the room were a family to me." He scratches at his day-old beard. "And now they're—."

My body shudders as I remember the massacre at the Witch House. "We don't need to talk about it."

"But I want to talk. Because for years I thought my mom was crazy, yet she did so much for me." His chin begins to quiver. "She was the one who got me to love books, to appreciate art, to be kind." He closes his eyes and takes several deep breaths. "I could have done more. I could have been more prepared." Jared's head bows.

"Truthfully, I think you did as much as you could have in Salem. Heck, you saved me."

"Again, thank my dad for that. He was a former marine—a real hard ass."

"So, your mom was a priestess and your dad was a soldier. You must have had an interesting upbringing."

"It was. My parents never married, but I split my time between them." He pauses, his fingers interlocking into a single clenched fist. "My dad's idea of fun was to spend every weekend in survival training camps, at gun ranges or shooting each other with paintballs."

"Sounds fun."

"Trust me. It wasn't. I hated every second of it. The worst part was that he made me do boxing for years. I can't tell you how many times I got my butt whipped."

"Yeah, that isn't good."

"But it was the strangest thing. At the Witch House, yes, I was afraid, but I knew what I had to do. It was like I was channeling my dad. His calm, get-shit-done attitude."

"Where is he now?"

Jared swivels away, but before he does, pain streaks across his face. "He passed away a year ago. Cancer."

"I'm sorry for your losses." I reach over, take his hand, and squeeze it. "Your mom was kind to me." He nods, and his smile improves my spirits a bit. Somehow my glass of wine is empty again—not sure how that happened.

A slow dance comes on and all the couples come together. The bride and groom rock together in a loving embrace.

A passing waiter fills my glass to the brim. My head swims, and I know I shouldn't drink anymore. Instead, I take another sip and ask, "Can you tell me something, Jared?" His blue eyes turn to me. "What's going to happen to me when I Ascend?"

He bristles, but doesn't let go of my hand. "It's not my place to tell you."

"Please," I say. "I'm scared, and I don't want to change. I don't want to lose who I am, and it feels like I've lost so much. I need to know what is the full price I will have to pay."

Jared shakes his head, and his tired face appears weighty. Finally, he says, "When you Ascend, you'll be able to channel your past lives."

"What do you mean?"

He leans forward and touches my forehead. Chills scamper across my skin. "You'll be able to tap into the knowledge and skills that your other lives had. For example, if you were a heart surgeon in a past life, you'll be able to perform open-heart surgery in your Ascended state.

"I wouldn't trust myself with a scalpel right now," I joke, spilling wine onto my *sari*.

Jared looks at me as if he suspects something. Then he says, "It's more than that. You'll have an understanding of human behavior and culture. Politics, logic, language, agriculture, warfare, literature. Imagine: in an instant, you'll know every realm of human knowledge."

Something clicks. It makes sense. "It was like when I was speaking a different language in Mumbai."

"You likely had a past life in India."

"But I don't think I was Ascended in that past life. You said I've been lost for thousands of years."

"It doesn't matter if the knowledge is from an Ascended or Descended past life. You'll remember all the wisdom from every past life."

"Wait," I say, a skeptical seed growing in my stomach. "Are you saying that—I'll have super powers or something?"

"Not super powers," Jared replies, his voice hardening. "It's all the experiences of a lifetime. Think about how much you learn in a single life. The Ascended are powerful because they can recall these experiences and know how to utilize this knowledge to their benefit."

I turn away and stare at the moonlight shimmering on the Arabian Sea. "In New York, I had a dream I was trapped in a prison. When I woke up, I was trapped in the tenement building. But it was like my mind knew that I was in trouble. If it wasn't for that dream, I probably wouldn't have escaped. It was like—the dream was giving me the tools I needed at that moment."

"Exactly," says Jared. "This is the power of the Ascended."

A gulp of wine doesn't sooth the doubt swelling inside me. "But the dream in New York and the experience in Mumbai were completely different. In Mumbai, I wasn't in control. Someone else was moving my body. Someone else was speaking for me." I remember the dream of walking to the salt flats, and I realize that the person in that dream was the person controlling me. Half the wine disappears from my glass.

Jared shrugs and offers only more doubt. "You're unlike any other god. You're stuck in a limbo state—halfway to Ascending but still Descended. You know," he speculates, "it might be that under intense stress, you can channel your past lives. But it doesn't sound like you have control. It's more like a defense mechanism. When you're in danger, one of your past lives takes control."

My eyes widen, and I quickly swallow the remainder of my wine, but it goes down the wrong pipe, sending me into a coughing fit. When I recover, I say, "I can't live my life with someone else controlling it." I flag down one of the passing waiters. He comes over with the wine bottle ready.

Jared takes the glass from my hands. "Maybe you've had enough?"

I give him an impatient snort and grab back my glass. The waiter fills it up again.

He raises one of this eyebrows and in a parental voice says, "The sooner we complete your Ascension, the sooner you will be in control." But this stale answer sucks. He glances at his watch. "We should call it an early night. We still have a long way to drive tomorrow."

The world spins. I swallow a mouthful of wine to calm my thumping pulse. "Yes, dad," I reply.

Jared crosses his arms. "Come on. Will you please be responsible?"

I pause, reconsidering my response. Screw it. I down the entire glass of wine. "Will you please stop being such a dick?"

"Excuse me."

"Why do you treat me like crap? Did I hurt you in some past life?" I stand up too fast and the glass slips from my hand and shatters on the ground. A group of guests shoots me dirty looks, but I don't give a damn.

"You've had too much to drink and you need to go to sleep," he says, grabbing my arm.

I break his hold and shove him away. "Don't treat me like a child."

"You're acting like a child."

"Not once have you treated me with respect. You never ask my permission. You do what you want and drag me along as if I'm a piece of luggage."

He lowers his voice. "That's not true, and you know it."

"Oh, you want to talk about truth now? What about the prophecy, Jared? What about the Purging? Are you finally man enough to tell me what those are?"

Through gritted teeth, he says, "This is neither the time nor the place."

"Exactly, never the right time, never the right place. You're pathetic," I say, "and you're a coward. You're afraid of what I'll do. Well, guess what? I'm not afraid. I don't give a damn anymore."

His body shudders, and he swallows hard before saying, "You have to settle down right now."

I look around and realize we're surrounded by wedding guests giving us shocked stares. I swing back to Jared and say softly, "Why don't you leave? I never wanted your help in the first place. I'm sick of you."

He stumbles a step toward me, but I back away. The color

drains from his face and he says, "You want to know why I act the way I do?"

There is a painful tightness in my throat. All the alcohol hits my head, and I rock back and forth. I want to apologize for everything I said, but it's too late.

"It's because I don't want you to die. When my mother and the others died, a piece of me died. I don't want their deaths to be in vain. I don't want you to suffer the same fate as them. I'm hard because I care for you, and it is the only way I know how to survive." He finishes his beer and slams it down on the bar. Then he turns and leaves me in a stunned silence.

Sitting back down, my shoulders slump as if the weight of the moon presses down on me. I didn't mean those things. Why did I say them? I want to run after him, but my feet are bolted to the ground.

I fight back the painful pressure of mounting tears, but it's no use. They come falling down.

The crowd of wedding guests disperses, and they avoid me like a bad smell. I'm the asshole, not Jared. I'm the one who makes a scene—makes a fool out of herself. I want to disappear and forget everything, but I can't, and the only person I have left, the only person who believes in me, I just insulted and belittled. I'm the horrible person.

I stand up, and the world spins and I grab onto the bar to stop myself from falling over. Taking off my glasses, I rub my eyes. I want to be clean. Maybe dipping my feet in the warm waters of the ocean will wash away the hurt? But when I glance up, a fuzzy flash of red appears.

My heart nearly stops. Reflected in the mirror behind the bar, leering over my shoulder, I find a blurred image—gigantic red mouth with rows of jagged teeth, a serpent's tail, and bulbous blackened eyes.

I stumble backward into a table, knocking over glasses and plates. Spinning around, I expect to find the demon ready to swallow me whole, but there is no one there.

The next moment, an air horn blasts. Someone pulls the plug on the music; it screeches off. People scatter in all directions as bright spotlights illuminate the entire beach. Utter chaos ensues as people jostle into one another.

With frantic steps, I stumble out of the bar searching for Jared.

Police officers in olive green uniforms materialize and rush forward with black batons raised. With a surprising savageness, they attack and tackle party-goers and slap handcuffs on wrists. It takes me less than a few seconds to realize that they're only targeting women.

I'm wanted for murdering my best friend, I remember.

Two police officers converge on me. I spin and sprint down the beach, but it's like running on a trampoline. My legs wobble, and I can't stand upright.

When they're about to tackle me, Jared appears and shoulder-slams the officers to the ground. They fall dazed.

"Run for the boat!" he yells.

I turn toward the sea. The last fishing boat pushes off from the beach, and I dash forward, leaving Jared.

I'm halfway to the boat when a police officer jumps from the shadows and grabs my wrist. He wrenches it behind my back and pain shoots through my arm. I gasp, and the man forces me to my knees, pushing me to the ground.

With a swift blow to the head, Jared knocks the man down. He lets out a grunt as he falls next to me.

Jared lifts me from the ground. Holding my hand, he drags me to the boat which is already floating away from the shore.

Crashing through the waves, I stumble through the surf and swim to reach the boat. The helmsman, frenzied and frightened, rows away from shore, while another man pulls the rope on an old engine. The boat glides farther and farther away.

We're not going to get there.

Jared swims past me with splashing kicks and powerful pulls.

He closes in on the boat and gets a hand on the side. As I swim, he shouts something to the helmsman, who hesitates long enough for me to reach the boat.

Jared pulls me up, and as soon as I'm on, the engine kick starts, and we accelerate, cutting through the waves.

I collapse near the bow, soaked to the bone, chest heaving. The engine roars, and we disappear into the night with chaos raging in our wake. I turn to Jared, my head wobbling and vision blurry, and ask, "Do you still care about me?"

CHAPTER EIGHTEEN
Place of Refuge

My mouth tastes like dog hair and my head is pounding when the train arrives into Trivandrum. Between bouts of nausea, I panic, thinking for sure the police will be waiting for us. Instead, we disembark, greeted by clouds of mosquitoes.

Jared, who I haven't talked to for the entire train ride, hails a yellow rickshaw. As we sit crammed together in the rear bucket seat, my neck and face feel burning hot. All I can think about are the things I said to him—the things I didn't mean to say. The two-cylinder engine kicks into high gear, and we are off.

Jared keeps his eyes focused out the back of the rickshaw as we weave down the road.

I cough to get his attention, but he doesn't look at me. I want to crawl into a hole, and never come out. "Feeling paranoid?" I ask, finally breaking the self-imposed silence.

He bristles, still not looking at me. "The attack in Goa was too well-planned."

Recalling the demon I saw before they attacked, my arm hairs rise up and a new wave of dizziness washes over me. Only afterward did I realize that the face in the mirror was the same one etched on Rava's temple in Mumbai. "How did he find us?"

Jared looks at me with annoyed eyes. "He was tracking us."

I hear the implication in his voice, and I know he is partially right. It was my fault Rava found us. My jaw clenches, and I push back the urge to feel sick. "Do you think we lost him?"

"No one appears to be following us." His expression loses a bit of its edge, as he probably realizes that I feel like roadkill. "Do you remember what Rava looked like?"

"A demon."

"No, his human form."

"Oh, no," I say, only recalling what a drunken mess I was. Every time I swallow, it's like I'm attempting the cinnamon challenge. I'm definitely going to be sick.

He touches my elbow. "Here, drink some water, it will make you feel better," Jared says, offering me his water bottle.

"Thanks."

The little rickshaw burps and hiccups forward. We leave the city and go deep into rice paddy fields. Few vehicles travel the winding road, yet I can't help suspecting that someone is following us. Maybe it's Jared's fear wearing off on me.

After an hour, I'm feeling a little more human. "Who is Rava anyways?" I ask.

"Likely an Ascended god," he says as if that's the end of the conversation.

"What was the deal with his temple in Mumbai?" I ask with chills running down my back. "I don't understand why anyone would want to pray to a demon like him."

Jared frowns and avoids looking at me. "Fear, love, respect, tradition. There are hundreds of reasons why people believe in a god or a religion. Rava has likely lived over a hundred lives. After that much time, he's become a master at exploiting mankind."

This is more than he's spoken in a day, and I don't want him to stop. "But why use this knowledge to harm people? Why not use it for good?"

He glances at me, surprised, and smiles like he did the other night. A soothing warmth radiates across my skin. "This is why you're important Mattie. Your first instinct is to help—not hurt."

I look away, belly twisting into granny knots. How can he still think this after what I said to him?

"But there are many gods in the world who are like Rava," Jared continues. "Their first instinct is to control. They want to be worshiped. They will lie, hurt, and kill anyone who stands against them."

Chin trembling, my heart aches as I remember Patrick, a victim of these gods. "So Rava is—is—what?" I clear my throat. "An evil god?"

"Well . . ." Jared pauses, his face creases revealing crow's feet at the corner of his eyes. "There are many gods, and they all desire different things. There are some, like Gurzil, who desire power. Some, like Caishen, who want wealth."

"Do gods offer anything good to mankind? Because it is sounding like all of them are kind of evil."

"They're not all bad."

"For example?"

"Well," he pauses and looks me in the eyes without blinking. "There's you."

My heart screeches to a stop. "What do you mean?"

"Mattie, you want peace and love. You want harmony in the world. This is the essence of your being."

Fighting back the urge to cry, I ask. "How can you believe that, Jared? After what I said to you last night?"

"Because I know that once you discover the part of you that has been asleep, you'll finally realize these things as well."

I feel my face glow a deep red. Thankfully, the rickshaw hits a pothole, and we pop into the air, giving me enough time to recover. "So," I say, "there's me and then there are the bad gods.

But, I still don't understand why they're chasing me. Why am I so important?"

Jared crosses his arm and grimaces. "Once we arrive, I'm sure this old friend of yours will answer these questions."

"I don't understand why you can't tell me things. Like, the prophecy? What's the big deal?"

He sucks in his upper lip, and sweat glistens on his forehead. "It's because I don't know. My mom only told me the part about you in Salem."

"Then, why didn't you tell me that?"

"I don't know," he says voice trailing, shaking his head and shoulders drooping.

My arms trembles as I reach out for his hand. "About the other night, I want to apolo—"

He pulls his hands away from mine and crosses his arms. "No need to say anything. You've been under a lot of stress."

"But Jared, I didn't mean—"

"Listen, I bet we're almost there," he says cutting me off again and turning away.

We travel down a narrow, pothole-studded dirt path. Mangrove forests surround us. The sun glistens through the leaves, and the only sound, besides the coughing rickshaw, is the squawkings of hundreds of invisible birds.

A large compound appears, and in its center stands an alabaster white temple shaped like a mutant Easter egg. The rickshaw stops in front of a metal gate, and a man in a red turban greets us with a head bobble and a burst of language I don't understand. He helps me exit the rickshaw in a departure reminiscent of clowns exiting a tiny car.

Passing into the compound, all my muscles relax and I let out a sigh. Something in the air drains my body of its accumulated stress. A peacock struts in front of us and spreads its elegant feathers, revealing a canvas of blues, greens, and purples.

Inside the walled compound, I find women in the midst of

cooking a meal. Laughing children run up to me and tug at my *sari*. Grasping our hands, they lead us toward the temple.

The air is warm, dense and inviting, like a steam sauna. Despite everything, all the horrors I've witnessed, I smile. "What is this place?" I ask.

"A place of refuge," Jared says.

A child runs up and hands me a flower. "Why are they so happy?"

"Because of him," the man in the turban says in English, pointing toward the egg-shaped temple.

Before entering, we take off our shoes, and the marble floor sends cool tremors through my toes. We enter a room with ceilings thirty feet high. A pool with crystal blue water takes up the center of the room, and floating on the surface, a creature stares back at me.

A smiling, exuberant creature who drifts on a lotus-shaped inflatable float. It's a man-sized elephant—with giant floppy ears, a twisted trunk, and shimmering ivory tusks. Bright golden rays of light extend out around his head like an angel. His eyes—alive and bursting—are deep ocean blue.

Before I can recover from my shock, the elephant opens his mouth and with a deep baritone voice, he says, "Come, float with me." He erupts with a tremendous laugh.

I swear that the foundation of the temple shakes.

CHAPTER NINETEEN
Prophecy

A moment later, the elephant apparition fades like a magician's illusion. Under the aura is a dark-skinned Indian man, somewhere between the ages of sixty and eighty. His wispy, white hair spills over his head. Deep-set wrinkles demarcate the trenches of an often-used smile.

The man—round and plump—wears a bright yellow bathrobe and turns in lazy circles, running his fingertips across the water's surface. His eyes fix on me like an archer's sight. "You seem surprised," he says with a slight British accent.

"Well, you were an elephant a second ago," I reply.

"Hmm," he muses drawing out the M until it sounds like he's hungry. "I wonder how you would react if you saw your own deistic form."

My eyes jump to my reflected image in the water, but everything is the same. "What do you mean?"

He ignores the question and points toward the edge of the pool. "Put your feet into the water. The temperature is marvelous," he says, drawing out each syllable.

With Jared shadowing me, I sit and put my legs into the water. It's as soothing as a deep tissue massage. I exhale a long breath, dispelling any remaining tension.

Maybe it's the affectionate cadence in his voice or the way his eyes penetrate me like an X-ray machine, but I have to ask, "Have we met before?"

He nods. "We knew each other very well."

"Knew?"

"In a past life. A long time ago."

"How exactly did you know me?"

He pauses for a few seconds, grinning as if enjoying a private joke. "You were my wife," he adds, dropping the comment like a ten-pound sack of potatoes.

My breath hitches.

"You seem surprised again."

I command my jaw to lift up. "I was not expecting to meet one of my ex's."

"You must understand, we were literally other people. Our bodies were different. Only our minds were the same."

Regaining my breath, I ask, "What's your name?"

"Hmm, interesting. You don't remember." He peers into my eyes, searching for something. "It's been such a long time since I've seen you." His expression makes me blush. It's the type that lovers exchange. "My name is Ganesha."

"Ganesha?" I repeat, the name sounding somewhat familiar. "Don't think I know you."

He pirouettes along the water. "It will be good when you fully Ascend. Many things will become clear." He stares beyond me, and a huge grin surfaces like a whale breaching the water. "Ah, Arjun, you brought chai and sweets. How kind."

The man with the turban presents me with a scalding metal cup of milky tea and a plate of golden pretzel-shaped sweets. I pick one up and take a bite. Impossibly, it is sweeter than raw sugar.

"Come, Protector," Ganesha says to Jared. "You can partake as well. "

"I'm fine for now," he says, standing close to me.

"So, Ganesha, are you a good god or a bad god?"

He chuckles. "A Hindu god—celebrated as a patron of the arts, sciences, and wisdom. But most importantly, I am the remover of obstacles. I find solutions where there are none."

"Great!" I exclaim. "Don't suppose you can stop Gurzil and Rava from trying to kill me?"

Ganesha shakes his head. "Unfortunately, there is no way for me to stop them."

"You're not much of a remover of obstacles," I say, sarcastically.

"What I can do is equip you with the necessary knowledge to not only keep them at bay, and one day, the gods willing, to defeat them."

I press my hands into my temples. "You're talking about the Ascension ceremony?"

He nods. "When you fully Ascend, you will be more powerful than you can possibly imagine. You still don't understand the concept of your true nature. Once you Ascend, all will become clear."

My body tenses. I'm sick of people saying this. "That's not a reason to complete this ceremony."

"Gaia, why did you first agree to undergo your Ascension?"

I think about my lost dreams and how they haunted my life. I blamed those dreams for my loneliness. Is the knowledge worth what I lost? "If I knew then what I know now, I would have never undergone the Ascension."

"Why?"

"I lost my best friend, and now I'm going to lose my identity. My body will be hijacked by another. I won't be me anymore."

"You will still be you," Ganesha reassures. "But you will be so much more. You'll have all your past lives residing within you."

"Yeah, and that sounds horrible. I don't want an orchestra of voices in my head."

"You don't need to worry," he says. "You will be trained in the art of channeling. We all learn to harness the voices inside of us. But the first step is for you to fully complete the Ascension."

I get up from the pool and let out an exasperated laugh. "How are we going to do this? Are you going to clap your hands, say the secret words, and I'll Ascend?" I stare accusingly at Jared, who avoids my eyes and rubs the back of his neck.

"I think we have a misunderstanding." I pause and turn to find Ganesha's apologetic expression. "I can't perform the ceremony. Only trained priestesses can complete your Ascension."

My headache comes back in full strength. "Then why did we come here?"

The man's eyes open wide, and he speaks as though he's addressing an audience. "There is something special about a pilgrimage. You are searching to discover truths. The act of travel is a purifying process. You need to destroy a part of you to allow space for growth. At the end of this pilgrimage, you will be prepared to accept the truths which will inevitably present themselves."

"So, to summarize," I reply, not hiding my derision. "Coming here was a gigantic waste of time."

Ganesha unleashes one of his deep-bellied laughs. I have an urge to grab and shake the man. "It's good that you have not lost your sense of humor after two thousand years." He wipes a tear from his eye. "Nothing in life is a waste, my love. You are here because I am a sign at a crossroads. I have knowledge that others do not possess. I know where to find the priestesses that can conduct your Ascension."

"You realize," I say, "there's this thing called Skype. We could have called you."

"No," says Ganesha, his face suddenly becoming as unyielding as granite. "You needed to come here. Secrets are only as valuable as the people who protect them. It's for the safety of the priestesses that others must not know their identities or location. Each coven of priestesses operates like individual cells. This way, if one is infiltrated, the others will still be safe."

The memory of the Salem priestesses surfaces, and a shiver runs through me. "Why do they do this?"

"Ever since the Purging, this has been the safest way for us to survive."

"The Purging," I repeat, my pulse jumping. "What is it?"

Ganesha exhales. He collects his thoughts like a hiker gathers supplies for a wilderness trek. "Why do you think there is another god out to kill you?"

"I have no idea."

"It's because they've always been trying to kill you."

Shoulders tightening, I can't speak. It's chilling to think that someone has always been seeking to kill me, yet, up until a few days ago, I had no clue.

Ganesha closes his eyes. When he speaks, sorrow fills his voice. "Before the one-god religions conquered the world, humans believed in two types of gods—female and male. Among the Ascended, we call these groups Father Gods and Mother Goddesses."

"Yeah, like Zeus and Hera," I say, recalling a seventh-grade lesson about mythology.

He shakes his head. "It goes deeper. The Mother Goddesses were the flip side of the same coin as the Father Gods. The woman played an equal role in the pantheon of gods as the man. They were meant to *share* power."

"OK."

"Have you ever wondered why the Mother Goddesses stopped being part of Western culture and many other cultures around the world?"

I shrug. "I guess people stopped believing in them."

"'Stopped believing' is a nice euphemism. That is exactly what the Father Gods want you to believe." His face glows flush, nostrils flare, and his voice deepens.

"What happened?"

He sighs and stares down at his empty palms. "There was a systematic annihilation of the Mother Goddesses. The Father Gods joined together to destroy us. Throughout much of the world, all goddesses were killed, erased, and forgotten. Not only did they kill the goddesses, but they also killed their priestesses. Do you know what this means?"

I shake my head.

"If you kill the priestesses, there's no way to conduct the Ascension ceremony. This means that the Mother Goddess stays Descended. They live ignorant of their true potential. This genocide we call the Purging."

My head tilts to the side. Something doesn't click. "How is it possible that a group of priestesses survived in Salem?"

"Not all places succumbed to the Father Gods. The world was a very large place back then. Here in India, the Mother Goddesses survived. Also, there were pockets of goddesses in distant lands. It was from these survivors that Westerners re-learned the secrets and traditions of our kind."

"But things have changed since the Purging?" I ask.

"Yes, within the past century, Mother Goddesses were able to Ascend in numbers that haven't been seen in two millennia. Many have come out of hiding and are teaching the old ways again. They're building up followers."

"That's good, right?"

His face appears heavy, and he sighs. "It is good, but the Father Gods cannot accept it. They must destroy it."

"But aren't you a Father God?"

"No." Ganesha's brow wrinkles, and he frowns. "I'm a Mother Goddess like you."

"But you're a man."

"Ah, I see why you're confused. Gender does not mean a

thing," he explains. "In this life, I am a man. In the next, I may be a woman. Both genders possess qualities of each other. Yin and Yang, so to speak. The term 'Mother Goddess' applies to something deeper, older, more eternal. We believe in balance for the world, harmony between species, and peace among people. Our existence is guided by love, kindness, and caring."

"The Father Gods are different?"

"Originally, the Father Gods represented rationality, strength, and understanding. But they changed and assumed the dark sides of humanity: fear, hate, jealousy, and greed. The Father Gods now desire power above all else. Their whole existence is fueled by their insatiable hunger to control, manipulate, and dominate."

"They're planning something, aren't they?" Jared asks, his voice startling me.

"Correct, Protector. They fear that the Mother Goddesses will regain power," Ganesha replies. "The most powerful Father Gods will purge the world again."

"Is that what I think it means?" I ask, as a pit grows in my stomach.

"They will murder every Mother Goddess and all their priestesses."

"Like before," Jared adds.

"But this Purging will not be the same. The scale of destruction will be a holocaust. The Mother Goddesses will not be the only victims. The violence and hate will spill over. The world will burn. Millions will die. Civilizations will crumble."

"Which Father Gods are behind the new Purging?" Jared asks.

Ganesha shakes his head. "That is a secret I wished I knew. I have heard rumors that a Father God has risen above all the others."

"Who are you talking about?" I ask. "Gurzil?"

"No, Gurzil is a young god. This is an Ancient, like you. He keeps his identity a secret, but like gravity, his force affects events around the world. Some call him the Shadow God." Chest tightening, I remember my talk with Caishen. Ganesha floats next to me and looks into my eyes. "This is why it's vital that you complete your Ascension, Gaia. The world needs you."

"But why me?" I ask, head spinning and pulse racing. "Why am I so important?"

Ganesha glances at me and turns to Jared and asks. "You haven't told her?"

My head whips toward Jared. "Tell me what?"

He steps back, defensively. "I thought it best that you told her. I'm simply her Protector."

"Can one of you please tell me what you're talking about?" The hole in my chest grows ever wider.

"My love," Ganesha says with a delicate slowness. "It's because of the Prophecy."

"What is it?" Hands trembling, a sour taste floods into my mouth.

Ganesha's eyes dim. The room chills, and my thumping heart reverberates through my body. When he finally speaks, his voice is leaden and heavy. "There are three parts of the Prophecy." I take a breath as if steadying myself for a doctor's shot. "The first part says that you will die and be reborn in the City of Peace on the day the dead rise."

My shoulders slump. "OK, what's the second part?"

With unblinking authority, he says, "You will lead the Mother Goddesses to subjugate the Father Gods. They will be servants to you. You will rule supreme. You, Gaia, will be the force that brings balance back to the world. You will halt mankind's destruction. You will prevent the coming holocaust. You will force peace between the Father Gods and Mother Goddesses."

The room spins as my muscles quiver and heart pounds. That's when it hits me, and I nearly fall forward. My fists clench tight. Jared knew about the prophecy the entire time.

He lied to me.

I spin around and face Jared. "You knew, didn't you?"

Jared opens his mouth, maybe to defend himself, but instead, he keeps his eyes focused on the ground. He doesn't even have the guts to look me in the face.

"Why didn't you tell me? I trusted you."

He reaches out to me, his hand seeking comfort. I push it away. Taking a step back, I shake my head. "You're a liar." I don't know why I felt sorry for him before. "I knew I should have never trusted you." I storm out of the temple to escape and disappear, my skin on fire.

CHAPTER TWENTY
Puja

My vision clouds white, and my feet carry me on auto-pilot. I don't care where they lead me as long as it's away from Jared. Nails biting into my palms, I steam out of the temple and am greeted by the searing tropical heat of midday.

I can't believe he lied to me. He's just another person who says that they'll be there for me, but who will inevitably leave. I will myself to push him out of my head, but it's like clearing a room of pollen when lilac trees are in bloom. He's everywhere.

My pace slows to a walk as I enter a quiet glen, shrouded by the broad leaves of banana trees. An elegant, golden statue of a goddess stands tall in the clean-swept center of the clearing. Silver chains drape the four-armed figure, whose face is frozen in metallic serenity.

I stare at the closed eyes of the statue, telling my heart to slow. Over time, the statue's silent expressions calm my nerves. Soon, the only sound is my own breathing.

But the peace doesn't last. My skin crawls as I realize that I'm not alone.

"It's called a *puja*," Jared says, coming up behind me.

My fists clench, and I tell myself to ignore him.

"It's a shrine. People pray to it. It's a place to meditate and re-flect. A place to unburden oneself of mistakes made."

I spin around. "Have you come to admit your mistakes?" I say, trying to mask my hurt.

"I came here to talk."

"Talk about what? About how you lied to me?"

"I didn't mean to hurt you, Mattie."

"Yeah, right." My voice comes out sharper than I mean it to be. "When were you planning to tell me the truth?"

A silence ensues, stretching on forever. Eventually, he walks up beside me and kneels down in front of the shrine. He's close enough to touch me, but he doesn't. He, too, stares into the eyes of the statue. "I should have told you about the prophecy at the start."

"You think?"

He scoops up a handful of the maroon-colored dirt and lets it flow through his fingers. "I didn't really believe any of this stuff either. My mom's plan was for you to complete your Ascension. You were supposed to already know about the prophecy. It would have come to you along with all of your other memories."

"Well, look how that plan turned out." Jared's breath catches, and I immediately regret the statement. It's an insult to the women in Salem who died because of me.

"I didn't even want to be there that night. My mom begged me to come. She said it was my responsibility to keep you safe and make sure you completed your Ascension. I never asked for this job, and there is no manual on how to do it." Sweat drips down his brow and his hands are clenched. "After they died and then your friend was murdered in New York, I decided you didn't need the added pressure of knowing that you are sup-posed to be some type of messiah," he pauses. "I was afraid it would scare you too much."

I place my hands on the ground and take a deep breath. "You don't need to handle me with kid's gloves. My world has been flipped upside down. At this point, I'm open to believing anything." Sorrow elbows its way into my voice. "I thought we were working together. How can I trust you now?"

He places his hand on my bare shoulder. The touch sends shivers across my skin. "You're right. I screwed up. I'm sorry."

I let out a ragged, heavy breath. Now that I have his apology I don't know what to do with it. A part of me wants to stay mad at him. "What else are you keeping from me, Jared?"

He stares at me long and hard, his blue eyes piercing. "Mattie, I'm all in. There's nothing left to hide."

My cheeks redden. "No, this is just a job for you."

"It's more than a job," he says, keeping his eyes trained on me.

I look away and stare up through the swaying trees. "This is why the gods in Amsterdam looked at me strangely. I'm different, aren't I?" Saying it aloud makes it real. After what I saw in New York and Amsterdam, and what happened in Mumbai, it's getting harder and harder to deny.

"It's not a bad thing."

I shiver and my body slumps. This realization, that the world is not what I thought it was . . . "It scares the hell out of me."

"You don't need to be afraid, Mattie." He reaches out for my hand and my breath quickens. "I'm here for you."

I pull away. "I don't want this and never asked for it."

"Sometimes we're not given choices. Sometimes our lot in life is prescribed, and all we can do is to accept its heavy burden."

"How am I supposed to make a difference?"

"Listen," Jared says. "Humans are on a collision course for their own destruction." Jared's expression hardens. "They need someone to save them."

"But I can't be that person," I counter. "At least, I hope I'm not. I can barely take care of myself. How am I supposed to change anything?"

Jared puts both hands around mine. "Let's take it one step at a time."

I stare into his eyes and warn, "Don't think I've forgiven you. I'm still angry."

"I wouldn't dare expect otherwise."

My back and shoulders straighten. I feel better. "Next time," I say. "Be honest with me. If there is something I should know, then tell me. I'm sick of lies. Can you promise me that?"

Jared nods and takes a step back. He points in the direction of the temple. "You want to go back? I know you have lots of questions for Ganesha."

"Like, when were we married?" Despite everything, I let out a sharp laugh. "I was thrown by that one."

"Get used to it," Jared says. "I'm sure he's not your first husband or your last, for that matter." He raises his eyebrows, and I turn away, my face burning crimson.

We walk back to the temple. It's afternoon, and the heat blasts down like a sauna. The gardens, bustling before with children and women, are quiet and deserted. It must be lunchtime.

Climbing the steps into the temple, I notice there's no wind blowing through the trees. Everything is still. No peeping birds. No sound except our footsteps. We turn the corner into Ganesha's pool room, and a chill runs down my spine. The premonition reaches me a second too late.

A black club swings down and smashes into the back of Jared's head. He crumples to the floor.

My mouth drops. I unleash a scream.

Jared lays on the ground, unconscious, a thin stream of blood leaking out of his skull. His eyes roll up into his head.

My screams pique with terror. Hands clamp down on my mouth, silencing me. Another pair of hands grab my arms and slam me against the wall. Pain shoots through my chest.

I push back and wrench my head free. Two men wearing police uniforms grapple me. "What the hell is going on?"

Neither man replies. One of them twists my arm. I gasp, incapacitated with pain, thinking my bones will break. They thrust me down the hallway toward Ganesha's pool. Two other men drag Jared behind us.

In the pool room, I find five police officers armed with pistols and black clubs. They stand at attention along the perimeter. The women and children huddle together—many of them crying. The mothers hold the small children tight to their chests.

Ganesha and Arjun kneel on the floor with their hands bound behind their backs. Ganesha's face remains serene and peaceful. He even smiles when I enter. The smile should have a calming effect, but my adrenaline surges.

My eyes jump from him to the creature holding court in the center of the room. I think for a second that my pounding heart will explode from my chest like a scene from a horror film.

I observe a demon's head—a monstrous mouth, serpent's tail, a blood red aura, and huge round devil eyes that burn with a putrid light.

In an instant, I remember where I last saw the face. It was etched onto the walls of the temple in Mumbai, and it was the same one reflected in the beachside bar in Goa.

The demon bares its jagged, broken teeth at me. "The goddess has arrived," it hisses.

I gasp like I've been punched in the stomach. "Rava," I whisper.

CHAPTER TWENTY-ONE
Similar Stories

Icy fear replaces the peaceful atmosphere in the pool room. The mothers bury their children into their sides to suppress sobs. Ganesha's face is somber as two guards restrain him. Rava's demon aura fades, and I'm shocked by the figure aiming a gun at me.

It's an old woman, skinny and bent like a swirly straw. Her high forehead plateaus to a clump of black greasy hair, braided into a thick rope, stretching down her back, and hanging a few inches above the floor. Her pinched and shrewd face studies me, feeding off my fear.

She tosses a portion of her *sari* over her shoulder, wades knee-deep into the pool, and sighs. Her sharp, hazel eyes inspect me as if I'm a cut of meat at a butcher's shop. "You're so plain looking."

I don't know how to respond, so I don't say a thing. I still haven't reconciled the image of the horned demon with this woman who would more likely be found haggling over fruit prices at a market.

She inspects her reflected image in the pool and grimaces. "I hate this body," she declares. "It is ugly and ungodly. In my next life, I will choose a vessel more fitting."

I try to swallow, but there is not a drop of moisture in my mouth.

"You shouldn't have visited my temple," she chides with tightening eyes. "I have watchers everywhere."

My feet feel bolted to the floor. There is no escape.

A penurious smile emerges, and she adds, "It's a shame what he will do to you."

"Why are you doing this?" I muscle the courage to ask. "We've done nothing to you."

Her hands clench into fists, and she speaks to the water. "There was a time when I was great. I had legions celebrating my existence. I was a king who commanded nations." A stream of blood seeps down her wrist from the nails digging into her skin. "You have no idea." She twists around with a manic energy in her face. "They lived in my name! They loved in my name!" Rava proclaims, and her voice drops to a whisper. "They died in my name." She walks up to me and runs her cold, long fingers over my cheek. "Our stories aren't so different, yours and mine."

I recoil as nausea accompanies her touch. But I realize she offered me something: an insight into my past lives. "How so?"

Her eyes become quizzical. She leans forward, and her nostrils flair, smelling something in the air. "You don't remember," she muses to herself. "How is this possible unless—" Realization lights in her face, and a creepy smile emerges. A smile she could have stolen from a corpse. "Ah, I see. You are Descended."

The ensuing silence confirms her suspicions. Finally, I say, "Listen, you want respect. Fine, you have my respect. Now, let us go."

"Let me educate you, goddess," Rava sneers. "Like you, lesser gods colluded, rose up, and betrayed me." Her body shakes with perceptible rage. "They routed me in battle and captured me. They made me watch as they murdered every one of my sons. They murdered my wives, my daughters, every relative who had a drop of my blood was destroyed. They killed off my priests. They burned the papyrus and broke the tablets that taught my Ascension. They wanted to make sure that I never Ascended again, and when I had nothing left," she pauses and leans close to my face, the smell of her patchouli perfume making me gag. "They drove a spike through my stomach, crucified me, and let the vultures fight over my carcass."

My heartbeats rattle like a snare drum. Was that what happened to me? Are these the type of memories that I'll remember when I Ascend?

Rava's face crinkles into an endearment usually shown by grandmothers. "Like you, my precious goddess, they wanted to erase me from history."

I have a sudden insight. Her insistence on our shared past may be the opening I need. "We're both victims of the same crime," I say, making it up as I go along. "There's no reason why you need to help them. Why perpetuate the violence and murder?"

She doesn't answer my question; her own past ensnares her. "The memories are so fresh," she mumbles, gripping the sides of her skull. "I still remember the treachery as if it was yesterday. That is the curse of the Ascended, you know." She rambles, a maniacal lilt in her tone. "Memories from a thousand years ago are so vivid they could have happened an hour ago. Dwelling too much on the past can cause a god to go insane."

That sends fresh chills through me. "What does it feel like?"

"I remember every time I was born. I recall every moment of every meaningless life and every uncelebrated death. Year after year. Life after miserable life. It didn't matter if in one I was a lowly beggar or in another, a rich lord. In the end, I died, and all knowledge was lost."

"How did you Ascend if they killed off your priests?"

The question punctures her bubble of madness. The dead corpse smile returns. "When my Ascension finally happened, those Descended millennia seemed nothing but a blink of an eye. I had so much work to complete. In one lifetime I had to create a new priesthood and a new religion. Fortunately, men and women are as naive as they were two thousand years ago. Human nature doesn't change." The glimmer of insanity re-emerges, and her hand tightens on the grip of the pistol. Rava tilts her head and points the gun at my chest. I swallow hard, thinking that this is the end. Instead of squeezing the trigger, she says, "You're very valuable to someone we both know."

I let out a jagged gasp. "Gurzil."

"Wrong," Rava says, annoyed.

"The Shadow God?"

"Good."

"But why work with him?"

"I will be given a nation in exchange for you. Maybe even a continent of followers. I will profit greatly from you. You are my bargaining chip."

"The only reason you're helping him is because you want his support?"

I cringe from Rava's impish smile. She paces toward the pool, kneels down, and strokes the water. "I will have a new ally. If there is one thing I've learned from being immortal is that you are either all-powerful or you have powerful partners. The Shadow God controls all. He is the ruler of all the others. By helping him now, he will reward me with new followers and territory. Soon, very soon, I will regain my legions. They will praise and shower me with glory. My name will once again be carved in stone and shouted from the rooftops. RAVA! RAVA! RAVA! I will regain my greatness, and then, I will exact my revenge."

"He will betray you," says Ganesha, who has until this point remained silent and still.

Rava spins toward him, and the gun finds a new target. "You know nothing, fool."

"You can't trust the Shadow God. He will destroy you because he must have complete control."

"Silence!" screams Rava.

"You will Descend again. You will be forgotten," replies Ganesha, his voice calm and assured, oblivious to Rava's inflating anger. "It is your fate."

Rava rushes over to Ganesha. She drags him to the edge of the pool with more strength than I thought possible. She kicks him down to his knees and forces the gun's muzzle against his head. "I want you to suffer through eternity like I did."

Ganesha's eyes find mine. They convey a message. Something I don't understand now, but maybe someday will. I force myself not to break his gaze.

Rava pulls the trigger, and blood splatters across the blue rippling water.

The women scream and break into sobs. My legs give out from under me as my body drains of energy. I'm catatonic. The guards keep me propped upright.

Rava drops the gun to the ground and marches out of the room. "Take them to the station. Including the women. I've heard that Gurzil sells them. We may be able to get a good price."

With guns to our backs, they force us out of the temple and into the blistering, soulless heat of the day. My heartbeat thrashes in my ears—my insides are empty.

CHAPTER TWENTY-TWO
Survive

"Jared, wake up!"

His eyes roll in circles like a cartoon character struck on its head by an anvil. He groans and rocks his body back and forth. I let out a relieved sigh. I thought he was in a coma.

I'm struggling to keep a brave face despite our desperate situation. The women and children huddle together on the chipped hardwood benches. Some pray. Others stare forward with the round, red eyes of loss. Arjun tries to comfort them, but his words do little to help. Reinforced steel armors the police van, while metal bars block the opaque, shatterproof windows. The door has no handle and can only be opened from the outside.

Jared closes his eyes and inhales like he's sucking up all his pain. His eyes open, and he takes in our surroundings in a long arching glance. "Well, this isn't good."

My eyebrows rise as if to say "duh."

"How long have I been out?"

"An hour or so. They're driving us somewhere. Rava mentioned a station."

He lifts his handcuffed hands, touches the back of his head, and flinches. "What about Ganesha?"

I give a quick shake of my head and hold back the tears. "She killed him."

Jared shudders while processing the information. He forces away the worry in his face and says, "We need to get you out of here."

"OK," I reply, my voice full of doubt. "But how are we going to do that?"

"When they stop and take us out, you're going to run."

"Are you kidding? You're handcuffed, and they outnumber us. How are we both supposed to get away?"

His expression hardens like freezing ice. "I'm not going any-where. I'm going to buy you enough time to escape."

"Wait, this is your plan?" I ask. "I can't leave you."

"Mattie, you have to escape."

I round on him. "First of all, we're in the middle of India. I don't know where to go. Also, I'm not leaving these women and children. I don't even want to think about what Gurzil will do to them."

Jared takes my hand and grips it tightly. "Don't you under-stand? Your life is all that matters. You have to escape and live. You need to complete your Ascension."

"But," I survey the confines of the police van as if searching for an answer. "How will I do that without you? I don't know where to find another group of priestesses."

"Listen, you'll figure it out. I know you will."

My voice lowers to a whisper. "I can't do this by myself." I know I can't. I won't even make it out of the city. "I thought you said you would never leave me."

"We don't have a choice," says Jared his eyes wavering. "I'm doing this to protect you."

"Doesn't feel that way."

"It is, Mattie. When the van stops, I'll draw away their attention. You run. If you don't escape, there's no hope for any of us."

I don't know how to respond, so I don't say a thing and stare down at the dirty floor of the van.

A moment later, the van slows, takes a turn, and stops. The engine turns off. Jared locks eyes with me. "Be ready, when I make my move, you run, and don't look aback."

I nod, but I'm full of doubt and fear. What about Jared? What about the women and children? How can I leave them?

The van rocks as our captors exit. There is an interminable silence. Blood pounds through my veins, and a cold sweat drenches my back.

I hear the door unlock. I turn to Jared, but he's resumed a closed-eyed, catatonic expression, his body limp. That instant, the door swings open, and light floods in.

Shielding my eyes, I soon discern four silhouettes; they're the same men who ambushed us at the temple. Two of the guards—expressions tense and ready—climb into the van.

This is not going to work.

They grab Jared by his arms, lift him up, and drag him out of the van. Despite the manhandling, Jared's face remains deadened.

A third guard points at me and commands something which I don't need a translator to understand. He grabs my arm and pulls me up from the bench. The fourth guard collects the women and children.

We're in a walled courtyard. Ten yards in front of us is an ugly, concrete government-style building. I know that once we enter, there's no hope of leaving. The guard's fingers tighten around my arm as if sensing my desperation.

We're halfway across the courtyard when Jared makes his promised distraction. Without any preamble, he jumps to his feet, lunges forward, and breaks away from the two guards. The flustered police officers react clumsily. Jared takes advantage of their surprise by driving his elbow into the guard's nose on his right. The guard collapses to his knees, gripping his face.

The guard on the left jumps at him, but Jared dodges him and swings his manacled hands over the man's throat. The man kicks out his legs and grapples to free himself of Jared's hold.

The man holding my arm releases his grip. He reaches down for the black club dangling from his belt and runs over to attack Jared, leaving me free.

This is my chance, but fear freezes me in place. These adrenaline-filled moments make me like a snail crossing an expressway after a rainstorm. Jared swings around. He's using the guard as a shield against the officer with the club. Jared's face blazes red with exertion, and his eyes shout at me: Run.

I snap out of my paralysis, spin around, and sprint in the opposite direction. Passing the van, in front of me is a long stone corridor. At its end is an open, busy street.

Freedom.

Pumping my legs, I race to the street. I don't look around because I'm afraid if I do, I'll lose all hope. The street is only twenty-five feet away. In a few seconds, I will be out and lost in the chaos of the city.

Almost there.

Ten feet more. I'm going to make it.

Then it's as if someone's jammed my ponytail into the gears of a machine. I'm yanked backward. I'm pulled so hard that I lift off my feet. I don't have a moment to register the pain streaking through my scalp, as I feel every follicle ripping out. The pull on my ponytail is so great, that I'm swung around—thrown through the air.

For a brief moment, I marvel at my own flight pattern, before I realize I'm headed for a face-first crash into the corridor's stone wall.

I lower my chin in time as my forehead takes the brunt of the collision. Stars and streaks of light explode across my vision. The pain is so much I'm sick to my stomach. The throbbing in my head is like a blasting tuba.

I fall to the ground and don't think I'll ever get up. Through my spinning vision, one of the officers—young and muscled, but face corrupt and grim—looms over me. His outstretched hand charges at me like an open jaw, ready to swallow me whole. The dizziness increases in intensity, and it's like I'm in a food processor. Everything spins faster and mashes together.

The hand looms toward my throat. I'm going to die from the pain, but hopefully, I'll pass out beforehand. The world spins so fast that the outstretched hand appears and disappears. It flickers, fades, and dissolves for good.

Everything goes white.

CHAPTER TWENTY-THREE
Gray Boulders

When I awake, I have no idea where I am. A second ago, I'd
been in the corridor, but now, I have no clue. My mind, slow
and groggy, deciphers the randomness. Gone is the guard. Gone
is the pain. Gone is the station. I don't think I'm even in India
anymore.

I'm alone, and the desolate wind blows. The whiteness, I realize, is snow. Plumes of fat flakes swirl in mini-cyclones and dust
the ground.

I turn, taking in my surroundings. Far beyond me, I see a valley filled with dark evergreen trees, swaying mournfully in the
howling wind. On the far side of the valley, a mountain range
stretches out like a dinosaur's spine. Snow-capped peaks rise in
the distance. How did I get here?

Zooming back in, I focus on my immediate surroundings. I
must be at the top of a hill or mountain because the ground
slopes away from me. Hundreds of gray boulders, painted dark
red and quilted with a thin sheet of snow, dot the land. I know it
must be freezing, but my body doesn't register the temperature.

A chill streaks down my back; something isn't right. My eyes fixate on the closest boulder. It takes me a second to realize that it's not made of stone. It's a body.

A corpse staring at the heavens. He's a soldier, dressed in a gray silk smock and coned helmet. One hand grips a broken spear, while the other lies at his throat, which is slit wide open. He lies in a puddle of frozen blood, face immortalized in pure agony. Around me, the boulders morph into thousands of dead soldiers. The dark red paint is blood.

Eyes widening, I feel that my throat is dry like the wind. It occurs to me like a lightning flash. This is a battle site, and I've been here before.

More than that, I've—I've—killed here before. A part of me is sick and full of fear, but another part is as calm as a sunrise.

I hear a voice above the howling wind. It's a deep, baritone mumble—like someone praying. No, not praying. Chanting.

I don't search to find the source. I feel my own lips moving, and it occurs to me that it's my own voice. The words are foreign. I shouldn't know their meaning, but I understand them nonetheless.

Glancing down, I wear a bright orange robe. My hands are different; they're callused, massive, and strong. I'm not surprised that these alien hands hold a polished sword with an edge so sharp it could slice flesh like hot butter. The sword lies across my lap, and in the polished blade, I notice my reflection.

The calm and composed face is not mine. It's a man with a shaved head and a round, wrinkled, Asian face. In the man's eyes, a crimson light blossoms into an all-consuming fire. The fire leaps from the reflected image into my own eyes. A wave of heat and energy flows through me. I convulse and stare at the heavens as the sky lights up into a brilliant red.

A thought awakens within me like a butterfly climbing out of a chrysalis.

An instant later, my eyes snap open. Not a second has passed since I hit my head.

The guard's hand still reaches for my throat, but time and space distort. Everything is in slow motion. I realize the man is off balance, and he's not protecting his right flank. His movements are clumsy and slow. He underestimates me. These thoughts occur to me as if someone whispers them in my ear.

As his hand is about to embrace my throat, my body acts on its own volition. My right hand strikes out and grabs his wrist. Without a second of hesitation, I bend the wrist and twist it with a sharp motion. The wrist snaps like a frail twig.

The guard's eyes bulge. He howls, falls beside me, and cradles his broken appendage.

With slow and steady balance, I stand. My head still hurts, but the pain diminishes, or maybe I'm ignoring it. I am myself, yet I am not me. I brush the dust from my sari with the hand that broke the wrist. I marvel at how natural it was to act out in violence. How did I know that I could do that to the man's wrist?

While I ponder the peculiar nature of my current state, the guard's hoarse screams attract the attention of another police officer. A giant of a man runs toward me from twenty feet away. He's armed with a black club, which he raises over his head ready to strike me down. Despite the man being twice my size, I don't panic. Instead, I wait for him, expecting him. Inviting him. I know exactly what I'm going to do when he attacks. By the time the guard gets within striking distance, he's panting—breaths heavy and sweat forming around his armpits.

I wonder why he doesn't control his breathing or conserve his energy. Then, I wonder why I think this when the thought of conserving energy has never occurred to me before. I'm still deep in contemplation when the cop swings the club at me.

He would have smashed my skull in if I hadn't taken a small step to the left. Only a half step. The club swings through empty space, and his attack results in him tilting off balance. His head dips down with the momentum.

Before he has time to recover, I drive my knee upwards. My knee connects with the man's nose, shatters the bone. A fire hose spray of blood shoots from his face.

The officer rears up, his eyes spike open, hands shielding his broken face. But by the time he rights himself, my foot arches like a pendulum through the air. It connects with the man's skull and drives him forward. After he hits the ground, his arms twitch and then lie still.

How is it possible that I can kick so high and with so much force? What has changed in me? Before I can confront the flood of questions that spring to mind, my eyes notice the black club on the ground. I reach down and pick it up. The heavy, blunt instrument feels more comfortable in my left hand than my right. Strange, because I'm right-handed.

One of the women screams, drawing my attention away.

I turn and sprint back to the place where Jared took out the first guard. I find the tables turned. One of the guards holds Jared from behind, while the other throws heavy punches into his midsection as if he is a slab of meat.

A second later, I'm behind the man throwing the punches. With a swift and sharp kick, I take out one knee. He collapses, shock shooting through the man's eyes. I swing the club. The man's front teeth explode out of his mouth like piñata candy.

Fear enters the last guard's face. While holding Jared in front of him like a shield, the captor brandishes a spear pointed knife.

He waves the knife at me, warning me off in a language I know is Malayalam.

I approach the man without hesitation. The guard throws Jared to the ground and lunges at me, aiming to stab me in the gut.

With a chop, I knock the knife from the man's hand. It jangles to the ground. The black club swings upwards and connects with his chin. He flies backward into the air and crashes to the ground.

I take a calm breath. I haven't even broken a sweat, yet all the guards are immobilized.

The Indian women stare at me with part amazement and part fear. Energy oozes out of me, and the black club falls from my hand. I survey the bloodied, beaten bodies of my captors. The screams of the man with the broken wrist have silenced. He must have passed out from the pain. Pain—such a strange thought; I feel none.

From the ground, Jared groans, and fresh bruises cover his face. He coughs up blood and stares at me with wide eyes. "What the hell was that?"

The world spins again—violent and unstable. My eyes flutter, and I know this time I'm going to pass out. Whatever or whoever was controlling me has departed. I look at Jared with no shortage of fear before saying. "I killed them. All of them." The throbbing in my head escalates, it's too much to bear, and I black out.

CHAPTER TWENTY-FOUR
Unexpected Reactions

I wake up and find myself in a huge bed. The cold air chills my nose and soothes my burning temples. I'm like a caterpillar in a duvet cocoon of high-thread-count cotton—safe and secure.

Then, the thumping in my skull makes me groan. Materializing by my side, Jared presses a cool, moist washcloth against my forehead.

"Oh," I exclaim, "that's heaven."

"How are you feeling?"

"Ughhhh." My headache diminishes to a dull beat. I'm somewhere between awake and unconscious. I clear my parched throat, and say, "Like I hibernated through the winter."

The bruises on Jared's face are a watercolor painting of greens, yellows, and purples. I sit up surprised, but the room spins, and I fall back to my elbows, breathing hard.

"Take it easy," he warns. "No need to rush." He offers me a mini-bar bottle of ginger ale. "Drink this. You're dehydrated."

The cold, sweet soda is liquid bliss on my tongue. I finish the entire bottle in a matter of seconds. "Thanks."

We're in a hotel room. There's another bed to the side and a flat-screen television muted to CNN in front of me.

"I want to stand up," I say.

"You need help?"

"I'll be OK." I rise, albeit more slowly than before as blood rushes from my head. Once I settle, I swing my legs off the bed. When my feet touch the carpet, a hundred pinpricks explode up my legs. The feeling passes after a minute. With Jared ready to catch me, I stumble toward the window.

When I throw open the heavy curtains, I see a desert lit up by a bright waning moon, dull light illuminating the sand in an ethereal blue. A lone date palm stands beside a puddle-hole oasis, and even farther out, a line of camels traverses the great expanse.

"Where are we?" I ask, unable to tear my eyes away.

"Dubai," Jared says.

My spine stiffens, and my mouth falls open. "Why?"

"We're traveling to meet a Mother Goddess who will assist with your Ascension."

"How long have I been out?"

"You've been asleep for almost twenty hours."

I stare at him as if he informed me that Martians have invaded. What happened? My mind is as foggy as a steam room. "How did we get here?"

"You can thank Arjun, Ganesha's Protector, if you ever see him again," he replies. "He helped to smuggle us out of the country."

Bits and pieces assemble like a jigsaw puzzle. "What about the women and children?"

"Arjun took care of them. In the event of his death, Ganesha had put together a plan. They will be fine. Arjun also told me where to go and who to meet to complete your Ascension."

The memory of what happened at the police station rushes back. Legs teetering, I collapse into an armchair next to the window. I turn to Jared, feeling desperate. "What happened back there? How—how did I do those things?" The images flash before me—breaking bones, shattering skulls, screams of pain.

Jared's eyes widen and he shakes his head, "That was amazing." His response makes me sick to my stomach. "We would be dead if it weren't for you."

"I wasn't in control of my body. It was like in Mumbai, but scarier." I stare down at my open palms—afraid of what I'm capable of. "I was hurting people, and I was fine with that."

"You saved us, though."

He doesn't understand. "Someone else was controlling my body. It was like I was watching them hurt those people. It was terrifying."

Jared comes up to me and puts his hand on my shoulder. "Before you started fighting, do you remember anything?"

I take a second to pierce the haze that my memories have become. "I remember being on a mountaintop. There were all these dead soldiers around me. I was speaking—I think—Chinese. I was a monk in orange robes, and I had a sword."

"You were a warrior in a past life."

I rub my temples. This is way too much to take in. "But I didn't ask for his help. I didn't want to hurt anyone."

"At the police station, you had a fight-or-flight moment. In that instance of stress, a past life took control."

"Oh, god," I reply. It's as if my world is a snow globe that's been shaken by a child. "This is really scary."

"What is?"

My shoulders slouch, as I slide toward a complete meltdown. At the very least, the responsible thing to do would be to lock me away in a prison and throw away the key. "Don't you understand? I can't control this." I wrap my arms around myself. "At any point, one of these past lives could barge in and take over. You don't know how it felt. When I was fighting those men, I was still there and watching. But I couldn't do anything. I was powerless."

Jared shakes his head. "I don't think you need to worry. Your past lives appear to take control only when you need them. Think about it. In Mumbai, you needed to express yourself. At the police station, you needed to defend yourself. Your past lives rescued you."

"But not having control of my body or mind . . ." I stand up from the chair and pace the room, my hands pressed to the side of my head. "What if I never have control?"

"What are you talking about?"

"Rava," I say under my breath.

"What about her?"

"She was insane, and her past lives made her that way. When I Ascend, that's what's going to happen to me."

He grabs my hand and sits me down beside him on the bed. "Mattie, Rava is a Father God, whose soul was corrupted by hatred and anger. You are stronger than that."

I survey the quiet and lonely desert. I don't know what to think or believe. I've never thought of myself as strong or brave. Just the opposite, I'm weak. "But—" I'm quiet for a second. "What if that doesn't happen?"

"What do you mean?"

"Do you realize how close we came to—" I remember Patrick and what they did to him. "What if I—" I can't finish the thought.

"What happens if you die?"

I recoil as Jared's words hit their mark. The thought sends shivers through me, and all I can manage is a nod.

"You'll be reincarnated into a new body."

"What do you mean by a 'new body'?"

"You'll be a newborn."

"I don't understand."

"Children are born every second. Your consciousness, your soul, will be transferred into one of them."

"So basically, I'll hijack a baby's mind. Sounds super."

"All souls move from one body to the next. That's the nature of birth and death."

"Except, I'll be able to remember all my past lives."

Jared shakes his head. "You won't remember any past life. When you die, you become Descended." He must see the confusion in my face because he says, "Take Ganesha for example. You saw him die?" I nod, feeling a shudder run through me. "But because he has followers, they will be able to Ascend him into a new body. He will be able to remember all his past lives. However, if he didn't have followers, then he would still be reborn into a newborn, yet he would be Descended and would not be able to remember anything."

"But I saw Ganesha die. His followers weren't conducting any ceremony."

"From what I learned from my mother, there is a short period of time between when a person dies and when they are reincarnated into a new mind. That's when the ceremony can occur."

"I don't have any priests or priestesses. In my next life, who will I be?"

Jared shrugs, which does little to inspire confidence. "It's completely random. You could end up anywhere in the world. You could die as a Mongol Shaman and be reborn as an Aboriginal. Die a doctor in Boston, be reborn a farmer's son in Africa."

"It's the lottery for human souls."

"Why do you think you've been 'lost' for over two thousand years? You have been cycling through lives the entire time without any clue of who you were."

As if I didn't need anything else to freak me out, my face flashes up on CNN. The banner on the bottom part of the screen reads: Police still searching for suspected killer Mattie Fisher.

Tears well in my eyes. My life is over. I wish I could reverse everything, see Patrick again, see my mom again. Body trembling, my head falls forward. Wanted by humans and gods alike. What's the point in living?

Jared notices my plunge into depression. He turns off the television and then wraps his arm around me. "Mattie, it's going to be OK."

I shake my head as the tears start to fall. "No, it isn't." He pulls me close to him and gently presses my head against his chest. I hear his heart pounding and can feel his skin radiating heat.

My tears taper off, but he doesn't let go of me. Instead, his fingertips dance softly along my arm. A breath shudders through me, and my heart races. I feel his body beneath his thin shirt.

I look up, and our eyes meet and my mouth goes dry. His breath comes shallow and fast and there's a spark of fierceness in his eyes.

Then, on some unspoken cue, we kiss. It's like the meeting of two rivers as our lips connect.

Tender and wild—the kiss banishes all thoughts. Jared is the only thing in the universe. His tongue, his teeth, the caress of his hands, the throbbing beat of his pulse.

Heart pounding against my own chest, fire lights up my entire body. My skin is as hot as a frying pan.

I'm no longer in the room. I'm hovering somewhere high above in a place I've only dreamed of.

Just as I'm beginning to enjoy this fevered high, I come crashing back to earth.

He pulls away—his gaze cloudy. Pressing his hand against his forehead, he shakes his head, fighting a thought in his mind.

Face flustered, Jared stands up, backs away, and rushes toward the door.

"Wait," I say. "You can stay."

He pauses, still looking confused. "Listen, get some rest. We have a long flight tonight. I'll be back in a bit." Then he disappears out the door.

Did I do something wrong? I'm left with a free-falling sensation, while at the same time, my lips tingle and buzz from the
kiss. What the heck just happened?

CHAPTER TWENTY-FIVE
This Old Church

Beautiful people surround us. I stand at the edge of Ipanema Beach, watching flawless women in string bikinis and handsome men in tight Speedos peacock across the white, hot sand.

High above, the statue of Christ the Redeemer praises the city of Rio de Janeiro. The sounds of samba—a strumming of loose guitar strings and fast drums—drift from some unknown direction. The smell of garlic, sizzling meat, and tropical fruit infuses the air. The clear sapphire ocean, warm as a bathtub, mesmerizes me. The sun blazes down, burning my shoulders red. At the airport, I had substituted my sari for a green sleeveless sundress; I must look like a Christmas wreath.

I take a moment to breathe in the air. I can't believe I'm in Rio, and before this in Dubai, India, and Amsterdam. I had never even left the US before, and in my wildest imagination, I could not have conjured up the last week.

Jared notices neither the beautiful people, the shimmering waters, the hot sun, nor the pretty dress that I picked out. His forehead wrinkles and sweat drips down his nose as he juggles a soccer ball with a group of kids on the beach.

I can't hold back a smile as he bounces the ball off his head and knees. I love that he joined their game.

He passes off the ball to a ten-year-old who keeps it in the air.

"You're not bad," I say, giving him a thumbs up.

Jared smiles. "Thanks." He puts his hat back on his head. "Let's go back to the church," he suggests. "Maybe we missed something."

On the plane ride from Dubai to Rio, I tried flirting with Jared, who seemed much more interested in taking sleeping pills than dwelling on the kiss we shared. Our taxi had dropped us off in front of an ancient church near the beach. The moss-covered marble edifice had aging sculptures of prophets engraved on its exterior. We looked inside but it was abandoned. We'd circled the same block for an hour searching for the Mother Goddess but came up empty.

When we get back to the church, I see a placard on the front of the deserted building which says it was built in the sixteenth century. "Are you sure this is the right place?"

He nods and pulls down the brim of a straw hat he bought at the beach.

"Who are we looking for again?"

"Hathor," he says. "She's a Mother Goddess—an Ancient like you."

We walk up the church's crumbling stone steps. Inside, the smell of musk and mold permeates creaking pews. The dirt-stained walls arch up to a domed roof where pigeons scatter at the sound of our entry. Any religious articles have long ago been removed.

We return outside and sit down on the steps, feeling defeated. The church reminds me of something Rava had mentioned. "Do Ascended gods have anything to do with religions?"

Jared snorts a laugh. "The Ascended created religions."

"You're kidding?"

He takes off his goofy hat and wipes his brow with the sleeve of his shirt. "Remember the main problem of being Ascended? Once you die, you're reincarnated into a new body. But this new body could be anywhere in the world, and you're Descended — you don't remember your past lives. But, with the help of priests and priestesses, the rebirth can be controlled. They can redirect your soul into a new body. The Ascended created religions to control their reincarnation."

"How exactly?"

"A religion is comprised of followers who believe in a higher power or set of views that give meaning to their existence. People sacrifice their lives for these beliefs. Harnessing the power of faith, an Ascended god maintains control. With the Ascension ceremony, a god doesn't lose his followers or power. Religion creates an infrastructure, a system that stays within a god's control. To this day, the tradition is still in play with Tibetan Buddhism and Indian Gurus directing their own reincarnation. The Pope is probably the best example."

My mind does a back flip. "The Pope?"

"Not every Pope, but certainly the majority."

"Why are there so many religions?"

"There are thousands of Ascended gods. Every new religion is an attempt by a god to either gain power, establish their power, or steal power away from other gods."

"Wait," I interrupt. "Gods can take over the religions of others?"

"Have you read about the split between the Roman Catholic church and the Eastern Orthodox Church?"

"Yeah."

"Well, in the beginning, there was only one church. You know what happened? One god usurped the power of another. They literally convinced half their followers to break away."

"I thought the break-up was for religious reasons."

"The Ascended cloak their movements and influence. But if

you pull off the layers, you find them there. They're always there. Influencing and manipulating the course of human history," he says, a bitter tinge to his voice.

"How many times has this occurred?"

"You mean the splitting of religions? Hundreds of times. The same thing occurred centuries later with Martin Luther and the creation of Protestantism. The split between Orthodox and reformed religions. The Ascended are constantly battling one another for believers and power."

"Rava had a religion, right?"

"Yes, but her religion was tiny. She probably walks a fine line because if one of the Ancient Father Gods discovered her position, they would crush her and take over her followers."

"What do you mean by 'Ancient' Father Gods?"

"Some gods are older than others. Often these older Ascended gods have more power and influence."

"This sounds less like religion and more like politics."

"In the beginning, the Ascended gods created religions, but they evolved with time. As religion lost influence to national identities, some of the Ascended became kings and queens. Divine Right was a concept created by Ascended gods. Henry the Eighth, Genghis Khan, Caesar. All Ascended gods."

I fall silent, contemplating the weight and implication behind Jared's words. The Ascended are more omnipresent than I'd ever imagined. I'm not ready or strong enough to take on the fate that the Mother Goddesses want from me. I breathe sharply as I remember Ganesha and something he told me. "What's the third part of the prophecy?"

"Huh?"

"Don't 'huh?' me. Before Rava attacked, Ganesha mentioned that my prophecy had three parts. The second part was the messiah business, but he never explained the third part."

Jared shakes his head. "I don't know. I only knew about the first and second part."

"I swear if you're lying to me again—"

"Mattie, I swear I didn't even know there was a third part."

At that moment, a bearded man in his late fifties walks between us. The man—draped in gold chains and sprouting a forest of chest hair from his popped collar shirt—gives us a quick nod, climbs up the stairs, and enters the church.

Jared and I exchange a baffled expression.

"Why did that guy walk into an abandoned church?" I ask.

"I have no idea."

We get up and watch as the man goes to the back of the church, past the rotting pews to the altar. He enters one of the confessional booths hidden off to the side. We wait ten minutes, and the man doesn't emerge.

"Wait here," Jared says. He walks over to the booth and pokes his head inside. A few seconds later he waves me over; we squish together into the small confessional. I feel Jared's breath on my neck, and my pulse jumps a notch.

A priest pulls aside a partition. Through the latticed wall, the man doesn't appear to be a priest. He wears a sleek, fashionable suit and no white collar. His hair has a little too much gel in it.

The man rattles off something fast in Portuguese.

"Sorry, do you speak English?" I ask.

The man bares a grin. "Ah, Americans, yes?"

We nod.

"Well, don't you have something to say?" the man prompts. "After all, you are in a confessional."

Jared's brow furrows. He turns to me and whispers. "I'm not Catholic. Are you?" I shake my head. "Bless me, Father, for I have sinned?" he asks, unsure.

The man let's out a sharp laugh. "Haven't we all sinned, my friend? Haven't we all . . ."

He flicks a switch on his side of the confessional. A mechanical grinding screeches. My hand shoots out for balance. The booth rotates one hundred and eighty degrees and comes to a jarring stop. Jared and I exchange a wary glance. Peeking my head out of the confessional, the decaying church is gone.

Dark velvet lines the sumptuous and rich room. A deep, throbbing ruby-red shag rug covers the marble floor. Golden candelabras light the room, and oriental perfume invades the space.

A barefoot woman waits in the center of the room. She wears a thin, black silk negligee. Her perfect body, I suspect, is most likely the product of Brazil's famous surgeons. I notice Jared staring and a sudden spike of cold shoots up my spine.

In the shadows, two suited men—hulking and immobile with roving eyes—stand with crossed arms.

"What is this place?" I ask.

The woman speaks in English, tinged with a heavy dollop of Portuguese accent. "We rarely receive American visitors." Her lusty smile disarms me. "Usually, our guests only come by appointment, but we can accommodate you for your first time. Come." She waves her hand for us to follow. I try my best to ignore the smile she throws to Jared.

The woman escorts us down a hallway, and we turn into another candlelit room, and I'm beyond confused. Ten beautiful women—all different ages, races, and sizes—stand in a line, dressed in lingerie that leaves little to the imagination. Their faces pout, smile, entice. Some demur, while others hold contemptuous stares.

Our guide spreads out her arms and declares, "Pick the ones you desire."

At that moment, I realize where we are. "I think we have a misunderstanding. We're not here to—um—to—ugh."

"Hire one of us?" our escort suggests.

"Exactly," I say, feeling my face burn red.

The woman tilts her head. "Then, why are you here?"

"We're here to meet someone."

"Who?"

"Hathor," Jared says.

The name has a sudden meditative effect on the women. Their faces assume somber and serious expressions as they drop their act.

Recovering a second later, our guide asks, "Why didn't you say so? She never receives visitors asking for her by her true name. Follow me." The woman turns out of the room. We go down a separate hallway lined with timeworn stone slabs and arrive at a massive teak door with a bronze heart-shaped rapper.

The woman knocks, and a voice responds on the inside. Our escort pokes her head through the door and speaks in Portuguese. Hearing a faint reply, she casts the door open wide. "She will see you."

In the room, light pours in through stained glass windows that depict biblical images. An Ascended goddess stands to greet us; a red aura blazes up around her body and her skin is as smooth as marble. A lustrous mane of red hair cascades over her shoulders like crawling fire.

The aura and image fade, and the olive skinned woman is as beautiful as her phantasmal image. Dressed in a black Versace dress, the woman is likely in her early forties. High cheekbones and pecan-brown eyes define her stunning face.

She walks around a glass desk neatly laid out with papers and a flat-screen computer, and opens her arms wide.

The woman approaches me, smiles, and gives me a strong hug. "Oh Gaia, it has been too long," she drawls in a heavy Mississippi accent. She kisses me on both cheeks and holds me tight. "I've prayed to the heavens that this day would come. Hallelujah!"

CHAPTER TWENTY-SIX
Betty Jean and Luisita

"Call me Betty Jean." Her heavy Southern accent completely contrasts with her features, and this throws me off. She takes an appraising step back. "My lord! You are ravishing," she says. "How in sweet peas did you find this body?"

"Luck of the draw?" I feel my cheeks burn. "You're Hathor?"

She raises her index finger and wags it. Her hips sway as well. "For our purposes, Betty Jean is what I'll be called." She reaches over and plucks a piece of lint off my dress. "What's your name, honey?" she asks. "Your *real* name."

"Mattie Fisher."

"Mattie. Mattie. Mattie," Betty Jean sings. "Short for Matilda?" I nod, and she bursts out laughing. "I love it!"

I glance at Jared, who looks totally confused.

"What a name," she continues. "A glorious name. Do you know its source?"

"Uh, no."

"Stems from the Germanic name *Mahthildis* meaning 'strength in battle.'" Her eyes shine with admiration. "Fits you perfectly."

I look around the room, my mind filled with questions. "We knew each other in a past life?"

She pinches my cheek. "You're so cute when you're Descended!"

I brush her hand away, but she doesn't take offense. "How did you know I was Descended?"

"Honey, I could see it in your eyes the minute you walked in. You were as surprised as a raccoon in a barbershop. You have no clue who I am." Her expression shifts to a faux sulk. "And we were once as close as sisters."

"Related?"

"Naw, but like two piglets in a pen."

A floral-designed Japanese fan materializes in her hand. Her eyes switch from me and land on Jared. One of her eyebrows makes an approving jump. "And who is this string bean?"

"Jared Stone, ma'am.," he replies, extending his hand.

Betty Jean walks over and ignores his hand. She raises her arm and slaps him on his ass. His eyes bulge with surprise. "Yes. You are rock hard." Her grip tightens, and his eyes pop. "You're Matilda's Protector?"

"Yes," he says, his voice higher.

Betty Jean releases her grasp and turns back to me. "I always love my Protectors. They are like best friends, lovers, and hired muscle all rolled into one convenient package!" She gestures to the woman waiting at the door. "Rosa has been my faithful Protector since I first Ascended. But don't for a second write her off because of her beauty. Rosa is a trained killer in six martial arts. She can paralyze you with her pinky fingers." Betty Jean winks, leans close, and whispers, "Which ain't always a bad thing in bed."

My cheeks are burning as Rosa bows. "I live to serve my goddess."

"Speaking of which," she says to Rosa, "would you mind givin' Mr. Stone a tour of our magnificent church? I wish to talk to Matilda in private."

Jared clears his throat and doesn't budge. "As you said, my job is to protect her."

"Oh, honey. Don't take your job so seriously."

"I'm afraid I will," he says, crossing his arms. "I'm not going anywhere."

"It's OK, Jared," I assure, eyeing Betty Jean with curiosity. "We can trust her." His mouth drops as if to say, '*You're sure?*', but after a few seconds and a reluctant nod, he follows Rosa out of the room.

When they're gone, Betty Jean flashes a conspiratorial smile. "You see. Feels good to boss men around. It keeps them on their toes and in their place."

"I think that was the first time I've ever given him a command that he followed."

"He may be a Protector, but he ain't the boss," she says in her no-nonsense manner. "You call the shots."

I file away that tidbit of advice for later use. "You mind if I ask you something, Betty Jean?"

"Oh course, honey cheeks, that's why you're here."

I run my eyes down the woman's voluptuous frame, long legs, smooth olive-tinted skin, and ask, "Why do you sound like a southern African-American lady?"

She erupts with giggles. After she's done, she says, "Now that is an excellent observation." She takes my hand and guides me to a plush purple sofa running along the wall. "You're goin' to need to sit down to hear what I gotta tell you." We sit down, and the scent of Jasmine wafts off her. "You see, I'm channelin' one of my past lives. I thought Betty Jean's voice may be less of a shock and put you more at ease."

Rubbing my temples, I ask, "Then, who is Betty Jean?"

"Why, Betty Jean was the sweetest soul this side of the Mississippi," she says, voice bright. "Her peach cobbler won the blue ribbon three times at the Neshoba County Fair. She had eight children and twenty-three grandchildren, and god knows how many great-grandchildren by now."

"So, she really was an African-American lady?"

"Now you're getting it."

"But . . ." I pause, not sure how to put it politely. "Betty Jean's dead."

"Well, yes," she concedes with a grimace. "Her body stopped livin' in 1953, but that don't mean that Betty Jean's soul disappeared. Why she's still as sassy as the day they nailed the coffin shut. She's almost mortified to death by your comment." She falls into more giggles. "Oh, she always has such a naughty sense of humor!"

"I think I get it. You can speak to me through any of your past lives, but you've chosen to use Betty Jean."

"Matilda, you've always been smarter than a bee sting." She flutters her eyes toward the ceiling. "I could be speakin' Hungarian or Bahasa if you so wished, but I felt that Betty Jean would be best."

"But who are you really? Who is Hathor?"

She raises her hands above her head and runs them down the length of her body. "Hathor is the name for the amalgamation of past lives that stands in front of you. If you're referrin' to historical mythology, then Hathor is most similar to Aphrodite."

"The Greek goddess of love?"

"More or less, in ancient Egypt, the peoples there gave me that name. They used to worship me in the matters of pleasure, beauty, and most importantly," she places her hand on my leg, "sex."

"Yeah," I say, removing her hand from my knee. "I figured that based upon the meat market you have out front."

"Don't be a prude and don't be judgmental." Betty Jean chastises me with a slight rap of her closed fan. "Luisita was not born into an easy life."

"Who is Luisita?"

"Luisita is the name of the person who was born in this present lifetime."

"Let me get this straight," I say, feeling even more confused. "This is Luisita's body, through which Hathor is channeling the past life of Betty Jean?"

"You got it!" she exclaims, fanning herself. "I love Luisita, but that poor girl did not have an easy upbringin'. She was born in the slums around Rio, and let me tell you, honey, her family was so poor the beggars gave 'em handouts. So, it ain't no wonder that by the age of sixteen, Luisita was a workin' girl on the streets, tryin' to scrape together enough change to put food on the table."

"That's horrible."

Betty Jean shrugs. "You gotta understand that life here is the same as it is in Jackson, Mississippi or any place for that matter. The same type of poverty exists everywhere, and girls face the same difficult decisions as poor Luisita."

"Still, to have no choice but to sell your body . . ."

Betty Jean finds my eyes and confesses, "I am not tryin' to minimize how horrible it is. I want to put it in perspective for you. Horrible things were done to Hathor throughout the centuries. I've seen the worst of humanity, but I've also seen the best."

"But, I don't understand," I struggle, "if you're Ascended, why did you end up as a prostitute? I thought the point of the Ascended was that they have thousands of years of knowledge. Couldn't you just, I don't know, use your infinite wisdom to get a job as a scientist or something?"

"Luisita only Ascended twenty years ago."

"Oh, I thought—"

"That I've always been Ascended?" Betty Jean shakes her head. "Like you, I hadn't Ascended for almost two thousand years." Betty Jean places her hand on my shoulder as if to comfort me. "The Father Gods Descended us during the Purgin'."

"When you say 'Descended', you mean . . ."

"Oh, they murdered us," she says, as nonchalantly as she would mention the weather. "You, me, most of the Mother Goddesses."

I'm confused again. Because if she was murdered and all her priestess died, "How did Luisita Ascend?"

Betty Jean's smile grows in size. "Luisita had a natural Ascension."

"What's that?"

"Her Ascension was not planned. It occurred without the help of priestesses," Betty Jean explains.

"Isn't that impossible?"

Her gaze drifts off out the stained glass windows. I realize the images depict the stories of Rebecca, Rachel, and Sara. "Luisita was twenty and still a prostitute. She knew that if she kept up with the life, she would die young. Being a streetwalker is dangerous. She never knew if the next man she'd sleep with would also be her killer. It was during one those frightening nights that she met the man who was to be her true love."

"You mean a customer?"

"Oh no, give some credit to the girl. She does have standards," Betty Jean says, emphasizing with another playful rap of her fan on my wrist. "He was a Catholic priest who had forsworn the flesh."

"She fell in love with a priest?"

"Well, not right away. Relationships evolve. Think about Mr. Stone; I'm sure you didn't immediately fall for him."

"Wait, I don't—"

"Oh honey, don't try to deny it. I see the way you look at him. Are you that surprised that he looks the same way back at you?"

It's like someone knocked me on the head. I wasn't actually aware he was looking at me any differently. Was he?

Betty Jean interrupts this chain of realizations. "Every night, that nice priest would go to Luisita's street corner and preach.

He accused her of sinnin' and bein' a Jezebel. You know, the usual nonsense. Luisita—sassy as always—would shout back that if he had a better idea of how to provide food for her family, then she was interested. Well, this went on for some time, and eventually, the shoutin' turned to talkin'. He would watch Luisita go off with her customers, and when she returned, he would still be waitin' for her. He kinda looked out for her."

"I guess love is found in strange places," I say with no shortage of skepticism.

"Amen to that," she says, fanning herself. "One night, it was pourin' snakes and lizards. She had no money for the bus back home, which meant she would have to walk several kilometers. The priest invited her back to his church to wait out the rains. They consummated their love in this very church. And you know what happened? In the moment that Luisita climaxed, she Ascended as well."

"Wait." A bashful smile cracks across my face. "She Ascended during sex?"

Betty Jean nods. "They say that the first gods and goddesses Ascended naturally. They knew the truth of their lives instantly, and they could remember all of their past ones." Luisita swirls her fingers through her rich hair. "Descended gods can have natural Ascensions only when they are in the act of their true nature. There are stories of war gods Ascendin' in the heat of battles. Gods of wine Ascendin' during a night of wild partyin'."

"Could this happen to me?"

Betty Jean shrugs. "Maybe, but it's incredibly rare. Yet, I know that it can happen. Luisita Ascended during her first orgasm. That priest literally brought her to a new level."

"What happened after?"

"Hathor is a goddess of love and sex. These are my tools and source of my power. Luisita knew that she couldn't leave behind her sisters who worked the streets. So we decided to create a place for them to do their profession in safety, without fear and where they could one day leave it behind."

"Wait, we?"

"Of course, Luisita wasn't by herself anymore. She had thousands of souls to help her."

"So the result was a brothel inside a church?" This was the best idea that they could come up with?

But Betty Jean doesn't seem put off. "This is a Church of Love, and all who enter are safe. Most women in the city, who have no other choice, eventually find themselves here or at one of the other churches we have around. All are welcome. The true purpose of these churches is to help these women transition out of this profession and find their true callin'."

"You're exploiting these women. You're a pimp."

Betty Jean wags her finger. "You don't realize, Matilda. These women have no other choice. Sex is their only weapon in this world. But, we've changed the model of the business. We've monopolized the sex trade in Rio. My Love Churches respect women. The women keep all their profits. The Love Churches eliminate pimps who control women with drugs, addiction, and violence. Women don't walk the streets in fear. They are safe here and all their families are taken care of. Before, under-aged girls were exploited. Now, you will never see a child on the streets. We run education programs to ensure they avoid this life completely. Everyone is encouraged to study, learn new skills, pursue their dreams in order to transition out of prostitution. Also, men who come here know that if they misbehave, they will not have another chance."

"Why?"

"Honey," Betty Jean holds up her index finger and makes a chopping motion with the fan. "We take their peckas if one of them touches a girl wrongly. We use the power we have over men and exploit it. Women don't need men. But men need women. We use that to our advantage. In our Love Churches, we've reversed the traditional world order. Women are in control here."

"What about the police and the Catholic Church?"

"They're some of our biggest customers. We keep videos of their exploits. The police chief, the mayor, even the archbishop. They know that we have them, and if they ever try to stop us, they'll soon find themselves out of a job or worse."

I think about Luisita's story, and wonder what I will do and what choices I will make if I Ascend. "Whatever happened to the priest?

Betty Jean turns away as her face clouds. "He is no longer with us. He passed into his next life. Someday, we may reunite." She holds back the emotion swelling her eyes.

"You've been expecting me, haven't you?"

She nods, and her hand takes mine. "I knew we would reunite. It was foretold you would Ascend again."

"Why am I so important? Why is there a prophecy about me?"

Betty Jean's faces assume a sympathetic demeanor. "Really, honey, I could start explainin', but these answers are already within you. You have to complete your Ascension before you can truly understand their importance." She smiles. "I have trained priestesses for you. Knowin' that one day you would come."

"Are they here?"

"No, I hid them in the mountains. They are part of the Pachamama faith—similar to Gaia in almost all ways. I will give you instructions on how to go there as well as provide all means of transportation to make sure you arrive safely."

"It feels like I never have answers. Only more questions."

"Don't you worry about that now," Betty Jeans says. "You've been traveling a long time. It is important that you rest."

I turn away, but there is one last question that has to be asked. "Can you tell me one thing? Ganesha mentioned there were three parts of my prophecy. What is the third part?"

A brief darkness falls over Betty Jean's expression, but she hides it quickly with a forced smile. "Don't worry about that for now, honey. It ain't important."

"If it's not important, why can't you tell me?"

She sighs and pulls me into a long embrace. "Once you Ascend, you will see your life not as livin' by the moment, but as a great unending chain stretchin' back to the beginning of time. This idea will set you free. The world will make sense, and so will the prophecy." She stands and offers her hand. "Come on, let's go find Mr. Stone. I can tell you miss him."

CHAPTER TWENTY-SEVEN
Church of Love

I exit Betty Jean's office and find Jared waiting. "You OK?" he asks, noticing my red face.

"It's nothing."

He opens his mouth to question me more, but Rosa interrupts. "Let me show you where you'll sleep." She leads us down a hallway.

As we walk, he leans over and asks, "How was your conversation?"

I feel his breath on my ear, and it takes all my effort not to think about Betty Jean's observations. "Fascinating," I reply.

Rosa pushes open a door to a dimly-lit room, and I stop dead in my tracks. My eyes grow huge. Moans of lust and ecstasy echo in my ears. It takes me a few seconds to process what I'm watching—to believe what I'm watching.

It's an orgy. Naked women and men interweave in every position imaginable.

A man buries his head between the legs of a woman. Two women embrace one another, while beside them, a man thrusts his hips into the backside of another man who yips like a chihuahua. The couples and groups rotate through positions like some swarming super-organism.

I force myself to stare at the floor. My overloaded senses attempt to block out the sound of slapping flesh and the overpowering ripe smell of lubricant. The cries, groans, and petitions to gods mix together into a symphony of desire and near-consummation.

Jared, also frozen in place, appears as stunned as I. He blushes and turns. Our eyes lock, and I force my stare back down at the floor. To my surprise and distress, a glow spreads through my body.

Rosa walks halfway across the room and realizes that we're still stuck in the doorway. Above the din of moans, she says, "This is the open room," she throws us a smile so innocent it could be in a Got Milk ad. "Some couples like to be with others while they enjoy themselves."

"You don't say," I reply.

Rosa waves us along. We weave our way through the twisting and rippling bodies. At some point, a hand caresses my leg—an informal invitation. I yelp and jump into Jared's arms.

"Sorry," I say, a little out of breath, disentangling my grasp from around his neck.

"No worries," he says with an awkward grin. His hand lingers a few seconds longer than necessary on the small of my back.

We finally leave the room, and I'm a little off balance and dizzy. It feels like it's a hundred degrees in here.

Rosa guides us down another long hallway. Behind the many doors, we hear more lovemaking. My heart hammers against my chest.

Rosa stops and fiddles a key into a door. "This will be your room for the night."

"One room?" Jared asks, his voice noticeably higher.

"I hope that will be OK. All the other rooms are in use by customers. Don't worry," she assures us, "the bed is very large."

My bone-dry throat prevents me from gulping. Rosa throws the door wide, and I realize that things will soon get either really awkward or really interesting.

Thick pink satin covers the walls, and lace curtains block the windows. Oil paintings of nude women hang in gilded frames, while an imitation bust of Venus de Milo takes up one corner. A gigantic heart-shaped bed with red sheets lounges in the middle of the room.

Rosa backs out into the hallway. "I'll send one of the girls over with dinner for you. For now, help yourselves to the champagne. Sweet dreams." As soon as the door closes, the plaintive cries of a woman next door echo throughout our room.

I avoid glancing at Jared who investigates the see-through glass shower.

After a minute of fierce screaming, the couple next-door fall silent. I exhale, but my pulse stammers like a broken car transmission.

"If you don't feel comfortable here, we can stay somewhere else," Jared suggests.

I shake my head. "No, this is fine."

"Are you sure? I don't think you've thought about the logistics of showering."

"It's OK." My eyes survey the room. "Want some champagne?"

One of his eyebrows jumps. "Really?"

"Yeah." The Venus de Milo statue rests on a built-in refrigerator. Inside, I find a bottle of champagne and chilled flutes. A hanging shelf next to the fridge holds bowls filled with condoms and massage oils.

When I pop the cork, it flies up and hits the ceiling. I fill two glasses and hand one to Jared.

I raise my glass. "Cheers."

"Cheers." We clink.

I smile. He smiles. I drink the whole glass of champagne. After noticing me finish mine, Jared finishes his as well. After a minute, the champagne makes me all melty inside.

Jared sits on the love seat in one corner, intensely investigating a fake Renaissance painting depicting voluptuous nude women. I am keenly aware of the way his body rests upon the couch, his thin frame sinking into the cushions. I sit down on an armchair next to the couch, twirling my champagne glass in my hands.

"This place is like an adult-themed Chuck E. Cheese," I say, hoping to break the tension that has suddenly filled the room.

Jared glances at me and smiles. "More like a Disneyland on Viagra," he replies.

"Lots of Viagra," I snort, taking a sip of my champagne, looking around the room.

When I turn back to him, his blue eyes are still sharply focused on me, reflective. "You know, Mattie, I didn't know what to expect when you came bursting into the door in Salem, but you're a remarkable woman."

My breath catches and the room suddenly feels hot and uncomfortable. "Thank you," I manage, "You're not so bad yourself."

He continues to stare at me, and I find it very difficult to breathe at all. "It's been quite the week," he murmurs, running his hand through his hair. There is sorrow in his voice and hesitation. A tear runs down his cheek and he glances away from me.

I place my champagne glass on the side table, and go to sit beside him on the love seat. I touch his hand, and my heart is beating uncontrollably. "Jared—" I manage, and he turns to me, his blue eyes searching my face. There is a longing there that I hadn't seen before. He slowly reaches and touches the side of my face where the birthmark rests.

"Mattie," he says, stroking my cheek, "you truly are extraordinary." He leans down and kisses me softly, and every sensation explodes within me. I am lost to all else as I kiss him fiercely back. His hand travels down from my cheek to my chest, gently tracing the outline of my breast. Lying back on the settee, I allow his fingers to dance along my body—sending tremors across my skin. But then he stops.

Jared reaches over and removes my glasses. He folds them and puts them on the side table, giving me a sheepish smile.

I can breathe again. Together, we rise, hand in hand, and walk to the bed, sinking into the velvet comforter. My hands scramble for his shirt. I lift it over his head—popping a button off in the process. In the dim red light of the room, his body cries out to be touched.

Pulse slamming against my chest and a fire burning up my face, we collapse together, the soft mattress pressing our bodies further together until I can no longer tell where I begin and he ends.

CHAPTER TWENTY-EIGHT
Those Feelings

When I wake up, I see Jared at the foot of the bed—fully dressed—tying up his shoes. "Good morning," I say.

"Hi."

Lying on my back, I extend my arms, stretch my whole body, and let out a deep yawn. It's like I'm a new person. "How long have you been awake?"

"A few hours," he says with a sharp clip to his voice. "You should get ready. We have to go soon."

"OK," I agree, chewing on a few strands of my hair. I wait for him to say something, and when he doesn't, I say, "I really enjoyed last night."

His body tenses, and his eyes break away. He runs his hand through his hair with an air of distress. "I'm sorry," he says, his voice metallic, "We shouldn't have done that."

My mouth gapes open as a coolness spreads across my skin. "What are you talking about?" I ask, sinking lower into the waterbed.

Jared stands up and walks over to the sink without glancing

or speaking to me. He turns on the water and washes his hands. As he reaches for a towel, he says, "My job is to protect you. It can't be anything else but that. It's important that I stay focused."

"I don't understand." My head shakes, while an unpleasant cold sweat crawls across my skin. "Didn't you like it?"

"I—I—I did," he says, his voice cautious. "But that doesn't mean it should have happened. I can't care for you too much because, if I do, then I will endanger you." He pauses, and he wrestles with a thought. "I can't have those feelings for you."

It's as if a frigid icicle has been thrust into my stomach. All the warmth I felt before leaks from me. "What do you mean by 'those feelings'?"

He turns away from the sink and walks toward the door. He avoids my eyes. "It can't happen again, and that's that."

A sickness spreads over me like a blanket, while one of my hands clenches my hair. I'm on the edge of yanking out a handful and screaming. Instead, I calm my shivering body and say, "OK, I see how it is." I lean over the bed and retrieve my underwear from the floor. "You have a job to do, and that's all that matters." I reason with a foreign brusqueness.

"It's not like that, Mattie."

"No, it is, Jared. You're right." I reach across the floor, holding the sheets close to my chest, and gather my sundress. Some broken glass skitters across the floor.

Jared frowns, and he appears to have an apology ready. For a second, I think I see the real him. The one I saw last night. I'm willing to give him another chance. Except, he ruins it. "Are we all good?"

I turn away. "Can you leave while I change?"

He nods but pauses at the door. "I'll be out front when you're done."

"Whatever." As soon as the door closes, I break down and tears soak the sheets.

After a long shower, I finally exit the room and find Betty Jean waiting for me. "Did you have a good night's sleep, or did you have a good night?" she asks with a wink. She must have mistaken my red puffy face for something else—maybe ecstasy. "Come on honey. Let's have one last chat." I nod, remaining silent. I try pushing Jared from my mind, but again, he's like pollen on a spring day.

Over a breakfast of sweet bread and strong espresso, Betty Jean says, "The priestesses are hidden in a small village in the Andes." She hands me a slip of paper with instructions. "Burn it after you memorize it."

I look down at the paper. "We're flying?"

"A driver will pick you up in the Amazonian city of Porto Velho. You and Mr. Rock Hard can trust him." The mention of him opens a chasm inside me, and Betty Jean notices the reaction. She places a comforting hand on my shoulder. "Old friend, your journey is almost complete. Don't be distracted from the final goal."

"I'll try not to be."

I finish my coffee and get up to leave, but Betty Jean's hand holds mine firm. "One last thing. Be careful. You must trust your Protector. Jared Stone could well be the only person who can keep you safe."

I nod, face burning bright, sick to my stomach, and lungs constricted so tight I can barely breathe.

The plane ride is silent. Even as Jared clenches his armrests with white knuckles, we don't exchange more than a glance the entire time. An oppressive weariness envelops me. I wish I had a bed to climb into and never get out of.

As soon as we step off the plane in Porto Velho, I smell the jungle. We exit the airport and find our driver, Paulo. He's a ruddy-skinned country guy—plaid shirt, beat-up jeans, and a trucker's hat—with a perpetual five o'clock shadow. He holds up a handwritten sign with our fake passport names on it. Paulo escorts us to an idling SUV, all the while talking on his cell phone.

Once inside, Jared asks, "Do you need to use the bathroom? It's going to be a long trip."

I glare at him. "I'm not a child," I snap. "Let's go." I turn away and stare out the window.

We leave the city, passing through sprawling slums—an endless expanse of corrugated metal roofs, coal smoke, and rainbow buildings. Then, the highway winds through oceans of sugar cane and wheat fields.

Every few miles, Paulo's cell phone rings with the sound of the "Macarena." I grow to loathe him and his incessant cell phone chats. And really, why is his ringtone the "Macarena?" Is Brazil that far behind the times?

After a few hours, we enter a dense forest filled with transcendent green foliage. It's late afternoon when we stop at a roadside cafe crowded with farmers, truckers, and the Brazilian equivalent of hillbillies. We congregate with them in an open-air picnic area and eat greasy portions of plantains, rice, beans, and fatty unidentifiable meat.

In the bathroom, instead of a toilet, I find a dark and fetid hole dug deep into the ground. When I return to the SUV, Jared checks the air pressure in the tires. "How much longer?" I ask, as my butt is already sore from all the sitting.

Jared turns and reveals the blue eyes that I fell for last night. I clench my hands into fists as my stomach rolls over.

"Don't know. We have to cross through a good portion of the Amazon to get to the mountains."

"Guesstimate."

"We're on the edge of the jungle. There's a highway that cuts through it. The trip usually takes twelve hours, but I spoke with one trucker who said that the highway was washed out in a storm. If that's the case, we'll take a rural road that winds through the jungle, and it'll take a lot longer."

"Great," I reply without enthusiasm. "Let me know when we get there." I get back into the SUV and close my eyes.

Two hours later, we come to a police car in the middle of the road. As anticipated, the officer notifies us that the road was washed out by a storm. We have to take the rural route, which is nothing more than a single-lane muddy road. It runs alongside a river. At times, the river is wide and shallow; other times, it converges on itself and transforms into a rushing tunnel of force and power.

We bump along at a snail's pace for the rest of the afternoon. We're able to drive only a few miles until it gets dark. In one of the rare moments when he is not on his cell phone, Paulo states, "Jungle not safe in dark." He pulls the SUV into a small motel dug out of the dense forest.

The proprietor of the motel, a round man with a goatee, makes us a dinner of more rice and beans, which I am getting pretty sick of. We eat in silence, while a soccer game blares on a television in the corner of the room. When I am done, I get up and go to my room.

As I lie in bed under a mosquito net, the cries of a thousand unseen birds and animals rise up like a chorus outside my window. Muscles sore and body burning, I tell myself not to think about Jared. In the end, though, he's all I can think about. Over time, the sound of the rushing river lulls me into a restless sleep that provides me little comfort.

CHAPTER TWENTY-NINE
Jungle River

I wake up to the sound of fat rain drops striking the corrugated metal roof of the motel. A thick cloud of insects buzzes outside my mosquito net, eager for a sip of my godly blood. The room doesn't have a shower. Instead, there's a faucet that issues icy water and a blue bucket with a bar of soap inside that has small black hairs embedded in it. I splash some water on my face, stare at the mirror, and sigh. This is as good as it's going to get.

My sundress seems ridiculous now. I change into a pair of jeans and a stylish black blouse that Betty Jean had packed for me. The rain diminishes to a drizzle by the time I leave my room. Jared and Paulo—each outfitted in yellow raincoats and tall boots that stretch up their legs—wait by the SUV.

"What's with the getup?" I ask.

Jared hands me a set of boots and a rain jacket. "You're going to need this today."

"Are we walking?"

"No," Jared replies, ignoring my sarcasm. "After heavy rains, the road becomes a muddy mess."

"So?"

"It means that we may need to push if we get stuck in a pot-hole."

I glare at him and then, resigned, my shoulders slump. "Whatever." I snatch the rain slicker and boots, and head for the SUV.

The day starts off the same as the day before. Paulo's "Macarena" ringtone never stops going off. His conversations have him either flirting with his lovers in low, sultry Portuguese or cackling to his friends.

But fortunately for my sanity, the further we drive into the jungle, the spottier the cell phone reception gets. Eventually, he gives up all attempts to answer his calls and focuses on the almost unnavigable road.

We drive for two hours before we get stuck for the first time. The middle of the road is a massive sinkhole. Paulo attempts to circumnavigate it by going along its muddy perimeter, but half-way around, the back tires slip downwards into the hole.

When he accelerates, instead of going forward, the rear of the SUV sinks deeper into the water, dragging the front wheels into the sinkhole as well. Paulo revs the engine a few more times but only succeeds in getting the SUV more stuck.

He turns to Jared and says, "Push."

Jared opens his door. "Come on," he says to me. "Let's do this."

With slow reluctance, I get out. But pushing a two-ton vehicle out of knee-deep water is anything but easy. When I step into the sinkhole, the muddy water floods my rubber boots.

We take up positions behind the corners of the SUV. If the rain isn't distracting enough, the army of mosquitoes swarming my face more than compensates.

On his signal, we push as Paulo taps on the gas. The rotating tires fling dirty water into my face. I wipe away the scum with one hand and shoot Jared an evil eye.

After twenty minutes, the tires find traction, and the SUV zips out of the sinkhole, but I'm off balance and fall face-first into the brown water.

When I raise my head from the mud, Jared wears a concerned expression. "Don't say a word." He comes over and helps me up from the sinkhole.

"Thanks," I say with an acid bite. I pull my arm from him as soon as I'm on my feet. Back in the SUV and exhausted, I find it hard to ignore my soaking clothes or the smell of sludge.

The light rain that began the day has turned into a heavy downpour. The river has risen several feet and is now a gushing torrent. I notice that the river sometimes divides into multiple pathways that spread out into the jungle. It see-saws between somber and quiet, and fierce and angry.

We don't pass any vehicles going in the opposite direction. The other drivers are smart enough to wait until the rains pass. "How much more time will we be on this road?" I ask, after another hour of what could generously be labeled progress.

"At the pace we're going," Jared replies, "it may take the whole day. Paulo said earlier that the road becomes pavement in another hundred miles. If we're lucky, we won't need to get out and push again."

But we aren't lucky. Three more times throughout the day, Jared and I have to get out and push the stuck SUV out of sinkholes that get deeper and deeper. Each time we leave the warmth of the SUV, a nervous itch of fear tickles the back of my neck. The jungle has a way of watching us. I fear that we'll never get to the other side. What if our SUV breaks down? We would be stranded in the middle of the Amazon.

In the afternoon, the road improves a bit, as does my mood. We are at least going somewhere. Paulo suggests that, if the road stays like this, we will be out of the jungle sooner than expected.

The SUV winds up a hilly peak through a series of switchbacks. The water rushes down the edges of the road without gathering in the middle. When we finally get to the top of the hill, I survey the scene, and my hopes plummet. The jungle stretches out forever into the distance.

Jared notices my crestfallen expression because he turns around in the front seat. "Mattie, I want to tell you something."

I ignore him and keep my eyes focused on our descent down the opposite side of the hill.

"I know you have no reason to forgive me. But I want to explain to you why it's hard for me to—" He releases a jagged sigh and his voice trembles, "Open up."

I feel one of my eyebrows jump, and my pulse begins to thump. I tell myself not to look at him, but I can't control myself.

Jared doesn't say anything immediately. Instead, he takes a deep breath and closes his eyes. When he opens them, they're red-ringed and swollen. "It's because of my mom."

"Why?"

"She warned me not to get romantically involved with you."

The memory of Gertrude's violent death comes shooting through my mind. A pit opens in my stomach.

He takes a deep breath and says, "She said that it would be harder for you. You would be dealing with so many new realities. It would be more difficult for you to be thinking about our relationship as well."

A cold shiver runs across my skin. "Is this the reason you've kept me at a distance?"

"Yes." He looks away, and says, "If I get too close to you, if I have feelings for you, you will die. You can't be distracted by me. This is why I can't confuse the boundaries between duty and love. I'm trying to protect you."

Head shaking and teeth clenched, I reply, "I'm so sorry that she said this to you, but I'm a grown adult and can make my own decisions. She shouldn't have put that additional burden on you." Then the dam breaks. "I don't like feeling used. I don't like when people play with my emotions, make me open up, just so they can rip out my heart."

"It's not you, Mattie. It's me."

"Don't cop out like that. God, Jared! I understand you're in mourning. So am I. Why can't you feel something for me? Who says you can't?"

Paulo jams down on the brakes. I nearly fly through the windshield. My seat belt yanks me backward. The SUV fishtails and slides sideways before coming to a rest near the side of the road.

"What the hell!" I cry. "Can't you learn to drive?"

Paulo and Jared respond with shocked silence.

I stare out the front window. Beyond the hypnotic fast rhythm of the windshield wipers, I see a massive fallen tree blocking the road, but that's not the thing that scares me.

What scares me are the ten men holding automatic weapons aimed at our SUV. A bullhorn-amplified voice shatters the silence. *"Salen del coche con las manos en alto!"*

I don't know what he said, but it can't be good. Fear courses through me like the wild jungle river.

CHAPTER THIRTY
La Macarena

My hands tighten on my seat's armrest. "What's going on?" I ask, a frantic tremor in my voice.

Jared keeps his eyes fixed on the men in front of us. "I don't know."

"Who are they?"

"That's what I'm trying to figure out," he replies, his voice cool.

I stare at the five men—faces hard and scarred—fanned out across the road. They wear faded camouflage army uniforms, none of which appear to fit well. Like they've been stolen from other men. They carry automatic rifles and have strings of grenades and bandoliers of ammunition crisscrossing their chests.

One of the men taking cover behind the fallen tree holds the bullhorn. Unlike the others, who wear camouflage bandannas on their heads, he wears a red beret.

"*Salgan del coche con las manos en alto!*" The man commands again.

"What's he saying?"

"'Get out of the car with your hands up,'" translates Jared. "Can you reverse out of here?"

Paulo shakes his head and raises his eyes to the rear-view mirror. I turn around. Three armed men materialize behind us. Their guns also aim at the SUV.

We're trapped.

"Who are they?"

"I don't know. It all seems too planned."

"How could this be planned?"

"I don't know yet, but it will be OK."

"Thanks for the positive encouragement," I reply, but my face says *Yeah, right*.

"*Salgan del coche o abriremos fuego!*"

"What was that?"

"He says that they will open fire unless we get out."

"What are we going to do?"

"Stay calm, Mattie," Jared replies. "Here's the plan. Paulo, you're going to get out slowly on your side. Mattie, you're to get out on my side. Don't make any drastic movements, and don't try to run."

"OK," I reply, doubting very much that I'll be able to do anything more than transforming into a statue of fear.

"Remember, do everything slowly and keep your hands up."

Following Jared's directions, I open my door and step into the fierce rain.

Once we're outside, the man with the bullhorn shouts something else. "*Acuéstense con las manos fuera!*"

"He wants us to lie down on the ground with our arms spread out," Jared says.

"Should we do it?"

"We don't have a choice. Do what he says."

But that's not how things play out. As if the Brazilian telecommunication companies are playing a sick joke, as I'm bending my knees, Paulo's cell phone beeps with service. A second later, his "Macarena" ringtone blares up, shattering the silent, tense moment. I glance over and pray that Paulo won't do what I imagine he'll do.

But he does.

Like Pavlov's dog, Paulo reaches to his side to grab the phone from his belt. In that instant, he realizes his mistake. One of the gunmen, likely thinking that he's reaching for a gun, aims and pulls the trigger of his rifle.

Three huge explosions come one after another. All three strike Paulo's chest and blood sprays out through the exit wounds in his back.

Still holding his cell phone playing the "Macarena," Paulo falls to his knees and observes his killers with utter shock. The next second, while I'm frozen in disbelief, Jared snags my hand and yanks me toward the cover of the jungle.

We're halfway to safety when I think for sure that they will mow us down. I hear the gunshots. The air moves around me. I expect this to be the end, but the bullets soar over our heads.

I finally breathe when we enter the jungle; my feet run on autopilot. More shots follow us. Some of the bullets splinter off pieces of bark from the trees. Our pursuers shout in Spanish, and their footsteps grow louder as they enter the dense jungle.

Jared drags me along, pulling me deeper into the forest. Massive ferns and vines block our way. We stumble through the growth, running blind through a maze of green, the men close behind us.

At that moment, I notice Jared's limping gait. His hand holds his right leg. We run another twenty feet when Jared pulls me down behind a fallen tree. From his jacket, he pulls out a revolver. Where or how he'd gotten it, I have no clue. Jared aims it toward the way we came.

He doesn't wait very long. Three seconds later, one of the men comes barreling through, following the path we'd taken. He doesn't have time to discover Jared aiming the gun at him. He pulls the trigger.

Two loud successive shots ring out, sending flocks of birds into the air. The guy cries out and crumples to the ground. A second later, he drags himself behind a tree.

Jared waits for more men to come, but a minute passes, and none come. Blood soaks through his pants. A bloody bulls-eye stains the back of his thigh, and the blood drips onto the ground.

"You're hurt."

"It's OK. I'll take care of it." But something in the way he says this gives me the feeling it's more serious.

Silence takes over the jungle. It is as if all the animals, birds, and even the trees watch us, holding their breath, awaiting our next move.

A cry comes from the commander's bullhorn. *"No mata la chica! No mata la chica!"*

"Shit," says Jared, his hand pressing down on his bleeding wound.

"What did he say?"

"They want you. He's saying, 'Don't kill the girl.' This was a setup. They knew that you were here and that means one thing."

"Gurzil," I say. "It's a trap."

"Yeah."

"What do we do?"

"You have to go. I'll buy you time to escape."

"No," I say, shaking my head, body trembling.

"You have to," replies Jared. "There are too many of them. It's only a matter of time before they overrun us, and I'll slow you down." The jungle rustles in front of us. They're close.

"You can't do that," I say, fighting back tears, while a sour taste floods my mouth. "Your leg isn't that bad."

He takes my hand. "Mattie, I won't make it a hundred yards.

You're uninjured. You can do it."

"But where do I go? It's the jungle."

His face bunches up. "Don't you see," Jared says, exasperation rising in his voice. "There is no other way."

Footsteps crunch leaves near us. Jared turns around and aims his gun. A head pops out, and he pulls the trigger. The gun roars, but the man pulls out of the way in time.

He turns back to me fast. "Time's up. You either go now or we're both dead."

"I—I—can't."

"Go," he whispers, a fierceness in his tone, and he pushes me away.

I take a few steps backward, and the forest moves from another direction. They're coming from two different angles. Jared has already turned around. He raises his gun in the direction of the new attackers.

I take one last glance at Jared, and my feet take on an energy of their own. I spin in place and sprint through the rain forest. Branches cut my arms and face as I stumble through the dense bushes, adrenaline coursing through me.

I'm so caught up in the moment that I don't even spot the man I barrel into. He's one of the camouflage attackers. We both fall to the ground, and the man's gun slips from his hands. The man, at first stunned, scrambles to grab my leg, but I spring to my feet and am off.

This time I have a predator on my tail. His footfalls gain on mine. I press myself faster. Sweat pours down my face, and my heart thumps like that of a rabbit being chased.

The man is larger and clumsier. I'm like a gazelle, sliding under thick branches and leaping over bushes. I'm putting distance between myself and him. I take a quick left and run through a clump of vines. A brief spike of hope lights up my being; there's a chance I might get away.

But then the ground disappears beneath me.

I free-fall—one second, two seconds, maybe three seconds of plummeting through the air.

I expect to hit the hard ground. Instead I plunge headfirst into the warm water. It takes a moment for me to realize that it's the river that has followed the road.

I've fallen over a ledge. High above, my pursuer stares down at me. Smiling, I think that I've escaped, but I soon realize that I have a bigger problem. Now that the river has me, it refuses to give me up. The turbulent whitecap waters send me cruising away fast.

My feet hit a submerged rock, and I somersault head over heels. I fight to keep my head above the water. Each time I go up to take a breath, I get a mouthful of water.

I grab onto the low-hanging vines, but they break each time.

My hands grapple for the algae slick rocks along the banks, but the river ushers me past them.

The next moment, I enter a vortex pool. I spin faster and faster. My time is up. I know it. I can't keep my head above the water for much longer. A second later, my head slams into something hard, and the world turns off.

CHAPTER THIRTY-ONE
Lost in Translation

I wake up like a newborn. Blinding yellow light pierces my vision, and my eyelids snap shut. Through half-cracked glasses, dark lines form into blurry objects. Birds caw, insects chirp, and water trickles.

I'm alive. This thought surprises me more than the shadow, which materializes over my head, blocking out the sun's warmth.

The shadow takes the form of charcoal hair, burnt umber skin, and the largest ears I've ever seen on a child. The boy floats over me as a disembodied head. His nostrils flare, mouth widening to a smile.

My eyes shoot open, and I sit up too fast. The world spins. My brain throbs. I collapse backwards, huffing from the effort.

The boy appears again. He leans over and presses something to my lips. Cold water hits my tongue, and I suck back until there is no more. I clear my throat. The boy's smile reveals a set of teeth in desperate need of a dentist.

The pounding in my skull abates to a dull conga beat. I negotiate my way onto my elbows. The boy squats in front of me and watches, his eyes curious.

Towering trees with broad leaves filter the sunlight. The air wraps around me like a terrycloth robe—dense, warm, and comforting. By my feet, a stream flows. I pick up a handful of sand and let it fall through my fingers.

The boy, I realize, is naked, and he doesn't think it's that big of a deal. I smile and wait for him to say something, but he remains silent. After a minute, I ask, "Where am I?"

The boy's jaw drops, and his eyes grow to ghoulish proportions. He spins around, scrambles up the banks of the stream, and disappears into the jungle.

"I can't look that bad."

I stand up, and my muscles cry out and bones crack. I wait another minute, but no one else comes. Eventually, I follow him into the jungle. After a short walk along a thin trail, I arrive at a clearing where small thatched huts pop up like mushrooms.

The men have faces smeared with red paint, and round stones hang from their ears. Women with black and dark skin wear coarse straw skirts. Their bosoms hang freely. All are either pregnant or carrying children. They busy themselves with general tasks—nursing, sewing, preparing food. I spot the boy with the huge ears as he cowers behind one of the women.

One by one, the villagers notice me. They stop what they're doing and all stare as if I am an exotic animal. Silence creeps over the clearing.

Finally, I say, "Hello."

But when I utter the greeting, it breaks the trance. The women scatter into the huts, while the men advance with spears.

A five-foot tall, squat man, with a skull shaped like a watermelon and a white curved bone in his nose, takes the lead. He stands two yards from me and screams in an alien language. Rage wrinkles his face. His drawn bow carries an arrow aimed at my heart.

I hold up my hands. "Wait, don't—"

But it's too late. His fingers let loose the arrow. It zips over my shoulder, nearly nicking my skin. A second later, he's ready with another arrow. I know that the next shot will not miss.

"Please stop! I don't know where I am!"

But my words only inflame his anger, and he barks out epithets like an enraged poodle. He comes within three feet of me. The sharp and deadly arrowhead aims at my chest, fingers slipping a little on the drawn string.

My head shakes, and my mouth opens in a silent plea. I can't believe I'm going to be murdered by this tiny man. I close my eyes, refusing to watch what happens next. But the arrow's death sting doesn't come.

Another voice overshadows the man's. An old woman waddles over from one of the huts. She hunches over a gnarled cane made out of jungle wood and comes toward us. Hair white as clouds and skin wrinkled deep like Martian canals, she dons an overflowing headdress composed of feathers and beads.

Her staccato outbursts halt and silence the watermelon-head man. He whips around and fires off a torrent of testosterone-filled speech.

The woman offers a soothing smile and makes a tsk-tsk sound. She hobbles over and places herself in between me and the half-drawn arrow. Then, in a voice that only he can hear, she whispers something. His face glows red, and he slowly releases the tension on the bow and aims the arrow to the ground.

I sigh, my muscles becoming weak, but my heart still slams a marching band beat.

The man's eyes narrow, and he holds his ground for a few more moments before swaggering back toward a long hut. All the while, he shoots a suspicious look at me.

He makes a declaration to the village. The other men—casting wary glances in my direction—gather around him. One by one, they disappear into the hut.

Before the watermelon-head man leaves, he fires off one last outburst. He points at me with a long, twisted finger and swipes it across his throat. He spins around and enters the hut.

The old woman turns toward me, a frown marking her face. Through cataract-misted eyes, she stares at me. The next moment, a brimming smile emerges, and her rough hands reach up and feel my skin. Clicking her tongue, she cries out something in her language. Coddling speech bubbles from her tooth-less mouth like water from a fountain. She reaches around and pinches my waist.

"Ouch!" I cry.

The woman lets out a deep belly laugh and murmurs something to herself. The women and children re-emerge from the other huts. With outstretched hands, they run their fingers through my tangled hair and along my mud-stained clothes.

They smile, and despite everything, I smile back.

"Where am I?" I ask the old woman.

She responds with a baffled grin.

OK, that didn't work. "Who are you?"

Again, a befuddled face.

Getting out of the jungle is what matters. I don't belong here. How far could have the river taken me? I could be miles from the road. I remember the men with the guns. Would they search this area? And what about Jared? Heart sinking, I remember how I left him with an injured leg and no hope of escape.

I spend the next twenty minutes pantomiming and gesturing all the ways to figure out where I am and how I can get back.

It must be a good show because, by the end, they're laughing and giggling. I give up. Until I figure out where I am, there's no point in wandering off into the jungle to get lost. The realization stings me like a wasp: I'm stuck here.

Rising discordant voices shock me to the present. The voices come from the long hut filled with men. The voices change to shouting and morph into chanting. War-like chanting. Something's happening, but I don't know what.

I turn toward the old woman for an explanation. She glances over at the hut and makes a sour face. She takes my hand and leads me away from the clearing, into the jungle.

CHAPTER THIRTY-TWO
A Fireside Song

We walk through the jungle for only a minute before we arrive at a smaller clearing. The old woman sits down with me in front of a crackling fire. The other women join us, encircling the blaze.

They pass around pieces of burnt barbecued meat and mashed root vegetables. The food makes my stomach rumble and mouth water. I'm too famished to refuse the meal. The meat is tender and delicious, but I'm pretty sure that I'm eating an animal that I never knew existed. Pleased by my appetite, the old woman grabs my hand and drops a handful of roasted grubs into it. Hmm, I'm not *that* hungry. I shudder and pass back the handful of bugs.

The women laugh and talk among themselves. We eat until I'm full and sleepy. After we're done eating, the women sing a song with arching melodies and complicated harmonies. One of the women accompanies with a drum.

The sun sets. They throw logs onto the fire, and the flames leap up and lick at the forest canopy. The drums and singing grow louder. A water gourd passes from one woman to the next. Each woman takes a few gulps and passes it to the next in line. The old woman beside me takes the gourd, gulps, and passes it to me. My parched throat yearns for water, so I lift it to my mouth.

The stuff inside hits my tongue, and I feel instant nausea. It's the consistency of thick sludge and tastes like a smoothie of top-soil, old leaves, and bugs. I push it away, but the old woman presses it to my lips and forces me to drink the remaining contents.

When I'm done, I lurch forward and dry-heave. I think for sure I'm going to be sick, but the next moment, the old woman shoves a piece of fruit into my mouth. A sweet citrus taste washes away the lingering bitterness. Shocked, I spin toward her. "What the heck was that?"

The woman responds with a quizzical smile.

The singing swells louder. I stare at the fire—quiet and contemplative. My chaotic mind swirls among my fears—lost in the Amazon, hunted by a sociopath who thinks I'm a god, wanted for the murder of my best friend, prophesied to be a messiah. I can't imagine things growing worse. The merry-go-round of fears gets stuck on one alone, like a skipping record.

Jared.

What happened to him? When I left, he was shot. Did he escape, or was he captured? If they have him, what are they doing to him? What if he didn't—I cut myself off. Shivers scampering down my spine, I can't face that possibility right now. I need to worry about myself.

The singing pushes away these fears. I fixate on the fire, and the music empties me of concerns until I'm at peace. The mesmerizing sound lulls me into a trance, a familiar tingling sensation emerging in my hands. It spreads through my entire body. All of the tension and fear ooze out of me, escaping like a poisonous gas.

Every sound sharpens. Every color brightens. My body tingles. The trees shimmer. My skin is as hot as the bonfire. Fear, worry, and pain disappear from within me. My mind melts into liquid peace as the singing fades away, and my eyes close.

In my mind's eye, it's as foggy as that first night in Salem. Images form in the haze. Repeating lights and movement. Someone's waiting there.

My body vibrates and breaths come fast and heavy—as if the oxygen is fueling a furnace inside me. The hyperventilating reaches a crescendo. An explosion of light blasts away the fog, and I discover what's hiding.

It's a woman.

A middle-aged woman with a soft, round, and loving face. She smiles. I recognize her, but I don't know from where. She has warm, trusting brown eyes. She's a nun—wearing a black habit, white coif, and black veil. In one hand, she grasps a rosary. Her other hand reaches toward me.

I step back, resisting. I don't want this, but the hand doesn't stop advancing. It grasps mine, and a jolt of hot energy shoots between us. My body rocks and shivers as her hand absorbs into mine. The nun's whole essence, image, and energy fuse with my hand, and she enters me.

I convulse forward. Images and sounds flood through me—a small white church surrounded by jungle, singing in Latin, close-packed pews, laughter, a child cradled in my arms, a man on the edge of death. I spoon clear broth into his withered mouth.

The sensations bombard and twist together as a cyclone, a tormentor of tremendous proportions. Then, as quickly as they come, they're gone.

CHAPTER THIRTY-THREE
Song of Souls

When I wake up, I'm in one of the huts, lying on a thatched mat. I'm by myself, yet, when I sit up, I realize that I am not alone. Someone else is here.

Mattie . . .

It's a whisper in my ear. I know the voice. It's the nun from my dream. I survey the hut searching for another woman, but there's no one else here.

Mattie . . . let me in . . .

The nun pleads into my ear. I spin around, expecting to find her, to catch her mid-speech. But she isn't there. "Where are you?" I ask out loud. "Come out."

I'm here, Mattie . . .

"Stop it," I demand, fear climbing through me. "Stop hiding."

I'm here . . .

I shake my head and cover my face with my hands. Am I going insane? My hands tremble. The hairs on the back of my neck stand on end. My eyes search the hut. Finally, I ask, "Who are you?"

My name is Sister Maria Luisa . . .

I'm totally confused. How is it possible I can hear her? She's not here unless she's—it occurs to me with a shudder. "You're inside my head."

I am here . . . Let me help you . . .

A frigid flutter, like falling dominoes, runs up my spine. "Have I Ascended?"

No, it is only me . . . the others aren't here . . .

Arms shaking, I shout, "No! Get out. I don't want you inside of me!"

I can help you . . .

"I don't want your help. Leave me alone!"

I can't leave. I've always been here . . .

Who is this woman? She tugs at my subconscious. She wants something from me. "Stay away. I don't want you here. I don't want you inside of me!"

In my mind, I build a brick wall, tall and impenetrable. Laying the red stones up until they tower into the sky, I know that the wall will protect me. On one side is my consciousness; on the other is this foreign woman. I wait for Maria Luisa to break through the wall, but there's only silence. A moment later, the old woman appears in the doorway of the hut. "Are you well, goddess?" she asks, her tone full of concern. "I heard you shouting."

"I'm fine. It was—" I stop, and my tongue hangs mid-syllable. I can't believe it.

The old woman's face breaks into a grin and she says, "The ceremony has given you the gift of tongues." She raises her hands into the air. "Praised be the goddess."

I shake my head, feeling breathless. This can't be happening. "How is this possible?"

The old woman stares at me, surprised. "The goddess understands all tongues."

The language comes as if I've always known it. I don't think about it. It just happens. The words appear as if they've always been there. I take a deep breath, attempting to calm my nerves and ask, "What did you do to me last night?"

"We still remember the old ways—the old ceremonies," the woman explains, giving me a toothless triumphant smile. "The Song of Souls always brings back our ancestors within those who carry the mark." She reaches out an arthritic finger and points at the jagged moon birthmark on the side of my head.

I recoil from her hand. "But what did you do to me?"

The woman appears confused. "We summoned our ancestors. For in our time of desperation, we need the knowledge and wisdom of their years."

I fall silent. Even though I now speak their language, it doesn't mean I am any better at understanding them. "Who are you?" I ask the woman, who stares at me with unrestrained admiration.

"My name is Pucu," she replies. "I am the priestess of the Black Stream people."

"The who?"

"The Song of Souls can confuse the mind." Pucu nods with understanding. "You answered our prayers. You came to us in our time of need."

Time of need? Talking with her makes me more confused. I must get out of this place and return to my world. "Where am I?"

She spreads out her arms, and declares, "You are in the land where the rivers become black streams, and the trees soar to the heavens and block out the great light."

So, I'm in the jungle. Well, I already knew that. "How did I get here?"

Pucu, eyes shining, grasps my hands. "You heard our prayers and lamentations. You caused the clouds to cry. Your tears flooded the water, and from the waters, you came to us."

My head spins. What did I get myself into? "You keep on saying prayers. What prayers? What are you talking about?"

"You don't know, my goddess?" The old woman withdraws, lips pursed. "Maybe you test us?"

I raise an eyebrow. "Do I look like I'm testing you?" I exhale, tempering my rising frustration. "Please. Tell me what you mean."

"Of course, goddess. We are here to serve you." The woman bows her head. "Tomorrow, our people go to war against the High Tree People. Many will die. Misery will reign."

"OK . . . What am I supposed to do?"

Pucu's unblinking eyes widen. "You will stop the bloodshed. You will bring us peace."

I'm dumbfounded into silence. She rises and offers her hand to me. "Come, we must move quickly." She takes my hand and yanks me to my feet. Despite her having at least fifty years on me, the woman is as agile as a twenty-year-old.

"Why?" I manage to ask.

"Because our village chief thinks you are a witch sent from the High Tree people. He believes that you are here to bring bad luck." She drags me out into the muggy, hot Amazonian air and adds casually, "He has promised to kill you this morning if you cannot prove that you are the goddess."

CHAPTER THIRTY-FOUR
Court is Adjourned

Before we enter the men's hut, Pucu leans over and whispers, "Do not speak until you receive my signal."

I nod, still baffled by her comment that yet another person plans to kill me. But, as soon as we enter the hut, I understand. It's like I'm a defendant on a daytime court television show. My jury, I realize, are the five wizened village elders, squatting on the ground, observing me with curious stares.

The chief—the man with the oblong watermelon-shaped head —is the prosecutor. He struts in front of us, puffing his chest out, growing red in the face.

He spins toward Pucu, who plays the role of my defense attorney. "Why do you bring this witch into the sacred hut?" he asks, firing off his first salvo. He swaggers toward us, jabbing his spear in our direction. "She will curse our tribe." He spits onto the floor and makes a sign to ward off evil.

Pucu replies, her tone quiet but confident. "You are wrong, Mapi." She steps forward as if to embrace his spear. She's shorter than him, but her voice carries weight. "She is the goddess who answered our prayers."

"Prayers? Whose prayers?" Mapi asks. "I didn't pray for a white witch to bring bad luck on us." He nods agreeably toward the jury of elders.

I'm about to lose control because these men will determine my fate. They will sanction my death if I can't prove something I still don't fully understand myself. I gulp as a dizzy spell overcomes me. I take one glance at Pucu and make a realization: I'm as good as jaguar kibble.

"She has come to bring peace," Pucu says, directing her voice to the elders. "She will stop the war between us and the High Tree people."

"Old fool!" Mapi exclaims, producing a vile smile. "The High Tree people are our enemies. Peace can't return to the forest until their blood waters the ground."

"Mapi, you are too strong-willed," Pucu chides, belittling him like a child. I don't think this tactic is wise and would like to petition the court for a new attorney. She continues before he explodes. "Your hate blinds you to the truth. You must believe in the goddess."

Mapi fumes at her tone and glares at me. "This witch can't help us. She doesn't know us. She can't even speak our tongue."

Pucu shoots me a satisfied smile. I hadn't realized it, but she waited for Mapi to entrap himself in his own logic. She gestures for me to make my case.

"Actually, I can," I say, astonished that Pucu had been planning this the entire time.

The effect is instantaneous. It's like a jolt of electricity shoots through the elders—their eyes widen as they mutter among themselves, pointing at me.

Mapi's eyes narrow, and his mouth twists into a snarl. His quick recovery surprises me. "Witch!" he screams, outraged that he's been tricked. "What sorcery do you use to steal our tongue?"

"Not sorcery," Pucu declares, her voice triumphant. "She uses the knowledge of our ancestors."

Mapi shakes his head and makes a foul face. He spins toward the jury to make his closing argument. "Witches are mischievous and cunning. Only when the High Tree people are destroyed will our ancestors be at peace." He swirls and points his spear at me. "We should begin by destroying this false goddess sent to us by the High Tree people."

Pucu straightens her back and stands tall. "You will do no such thing. She speaks our tongue. That is proof enough that she is one of us." She turns to the elders, awaiting their final verdict.

I hold my breath, heart pounding and sweat drenching my brow. The elders huddle and talk among themselves. After a minute, they nod in my direction. Pucu smiles. She just saved my life.

Mapi bears his teeth, face brimming with anger. "It makes no difference. By the next sunrise, we will go to war." He shoots a malicious glance at Pucu. "The women of this village need to learn their place!" he shouts and marches out of the hut.

After he leaves, I hear Pucu whisper, "Son of a monkey's ass . . ."

She then bows to the elders. I bow as well. Pucu takes my hand and leads me out of the hut. Once we're far enough away, I pull her to the edge of the jungle and confess, "I'm not a goddess."

She recoils and shakes her head. "Of course you are."

"No, I'm—I'm a teacher." But what does a school teacher mean to this woman? As far as I can tell, there are no schools here.

But the woman dispels any doubts. "Yes, you are a teacher."

Stomach tightening, my body goes rigid. Where is Jared? He would know what to do. No, I can do this by myself. I don't need him. "I need to return to my people and my world."

Pucu pauses, her eyes fall downcast to ground, and she nods.

"If you wish to go, you are free to do so."

I exhale, glad that I am not a prisoner. "OK, where is the nearest village?"

"The High Tree people's village is closest to us. They are a half day's walk away."

The High Tree people! She's got to be kidding me. They're the ones that the psychopath with the melon-shaped head is hell-bent to murder. "Ugh," I moan.

Pucu places her hand on my shoulder. "When I was a small girl, and there was peace between our two peoples, I remember that they had magic which allowed them to speak with the spirit people."

My curiosity lifts a bit. "How?"

"They had a vessel that gathered voices from the wind."

I take a few seconds to decipher what she's saying. And then, it occurs to me in a flash. "Wait, they have a radio."

"A what?"

"Um, a vessel which allows them to speak with people far away."

Pucu gives me an encouraging smile. "Yes, yes, yes. That is what they have. With it, they can speak with spirits in the air."

They have a radio. It's like a sunbeam of hope. If I can use that radio, I can get out of here. "I need to go there right away. How do I get to them?"

Pucu's face drops, and she shakes her head. "You can't go to their village."

"Why not?"

"Because we are at war with them. The men will go there tomorrow and burn their village to the ground. They'll destroy everything and take back slaves. Many will die. There will be much misery."

Crap. Double crap. Triple crap. "How can we stop this?"

"You are the goddess. You should speak with our ancestors. They will tell you what to do."

She is right . . .

A jolt goes through my body as Maria Luisa speaks to me. My stomach clenches into a tight knot. Even though I created a wall in my mind, her voice floats through it.

Go away, I think. I don't want you here.

I'm here to help you . . .

"Stop it!" I shout out loud, gripping the sides of my head.

Pucu appears surprised, but her eyes narrow. She knows what's happening to me. "Why do you resist our ancestors?"

I consider her words while feeling every breath enter my body. While it's true that Maria Luisa is not like the other souls — the Chinese warrior or the Indian — I still resist. The other past lives made me into a backseat driver for my own mind. "I don't want to lose myself. I want to be in control," I reply.

You are in control, Mattie . . .

I can't trust you.

Mattie, let me help . . .

"How can you help me when I can't even help myself?" I yell, meaning for it to be a thought.

"What do you mean?" Pucu asks.

"I mean, there's someone in my head. She is trying to control me."

Pucu smiles. "This is good. The ancestors want to help you. You must open your mind and allow them to help."

She is right . . .

"No! I can't. I won't. It's my mind. I will not share it with another."

A bloodcurdling cry rips through the village, and my head jerks toward the source. One of the women collapses onto the ground and wails. We rush over to a growing circle of villagers.

In the center, we find the small boy with the giant ears; the one who found me yesterday. He's laid out on his back. His sallow skin has the color of curdled milk.

"What happened?" Pucu asks one of the women.

She gestures toward the dying boy. "Tari was playing and was attacked by the High Tree people. They put a curse on him."

The boy breathes hard and fast, and sweat pours down his forehead. He could die at any moment.

Mapi breaks into the circle. He stares at Pucu and declares, "Is this the peace you were expecting?" He turns to the other villagers and screams, "They attacked the boy outside the village! We are not safe anywhere!"

"Why would they injure a boy? Why not raid our village if they are so close?" Pucu asks, staring back with defiance.

"They are cowards and fear the warriors of Black Stream," Mapi retorts, pounding his chest. "They heard me coming and ran like mice." Despite the dying boy, Mapi wears a proud smile.

"Something isn't right."

"You are correct, old woman. It's not right. But Tari is not doomed to death." Mapi points at me and says, "This witch is a goddess. She'll be able to save Tari from death's hands."

All the villagers' eyes turn toward me.

"Come on, witch," Mapi taunts. "Prove your powers."

A grumbling of agreement comes from the other villagers. Mapi turns to the elders, who now stand arrayed to one side. They all turn their expectant gazes on me.

A cold drip falls down my spine as the villagers wait for my next move. I lean to Pucu and implore, "What do I do?"

Pucu's brow furrows, furious at being outmaneuvered. "My fellow villagers want to see your powers." She glances down at Tari. "You must heal the boy."

A path clears for me with Tari at the end. Mapi stands to the side, a cruel smile plastered on his lips. "What happens if I can't heal him?" I ask.

Pucu turns toward me. "They won't believe you are a goddess, and you will lose my protection."

Translation: jaguar kibble.

She points to the boy. "Go, you must heal him. You must show that you have the knowledge of our ancestors."

With hesitant and slow steps, I walk toward the boy and crouch on the ground beside him. His breaths are heavy and rattling. His glassy eyes gaze up toward the sky. I've never had any medical training in my life except a day-long CPR certification. How am I supposed to heal him when I don't even know what I'm supposed to do?

Put your hands on him . . .

Maria Luisa whispers over the wall. No, I think, shaking my head and ignoring her, but her response shocks me.

What choice do you have?

I bite my lip and grimace. She's right. If I don't heal him, I'm as good as dead. I either do what she says, or I'll soon be a voice in some other poor person's head.

I reach out and put my hands on the boy's chest, feeling wild heart beats. He's burning up. His energy courses through me.

Poison . . .

OK, I think. What type of poison?

Look for the source . . .

The source? What do you mean? Maria Luisa doesn't reply. I inspect Tari's entire body, but I don't find where the poison came from. The boy spasms, barring his teeth. He's fighting for his life. I don't need a doctor to know that he doesn't have much time left.

Look closer . . .

I search again, closer this time. I feel the blood pounding through my head. The villagers stare at me; I have to do this. I don't have a choice.

But there's no source. No poison. It's like I'm falling off a cliff. Maria Luisa is wrong, and I'm as good as dead.

Then I notice something.

Tari clenches his right hand while his left hand remains

opens. His fingers have assumed a rigor mortis state. I reach over and pry open the fingers on his right hand, finding a thin dart with red and white feathers hidden inside his palm. The dart has a dark brown sticky substance on its tip. I remove the dart from his hand.

Smell it . . .

It has an aromatic and tarry odor.

Mortar, pestle, and clean water . . .

I spin toward Pucu. "Get me a mortar and pestle, as well as clean water."

She hurries off into one of the huts.

Go into the jungle . . . find the plant . . .

I jump up and sprint into the jungle, searching for the plant. I don't know which plant, but Maria Luisa's presence guides me. I'm not stumbling blind; she pushes me in the right direction.

After about a minute, she whispers, *Stop . . . gather the red leaves . . .*

My eyes shoot to the ground, and sure enough, by the base of a tree, there's a small bush with red leaves. I pull up the entire plant—roots, stems, and leaves—and run back to the clearing.

When I return, Tari makes thin gasping sounds that make my skin icy. His throat closes, his face knotting in pain, but Maria Luisa tells me what I must do. I hand the plant to Pucu. "Make a mash out of the leaves with water."

With deft and quick movements, she turns the leaves into a thick soup.

The boy's face turns blue from his blocked throat. He's asphyxiated.

She hands me the mortar filled with the liquid. I pull open Tari's mouth as if he's a doll and pour it down the boy's throat. At first, he gags and spits it up.

Please—please—drink it, I pray.

The soup puddles in his mouth, refusing to go down. I wait a few seconds only to see his face become bluer. He can't drink it.

It's too late.

Tari's body goes still. No more breaths come from him, and I don't feel his pulse anymore. His heart has stopped.

No! I clench my fingers, raise my fists and pound down on the boy's chest.

Tari convulses and by some miracle, a little of the liquid loosens his esophagus. Then, the puddle of mush drains down into him. Pulse racing, I force my hands to stop shaking as I pour more of the liquid into him. He drinks it.

Within seconds, he takes a gasping breath as if his head was under water. Blood rushes back into his face. His chest heaves and expands outwards. He looks up, smiles, and then he closes his eyes and falls to sleep.

You did it, Mattie . . .

I can't believe it. We saved the boy. He was as good as dead, but we saved him together.

I'm here to help you, Mattie . . . You can trust me . . .

Pucu unleashes a triumphant joyous cry. "The boy is saved! The goddess has proven herself again."

The rest of the women match her happy cries. Overwhelming love flows through me. We did it. We saved him!

"Silence!" Mapi screams, shattering the hopeful cries. "Foolish women! You celebrate, but you already forget the injustice. We were attacked. One of our children almost died. This can not go unpunished." His malicious eyes explode. "We must kill them all. We must destroy the High Tree people. Only then will we be safe. Tonight we should raid their village and burn it to the ground." He raises his spear into the air and cries, "Blood for blood. Blood for Blood! Blood for blood!!"

The village men take up the chant. Gone is the hopeful love. There is only the war cry, which fills me with dread. Pucu grabs my arm and leads me away. "Come we must talk with the elders again."

She tugs at my arm, but before I twist away, I notice something. As Mapi jumps up and down with fury, the pouch on his side has come undone. Inside, arrayed like teeth, are blowgun darts. They all have the same red and white feathers.

My stomach hardens. The war chants grow louder even as we retreat further away.

CHAPTER THIRTY-FIVE
Field of Death

We walk through the remnants of an old battlefield in the black of night. Torches light our path. Scraggly bushes spring up from the dying, yellow grass and barren earth. Death permeates the ground. Broken human skeletons pepper the ground. Bashed skulls. Snapped femurs. The bones are blanched white by the hot sun and picked over by scavengers. A field of death.

Pucu whispers, "This is where our ancestors came to battle and die."

Mapi spins around and gives her a harsh glare. "Quiet, you old fool, or we'll leave you here." The men carry heavy clubs and sharp stone knives. Their faces glisten with smeared blue paint, sweat, and malice.

It is by some miracle that Pucu and I have made it here as women are not permitted on these expeditions to battle. While Mapi whipped the men into a mad frenzy, Pucu petitioned the village elders to allow us to accompany them. She argued that victory would be assured only if I, the goddess, were present. Despite Mapi's protests, they allowed us to join them.

As if Mapi is privy to my thoughts, he turns and raises his stone knife. He sticks out his tongue and runs the knife down its center until he draws blood.

"Blood for blood," he whispers. A few of the men repeat the phrase as if enchanted.

We walk for another hour and enter a part of the jungle where the trees soar high above us. They block out the stars, so the sky is a canopy of leaves. Extinguishing their torches, the warriors navigate the darkness by memory. The warriors' footsteps are silent. I place one foot in front of the other, praying for noiselessness with every step. The snap of a twig could mean my banishment.

Without warning, Mapi raises his hand into the air; on the signal, the other men freeze.

At first, all I hear is the jungle's song—insects chirping, frogs croaking, birds cawing—but as I listen more closely, the sounds of humans greet my ears. A woman sings. A child cries out. A man laughs.

Mapi and his warriors crouch and creep forward, knives and clubs at the ready, for thirty feet through the foliage. I discern shadows dancing around a clearing. A mother carries a sleeping child into a hut, and a family shares a late meal around a dwindling fire. None of the men have weapons nearby.

It occurs to me then that the High Tree people have no idea what's coming. They have no idea that the Black Stream warriors will soon descend upon their village. They have no idea that their lives will soon be destroyed and everything burnt to ashes. The scene unfolding in front of me is not one of wartime preparation; we are part of an ambush that may be unprovoked.

You can't let it happen . . . Maria Luisa whispers.

I know, but what can I do?

You must do what is right . . .

How?

Let us become one . . .

A spike of fear makes me cold inside. No, I can't let you take control.

What are you afraid of?

I'm afraid of what you will make me do. I'm afraid of myself and for myself. I'm afraid for Jared. If I lose him, I will lose a part of myself. What if I change into someone he won't recognize or love?

Please, Mattie . . .

Mapi raises his club high into the air. He signals for his warriors to spread out and surround the village. Seeking to ensure that the massacre is complete, he doesn't want any of them to escape into the jungle. I know that when he gives the order, the warriors will attack without question, pause, or mercy. Filled with hate, they will murder and kill. As the warriors assume their positions, Mapi turns and grins at me. "Watch, witch," he whispers.

It occurs to me that I've seen this play out hundreds of times. Through my many lives, I've seen the battles, the death, and the loss. The result is always the same. More misery, anger, and hate. When the Father Gods rule supreme, the end is always war. What is the purpose of bloodshed? Why can't there be peace?

You are the key . . . you can prevent this . . . let me in . . . let us become one . . .

Pucu's face is drawn and long; she already believes we have failed. We can't prevent the coming bloodshed. I sigh and stare at my hands, realizing that I have to do something, and there is only one thing I can think of to do. OK, Maria Luisa. We will become one, but you must promise to stop this.

We can do it together . . .

I close my eyes and picture the wall. A deep crack suddenly runs up its length. The bricks topple over. On the other side, a glowing light waits for me.

The next moment, she flows through me. It is like a sauna inside my body. Everything warms and slows. As Maria Luisa and I merge, her life flashes through my thoughts: a young girl appears, the daughter of Spaniards. She's a loving, kind soul. Her parents want her to marry a rich trader, but instead, she renounces the colonial life to be a nun who cares for the indigenous tribes. She learns to be a healer and discovers the secrets of the jungle. She masters the many languages of the jungle people and advocates for their lives and traditions.

Her thoughts, memories, and emotions flood into me like water filling a jug. Steadying myself, my hand jumps out to a tree. Her soul continues to flow into me until I feel I'm going to burst. When it is over, I waver on my feet. Everything is clear now. Gone is my uncertainty, self-doubt, and dependency, as I know exactly what must be done.

The muscles on Mapi's back tense as he waits for his last warrior to get into position. He holds his club with white knuckles. He's too focused and excited about the oncoming slaughter to even notice Pucu and me behind him.

Crouching, my hands search the ground and find what I need. Maria Luisa knows how to walk as silently as the jaguar; together, we approach Mapi.

He senses me as I'm behind him. He spins, his knife ready to slash my throat, but my hands remain steady and strong. I slam the rock into the back of his head, and there's a sound like a kicked soccer ball. He crumples to the ground, unconscious.

Pucu's mouth drops open, and she stares, shocked. She recovers, and asks, "Goddess, what are you doing?"

"Preventing a war," I reply.

I step over Mapi's limp body and walk forward, Pucu following after me. I enter the village of the High Tree people with Maria Luisa guiding my feet. The village is almost identical to the Black Stream village—a small clearing surrounded by mushroom-shaped huts. The High Tree people react the same way as the Black Stream people when they see me. The women grab the children and huddle together near their huts. The men tense and reach for weapons.

"I wish to speak to the chief of the High Tree people," I announce.

The trance breaks, and there's a rustle of movement. The men tighten their grips on their spears, and a child starts to cry.

After a minute, a man limps forward. He has graying hair, an arched back, and a curved face. He approaches, supported by a gnarled stick, and halts in front of me. "Why do you come to the High Tree people?" he asks.

"I wish to stop a war."

The chief's eyebrows jump, and he raises a trembling hand. "What war?"

Maria Luisa already anticipated his response. "The war between the High Tree and Black Stream people."

Crossing his arms, the chief's eyes narrow. "We are not at war with them."

"The Black Stream people have surrounded your village. They are planning to attack you at this very moment." As I say this, scared cries erupt from a few of the women. "But I can stop this battle. We can stop this. But you must promise me one thing. You must promise that you will not harm any of the Black Stream people. Do you promise this?"

The nervous chief observes his people. He turns back to me and gives a stern nod. "Hear me now, High Tree people," he declares. "You will not harm any of the Black Stream people."

I turn toward the jungle and shout, "Black Stream warriors! Put down your weapons and enter the High Tree People's village in peace."

The woods remain silent. After a minute of indecision, the foliage rustles. One by one, the Black Stream warriors emerge from the darkness.

The High Tree people reach for their weapons, but I shout, "Remember your promise." This relaxes them. At the same time, the Black Stream warriors come closer, many still holding clubs and knives. "Obey your goddess, Black Stream people. Put down your weapons," I say, while watching each warrior place their weapons on the ground. Both groups stare at one another —rigid and skittish.

The chief points to the fire. "Come, let us sit and speak."

We gather and sit on logs with both tribes sitting opposite one another. I turn to one of the Black Stream people and ask, "How did this war begin?"

The man shuffles with eyes pointed to the ground, but finally says, "The High Tree people have been hunting on our lands."

"Is it true?" I ask the chief.

He shakes his head, "No, we have hunted where we have always have. It is the Black Stream people who have been hunting in our lands. The Black Stream people violated a sacred pact between our two tribes. The hunting grounds where the two rivers break and flow to the jungle has always been our hunting ground. But, in the past six moons, the Black Stream people have been hunting and killing our animals. Our children go to sleep hungry. Our wives cry because we do not have enough to eat."

Some of the Black Stream warriors protest and grumble. "Is it true? Have you been hunting in their grounds?" I ask.

The men avoid my eyes. "It is true," one of them answers. "But Mapi told us that the gods gave us permission to do so. He says that those lands were taken from us by the High Tree people."

That confirms my suspicions. "Hear me now, Black Stream people. Mapi lied to you. You have been breaking the sacred pact. The High Tree people are innocent. There will be no violence. No blood for blood."

"What about Tari?" One of the Black Stream warriors asks. "The High Tree people attacked him."

"Is it true?" I ask the chief. "Did you attack a boy in their village today?"

The chief shakes his head. "We did no such thing."

The same warrior asks, "If it was not the High Tree people, who wounded Tari?"

"Witch!" screams a voice from the jungle. All eyes turn, and Mapi emerges from the treeline, his head matted with blood. "There will be no peace. Not now or ever!" he screams, running straight at me.

I don't run from him; instead, I rise and walk toward him. Mapi, his face distorted with rage, races toward me. He raises his battle club over his head, bloodlust filling his eyes.

When he is a few feet away, Maria Luisa reaches deep inside of me and calls out for someone. An instant later, a new force flows through my muscles. Another past life takes control.

Mapi swings the club down, aiming for my skull.

Possessed by some new force, I leap forward and drive my knee into his groin. The club drops from his hands, and he collapses to the ground. Staring at me with pain-filled eyes, he fights to stay conscious, but he passes out.

The soul retreats out of me like the tide rushing back to the sea. Maria Luisa and I are back in command.

"Mapi is the cause of these problems," I say, reaching down and taking out the poisoned darts from his pouch. I display them to the Black Stream people. "Look at the feathers on his darts." I take the dart from my pocket. "They are the same as the dart that wounded Tari." I point to Mapi. "He was the one that wounded the boy and fostered hate and anger between your two tribes. He wants you to battle because he feeds on power."

The Black Stream warriors appear at a loss. Hate and fury have been replaced by confusion. "What do we do now?" One of the warriors asks.

I spread out my arms. "This is your chance to resolve your differences. This is your chance for peace. Talk. Let love be more powerful than hate."

CHAPTER THIRTY-SIX
Departures

Back in the village of the Black Stream people, drums beat and voices sing. The High Tree and Black Stream villagers gather to celebrate peace. Children of both tribes run and play together.

Despite the celebrations, I'm in no mood to party. In front of me are the ruptured remains of a rusted brown radio with a mess of frayed wires spilling from it like disemboweled organs. The High Tree chief gave it to me as a present, but there is no way it will ever work. I still haven't faced the fact that I'm stuck in the Amazon, and I may never leave.

Pucu comes over and hugs me, attempting to cheer me up. "Goddess, you did it. You prevented bloodshed."

I give her a halfhearted smile. "For the time being."

"You don't need to worry. Mapi has been banished from the tribe. He will no longer control us."

"I'm glad you have peace."

There is a glint of pride in her eyes. "I knew you had the power."

She is right . . . whispers Maria Luisa.

I know she's right.

You realize the power you have . . . we are not here to hurt you, Mattie . . . we are all one . . . we've all been where you are . . .

Why didn't you take control and do what you wanted?

That's not how it works . . . You must want our help . . .

Well, I'm glad you were there, Maria Luisa.

I'll always be here . . . no matter what . . . I'm here for you . . . We are all here for you . . .

Pucu takes a stick and pokes the radio as if it were once a living animal. "You know, you can always stay here with us," she suggests. "We need your wisdom. You can find a husband, have babies, and live happy."

Her comment makes me smile. I briefly imagine what it would be like staying in the village. Growing old with these people. Not worrying about paying the rent, shopping for groceries, and getting fired from jobs.

But something would be missing. Something that I didn't even realize I needed. An ember inside my chest grows hot, and my body and mind desire one thing.

It's OK to love him, Mattie . . .

I grimace and bite my lip. Maria Luisa, why don't you tell me these things in the first place if they are so obvious?

Because you need to discover them for yourself . . .

It's a funny type of relationship that you and I have.

I turn back to Pucu and say, "Thank you. Your offer is very generous, but I must return to my own people. There is someone I have to find."

She nods. "In that case, come with me." Pucu takes my hand and leads me back to the stream where I was first found. On the sandy banks, five of the village warriors wait, ready for a long journey with satchels filled with food and supplies.

"The men of our village will bring you back to your people."

My mouth falls open; I can't believe it. This is my way out of the jungle. This is my way back to the life I left behind. "You know about my people?"

Pucu nods and adds, "Long ago, your people came through the jungle. They told us that we must believe in one god. We refused. They left and haven't returned yet." Pucu hugs me, and whispers, "We will always remember you and the peace you brought us."

A part of me is sad to leave. These people believe in gods and goddesses. They believe in me, and my ability to change their lives. In the modern world, where there are so many false gods, I don't know if I have a place. But I also know that I don't belong in the jungle. It's time for me to discover my role in the world. It's time for me to find the one person who knows me best and also truly believes in Gaia.

CHAPTER THIRTY-SEVEN
No Longer Alone

The multi-colored bus jams to a grinding stop, and my head nearly slams into the seat in front of me. The bus driver nods to me in his rearview mirror. The woman sharing my seat wraps her arms around me in a farewell embrace. Walking down the aisle, I'm the only one who gets off at Acobamba.

The brisk Andean air bites my lungs, and a chill breeze makes me shiver. I made it, I realize. The sun's last glimmers peek over the mountains; it will soon be nighttime. My knitted sweater will not be warm enough at this altitude. I must find the priest-esses.

I've been traveling for a week. My entourage of Black Stream warriors escorted me through the jungle. We split paths at a rundown village connected to the rest of the world by a mud road. A short embrace, an exchange of goodbyes, a few tears, and they melted back into the jungle like ghosts.

But I was still not alone even after they left.

For the days since, Sister Maria Luisa and I have been learning how to live with one another—like a series of first dates. I've come to appreciate and welcome her quiet whispers. They're often more helpful than not.

Although she speaks Spanish with an accent from a few hundred years ago, I can still communicate with pretty much anyone. Her knowledge of medicine—especially medicinal herbs and natural remedies—has helped us barter for rides, food, and lodging. We cured the rattling cough of a taxi driver and the fever of a hostel owner's baby. We've journeyed from the green lowland basins and rivers of the Amazon to the brown, rocky peaks of the Andes. We've lived through Peruvian bus drivers, who drive like they have nothing left to live for. We've watched the people change as well—becoming taller and stouter, as layers of clothing increased.

But more than anything, I've found comfort in her story and life. She was never Ascended. She never knew what it was like to share one mind with another past life. Yet, I've found a connection and meaning in her life, which resonates with me. I discovered slivers of my own existence—of who I am, who I want to be, and who I will become—through flashes of memory and shades of emotion. Despite being separated by hundreds of years, a different language and culture, we share more similarities than anyone I've ever met.

And finally, we're here.

I survey Acobamba, a small village nestled at the base of two mountains. The single-level buildings appear one winter away from collapse. Twisted rebar extends like weeds from cement roofs, and white plastic bags and old food litter the streets, attracting fat, loud flies. No one's around as I walk down the only road in town. It's dinnertime, and I imagine families huddled together eating. My stomach grumbles. I'm sure the priestesses will have food.

Betty Jean mentioned a church in her note, but a quick walk down the road reveals nothing but silent buildings. I'm beginning to get cold and frustrated when I catch a flash of movement out of the corner of my eye.

I turn and a curtain falls back in front of the window of a bodega. The store's glass display case has a meager stock of gum packets, Cheetos snack packs, and travel-size shampoos.

I knock on the door, but no one opens. I knock louder. "*Buenas noches*, is anyone there?" I ask in Spanish.

A rustle of movement and I hear people arguing in hushed tones.

"Sorry to disturb you. I only have one question," I continue.

The arguing stops, and I hear a bolt slide. The door opens an inch, and a round, brown face stares back at me. She's maybe fourteen, and her tense eyes are the same as those of a cornered animal. She's struggling to maintain control, but she's afraid.

"Where's the church?"

The girl exhales a ragged breath and points with a shaking finger down a thin path leading away from the village.

"*Gracias—*"

The girl slams the door shut and returns the bolt to its place.

Staring at the door confused, I turn and go down the path. I wonder what the girl was afraid of. The path travels out of the town and down the side of a hill. The last of the sun's rays bend over the mountains. The path winds around a rock cropping, and a simple church, surrounded by small, squat buildings, comes into view at the base of a valley. Off to the side, a herd of alpaca grazes on a steep field.

I can't believe it. I have traveled so far: from Salem to this small village in the Andes. My journey has changed me. I no longer fear who I am or who I will become. I'm excited to learn that I'm special and important. I can make a difference in this world and change people's lives for the better, and most importantly, I am no longer alone. I'm ready to accept my destiny. The world needs me, and my own fate will not be complete until I fully understood myself.

In short, I'm ready to Ascend. Maybe this was what Ganesha

meant when he said that I had to complete this pilgrimage by myself.

I do have one hope, which is counterbalanced by one huge fear. Will Jared be there? I pray now that he will be. Part of what has given me energy over this past week has been that hope. I play over a fantasy in my head: I will fling open the church doors to find him waiting with a smile. I can't 't think about the alternative.

There's a small school next to the church. But something is not right about the scene. No children. Balls and toys scatter about as if the children were there and then vanished mid-game.

There's no writing on the outside of the church, but a light burns inside. The priestesses must be waiting. I climb the steps, and my breath catches. A jagged crescent moon—the same as my own birthmark—is etched on the outside of the wooden door. This is the place.

I grab the metal door handle and push open the doors, ready to accept my fate.

But I'm not ready for the smell. Fresh, tangy, and nauseating —the smell is as thick as the buzzing clouds of flies. I know this smell because it holds a dark familiarity. It is the smell of death.

My eyes grow wide, and my hands jump to my mouth to suppress a scream. Blood and bodies cover the floor. The victims are all women, and their corpses scatter among the seats, on the floor, and on the pulpit. The bodies—shot, violated, and mutilated. One of them is a young woman about my own age.

The room spins as I stumble to the middle of the carnage, careful not to step on a lifeless hand or foot. Why? I gag as the bile in my stomach rises up my throat. Leaning forward, I'm on the edge of passing out. My skin is as cold and slimy as a reptile. Who did this to them?

It suddenly occurs to me. These are—were the priestesses. These were the women who were to complete my Ascension. Just as the weight of this realization comes crashing down, I hear movement behind me and turn.

I'm greeted by a man wearing a long black coat. He has eyes the color of charcoal, a black widow's peak slicked along his forehead, and a trimmed goatee. I know who he is by the blood-red aura surrounding him, the monstrous bull's head, and blood-stained horns.

"Welcome Gaia." Gurzil grins, baring his canines. "We've been waiting for you."

CHAPTER THIRTY-EIGHT
Dog of War

Four rough-faced men, dressed in combat fatigues and black berets, rush into the room brandishing automatic rifles. Their black boots splash through puddles of blood as they take up positions to the left and right of Gurzil and point their rifles at me.

Gurzil smirks with his arms across his chest. He wears an immaculate, designer black suit and a collared shirt. His eyes gleam in the candlelight that illuminates the church-turned-crypt. All the while, his aura burns brighter, and his deistic form is terrifying.

He waits, studying me as his aura transforms to a blackish green. His upper lip curls into a sneer. "Finally, we meet in person."

My eyes jump from the murdered women to Gurzil. The double shock of the trap has left me speechless. I stare back, a cornered animal, with nowhere else to run.

He senses my trepidation and walks toward me. I shudder as the sound of his steps compress the chest of a dead woman. Stopping a few feet away, Gurzil's eyebrows furrow and his nose wrinkles. "So, you're the girl," he says, squinting his eyes. "Tell me one thing. I'm a wee bit curious." He tilts his head like an owl hearing a mouse. "What makes you so special?"

"Special" has never sounded uglier.

I endeavor to contain my wild, beating heart, but all I succeed in accomplishing is inhaling a fear-rattled gasp.

"You're completely unremarkable." Gurzil continues, his tone reminding me of one of the judges on American Idol. "You're not that pretty." He paces, a shark circling his prey. "You're not that smart. Otherwise, you wouldn't have come here." He reaches down and plucks rosary beads from the hands of one of the dead priestesses. "Yet, you've done remarkable things. Before I slit Rava's throat, I heard about what you did to her men. That was incredible. I was even afraid that you had somehow completed your Ascension."

With his two hands, he snaps the rosary. I jolt as the beads clatter to the floor and fall in between the cracks of the floorboards. "The very fact that you're standing in front of me is a miracle unto itself."

My eyes widen to the size of kitchen saucers, and my arms wrap over my shoulders.

His smile disappears the next moment, and his eyes burn. "I asked you a question." His hands shake. "What makes you so special!" he screams, spit flying from his mouth. Two of the guards exchange wary expressions.

I stare down at my mud-stained boots. "I don't know," I whisper.

Gurzil's face contorts with disgust. "As I thought," he says with a dismissive wave. "The only reason you got this far was because of the remarkable abilities of your friend."

My head perks up and eyes alight. My friend—maybe that means he's alive. If so, there is a chance.

Gurzil notices my reaction. "You should have heard his screams," he says with a malicious laugh. He reveals nothing more, and my stomach hardens.

Stay strong, Mattie . . . Sister Maria Luisa urges.

I'd forgotten she is here. I'm not alone, and I'm not through yet. Her presence reminds me that I've come too far to give in so fast. "Why?" I ask, my voice strong and clear. I push all my disgust and outrage into the question. "Why did you kill them?"

Gurzil recoils as if stung by a bee, but the smile re-emerges. "Look who has some fight still in her? You go, girl." He snaps his fingers three times with manic energy. "Why?" He leers at the women and spits on one of them. "Because I can."

"You didn't have the right to take their lives."

"*Au contraire, mon cheri,*" he oozes, "not only do I have the physical right, as a superior being, but I have the divine right." He points to the bodies, swarmed by flies. "They were sacrificed to my glory. Each of their deaths was a tribute to me." He kneels and runs the back of his hand through the tangled hair of one of bodies.

Disgust ripples across my skin. Hands clenching into fists, I search for an exit or a weapon.

But Gurzil dispels any notion of escape. "There is nowhere else to go. Your story ends here."

Muscles tensing and raising a fist, ready to fight if need be, I say, "It will never be over. You may have killed these women and you may kill me, but I'll come back. In one generation, two generations, I'll keep on coming back. The teachings will be passed on. New priestesses will be taught. Even if it takes another two thousand years, I'll still be here."

Gurzil pauses, his face collapses into defeat; it appears as though he'll weep. But, a second later, he's smiling again. He erupts with a deep laugh. "Why do you think I wanted you alive?" he asks. "You know, I could have killed you a half-dozen different times."

His question makes me stop. Up until this point, I hadn't even thought about it, but he's right. He could have killed me on the first night in Salem with an assassin's red dot on my head. He could have had Rava kill me or his men in the jungle.

"Tsk, tsk, tsk," he chides. "You don't even know. Just goes to show how unremarkable you are. How unworthy you are of eternal life."

"What are you talking about?"

"You didn't realize that I wanted you in a limbo state. It was my will that you were half-way between Ascended and Descended."

I can't stop myself from asking, "Why?"

His grin disappears, and his face is as serious as a funeral. "I needed you alive because you must complete a ceremony which will permanently Descend you."

Sweat breaks across my skin. "What ceremony?"

"You'll know the details soon enough, but in short, the ceremony will result in breaking the chain of reincarnation. It will snap the continuity of your past souls. Once the ceremony is completed, you will never Ascend again. You'll never be able to access your past lives. No priestess or god will be able to help you. When you die—when *I kill you*—your death will be permanent."

My stomach lurches as if punched in the gut. My mind spirals, grappling for a rebuttal as if it were a life-vest. Staying strong is what matters, but his words are like two cold hands throttling my throat. "You're lying," I say, my voice weak.

"No, he ain't," Tatiana replies, appearing in the doorway, her black high heels click a march on the hardwood floor. She walks over and wraps her arms around Gurzil's neck. She extends her head and nibbles on his ear. "I told you she was still alive."

He groans like an aroused predator. "I never should have doubted you, babe."

"Sometimes all you need is a woman's intuition," she quips and spins away like a ballerina, deftly dancing among the dead.

My nerves slip away. Is it true? This ceremony, does it even exist? Tell me, Maria Luisa. Tell me now and don't lie.

It does . . .

A heaviness weighs down my body, and my breathing slows to a shallow gasping. Maria Luisa's acknowledgment scares me to the core. I had come to think of her as my rock. I have depended on her to give me hope.

Don't give up, Mattie . . .

But how do I fight? I don't have any weapons. They hold all the cards.

Keep fighting . . .

This obstinate old past life is going to be the death of me. I bite my lip. Stay strong, stay contemptuous. "How did you know I would be here?"

"Oh . . ." Gurzil smiles. "Don't play dumb. You already know."

I swallow, but my throat is as dry as sandpaper. Is he alive?

"Would you like to see him?"

I hold my breath, and my heart flutters. He's been the fuel that's kept me going. The thought of him has kept me hopeful through my darkest moments.

"Of course you would," Gurzil answers. He turns to a side entrance. "Bring in the prisoner!" A few seconds later, Brutus and Malachi enter—grinning and evil. They haul in an unconscious Jared.

He's tied to a chair, and his pallid skin stretches over a gaunt frame. A collage of purple bruises crisscrosses his face. His fingers are bandaged. Old blood stains his shirt and pants brown.

"Doesn't look healthy, does he?" Gurzil asks. "But, if he had simply told us where you were going, then his stay with us would have been much more comfortable."

I stare at Jared's closed eyes. He must have endured such unspeakable pain before he finally broke.

A heat grows inside of me. Jared is still alive, barely. We still have a glimmer of a chance.

Gurzil's harsh laugh brings me back to the present. "You love him, don't you?" When I don't respond, he continues, "That is touching. Love is beautiful. It's too bad that only the weak believe in the power of love."

"Only the fearful believe in the power of hate," I respond in a calm tone, my eyes not leaving Jared.

Gurzil pauses. "Fearful? You have to be kidding. I'm not afraid of you."

I turn and face him. "Not only are you afraid of me. But you're afraid of all the people you have ever hurt in your pathetic life. You were afraid of the women you killed in Salem. You were afraid of the women you killed here. Yes, you're afraid of me. Your fear fuels your hate. Because of this, I pity *you*."

Gurzil's jaw drops and anger flares up like a napalm bomb. "Save your pity, bitch!" His face loses the mask of cordiality and mirth. Now it's only the demon. "You stupid whore," he spits. "I don't fear anyone. If you lived even a day in my life, you would realize that fear is only what others feel toward me. I'm not afraid of your women. I killed them because they were in my way. A god of war fears nothing."

My voice—calm and tinged with pity—replies, "I feel sorry for you. You have known nothing but anger and hate your entire life. Hate corrupted you, rotted you from the inside. Hate twisted and mutated your soul."

"Silence!" he screams, spittle flying from his mouth, a vein pulsing on his forehead. "I am a god!"

"A god of what?" I ask. "How are you different from mortals?"

"I have the knowledge of over a thousand lives. Each more powerful than the previous."

"And what do you do with that knowledge? You kill, you hurt, and you destroy. You don't listen to all your past lives. I wonder what it's like in your head. Do you listen to the past lives that advocate for love and peace? Or do you ignore them and care more about the words from the older souls? The ones that call for blood and sacrifice. The ones that feed on human life. Are you really a god, or are you a slave to greater demons?"

The muscles and veins in his neck bulge. "I fought for this life. I earned this life. I won the right to be a god! He gave me the right!" he declares with triumph ringing in his voice.

Something is off about his declaration. He appears to be talking about an actual person. "Who gave you this right?" I ask.

Gurzil's reaction to the question is odd. He falls quiet and sullen like a child confessing an error.

"There is someone else. Isn't there?" I press harder, remembering the Shadow God. "Someone has set you on this path."

Tatiana rushes across the room to him. She stands up on her toes and says into his ear just loud enough for me to hear, "Stop listening to her. Let's finish her off."

But Gurzil smirks and with a rough shove, pushes her away. "What are you worried about, babe?" he asks, glaring at her. "Afraid your puppy is going to make a boo-boo? A little mess on the rug?" He shakes his head. "She's not going anywhere."

"You're right," I say. "I'm as good as dead. What's the harm in telling me who a god of war serves."

"I serve no one," Gurzil growls. "I am the master of my own destiny."

Suddenly things become clear. "Then why are you doing his bidding? Why is it so important that I die? Why have you been his lapdog chasing me around the world?"

"I am no dog!" Gurzil shouts.

"As you say," I reply, scowling with hands on my hips. "Yet, you do his work. I hope you will be compensated well."

"Oh, don't you worry. My prize is well-worth my time."

"Silence, fool," Tatiana interjects. "You made an oath."

He spins on her, madness glowing in his eyes. "Shut up, whore! Corpses don't speak."

"Come on, *babe*," I taunt, "who did you make a deal with?"

Gurzil laughs and his face withdraws. "I still remember the day you found me," he says to Tatiana. "I didn't believe a single word out of your mouth."

"He would not approve of this. You know that," Tatiana warns, and I detect a waver in her voice.

"I always knew I was different. Those dreams that I could never remember. You know how it feels," he says to me. "I knew I was greater in my sleep than I was in my reality. I knew I was something more. He allowed me to fulfill my true potential. The deal was simple: for immortality, complete the ceremony and kill you." He stops, a sliver of hate exploding into a raw, murderous glare. "Once I'm done with you, he will be next." His vicious eyes turn to Tatiana. "You hear that, whore! I'm coming for your real man." He laughs like a hyena. "In the end, death and war will rule supreme. My wrath will sweep over the earth. It will be all-consuming, and nothing will block its path. My power will swallow this world. It will swallow all of you, and I will be king."

Tatiana is white with fear. "As you say, so shall it be."

"*Bla, bla, bla . . .*" he mocks, eyes plowing into me with drill-like precision. "Bring me my knives."

CHAPTER THIRTY-NINE
The Game

Tatiana, anxious fear reflected in her dark eyes, fumbles at a bag by her side. She retrieves a roll of purple velvet. With shaking hands, she passes it to Gurzil who snatches it away from her. The rolled fabric spindles down, unfurling to reveal a half-dozen knives. His upper lip raises like Elvis's. "Now for some real fun."

He studies the knives. He grasps one with a detailed bone handle and withdraws it from the sleeve. Its curved edge glints sharp in the candlelight.

Gurzil holds the knife with a delicate grace as if it were a living thing. He stares into the blade's reflection, a mad excitement dancing in his eyes. The guards, on some unspoken cue, all take a step away from him against the back wall of the church.

"Are you ready for the game?" he asks.

"If you're going to kill me, just do it," I reply. I'm not going to give him the joy of seeing me squirm.

A taunting smile breaks from his serious expression. "Not so fast." He tosses the knife from one hand to the other and spins it with well-practiced skill. "Let me explain the rules." He points the knife at me. "You are Gaia—the goddess of the earth. In a sense, you are the mother of mankind and the spiritual embodiment of humanity. Agree?"

I nod, unable to speak.

"Ergo, the mother loves her children more than anything. The mother is kind, compassionate, and above all else preserves and protects the innocent. Are you all those things? A teacher, someone who cares for the young." He slashes the knife through the air, and I wince, my insides turning to solid ice. "So what do you think happens when you commit a crime that is so atrocious, so despicable, that it goes against your very nature and being?"

I shake my head. I don't like where this conversation is going.

Gurzil bares his teeth in a wolfish smile. "The Shadow God told me one thing. If you, Gaia, murder someone who is innocent, then you will no longer be Ascended. The chain of reincarnation will be broken because all your past lives will revolt against you. They will leave you, and you'll never reincarnate again." His face twists in sadistic glee. "What do you think? You want to give it a try?"

Gulping, my hairs stand on end and heart pounds in my chest. "What do you want me to do?"

Gurzil walks up to me. I smell expensive cologne wafting off his skin. He holds the blade in his hand. I see him pull back his arm and expect to feel the cold steel plunge into my stomach.

I close my eyes, chills spreading throughout my body. I ready myself for death.

But instead, Gurzil grabs my hand and places the bone handle in my palm. His icy hands close my fingers tight around it, and he steps away.

I hold the knife and look down at it as if it were an alien artifact. Turning back to Gurzil, my mouth drops open, but no words emerge.

His eyes flare with malice and determination. "Bring them in!" he shouts.

Through a side entrance of the church, they march in single file. About a dozen children, ages five to nine. I remember the empty school playground and the fear-filled eyes of the girl in the bodega. The children. They were taken, and now they're hostages in his sick game.

He winks, and he shoots his eyes in the one direction I was praying he wouldn't. My body trembles, and I fight to stay on my feet.

Gurzil's cruel smile grows larger as I put together the pieces. "Yes, that's right. Now you understand." He points to the children. "You need to make a sacrifice to my glory—a child, an innocent."

A wave of nausea courses through me. My hands shake and lower lip quivers. "I can't do it. I won't do it."

"Oh, yes you will," Gurzil replies. "Or the consequences will be even more terrible."

I close my eyes, take an icy breath, and ask in a quivering voice, "What consequences?"

"I will make you watch as I kill them all."

"You can't kill them," I plead, eyes bulging. "They're just children."

Gurzil crooks his head like a serpent. "You still don't get it." He takes another knife out of the velvet roll and walks toward the children. "I can do whatever I want." He brings the knife's edge against the throat of a six-year-old girl in a pink dress with ribbons in her hair. She begins to cry.

"Stop! Don't!"

His hand halts. "Oh, Gaia. Look what you're doing to them. Look into their eyes. Their lives depend upon what you do. Are you going to let them down?"

"Please."

"Oh, you pretty young thing." Gurzil caresses the girl's cheek.

She sobs with tears. "You will, because if you don't, I will slice each of their little throats. And I will make you watch while their innocent faces squirm and twist with pain."

I'm now crying. Please, Maria Luisa. Help me figure something out. I need you now more than any other time. I wait and hope.

But for the first time, she's silent and gone. I'm all alone.

"If you don't do what I command, then I'll find more innocents. I'll find more children, and I will kill them. I will continue killing until you fulfill my wishes."

I'm shaking with fear and anger. Icy sweat pours down my back.

"For I am the Lord your God, and I command it," Gurzil intones. He pulls the little girl to within a foot of me. She squirms and fights to free herself, but he holds her with an ironclad grip.

My grip on the knife loosens, and I look over at Jared, but he's still unconscious. I need his help.

When I stare into the little girl's brown eyes, I shake my head. My body feels like it will collapse. "I can't," I whisper. "I can't hurt her." To kill her would be to kill myself.

"You must," Gurzil says, voice hardening. "Come toward me," he commands. Like a puppet, I walk toward him. Each step is a heavy blow. I'm now standing in front of him and the little girl. "Raise the knife."

I bring the knife slowly up and rest it against the tender skin of her neck.

My tears splash onto the ground. The blade quivers against her throat, and I fear my hand will slip by accident. "I can't do this," I confess.

I hope for a miracle—anything to save me from this moment. Where is the Chinese warrior? The Indian? Maria Luisa? Where are any of the past lives who are supposed to be inside me? Aren't they supposed to come rescue me? Aren't they here to protect me? I pray for them. Willing them to save me. I need you now. Please!

But in the end—silence.

I imagine jamming the knife into Gurzil's stomach. I want Jared to jump to his feet and save the day. I want the police to come in and stop it all. But there's no cavalry. There's no rescue.

Gurzil releases the girl, who remains petrified in place. He walks up behind me. His hands grab my waist, and he pressed his hips against mine and hisses, "Kill her."

"I can't."

"You can, and you will," Gurzil assures. "It's the only way to save more lives."

"But I—I—."

Tears streak down my cheeks. I force my hands to stop shaking. I take a deep breath, and I know what has to happen. There's only one way out.

With a movement so swift that Gurzil will not be able to stop me, the blade leaves the girl's throat and finds my own. The blade's cold edge sends shivers through my body.

I will take my own life. In the end, it won't matter. I will be reincarnated into someone new.

I will sacrifice myself. Yes, it is selfish, but I won't kill an innocent. My rebellion might not save everyone, but it will prevent me from killing a child.

However, my hand doesn't budge, and the knife remains in place. I can't swipe the blade across my throat.

Gurzil's grip on me loosens, and he whispers in my ear, "Careful how you tread. I will still kill them all even if you don't do it. Look the children in their eyes before you slice your own throat. Because their blood will still be on your hands."

I turn to the children in the room. My heart beats fast. I do as he says and look them in their eyes—frightened, crying, innocent.

While staring into their fragile faces, a painful pressure builds inside of me. My breathing quickens.

In that moment, something ignites. It's a realization that sets my heart soaring.

I love them. I love all of them. This love explodes inside me, filling me with burning heat. This love destroys the fear that had gripped my heart. It destroys the hate and anger that I thought I needed. My love encompasses all. This love ignites a flame inside of me that starts to grow.

I feel love for the Black Stream people. Love for Luisita. Love for Ganesha and his followers. Love for all humans. Love for the forest. Love for the sea. Love for all creatures—animals, birds, insects. Love for Jared. I even feel love for Gurzil, a man who is driven mad by his determination to kill me.

Then things get weird. Time slows to the beating of my heart and then, stops altogether.

The faces of the scared children freeze. Gurzil's face—twisted and smiling—is a statue. The men with guns are afraid and under his spell. A fly's lazy path stops in midair.

Time refuses to move forward. Then, a small flame lights within me. A mini eruption. An odd tickling sensation at first. It begins below my naval. A series of more bursts become a burn. Not a painful burn but a purifying one. The flame inside of me grows. Destroying something that latched onto me like a virus, and it grows like a bonfire. A moment later, this burn spreads throughout my entire body. It burns off my clothes, my flesh, and my bones. Burning away the vestiges of an old life, the fire sets me free. My own body can't contain the fire, and it shoots forth through the entire room, blazing out in a bright yellow light.

This all-consuming fire encompasses the room. It fills the church. It devours the village. It engulfs the continent and swallows the world.

I convulse from the explosion feeling the radiant energy flow out of me. Out of my fingertips. Out of my eyes. Out of my chest. I feel the entire life energy of the planet—beating, growing, living inside of me.

As quickly as the fire engulfed me, it disappears a moment later. Everything goes black. A familiar black from a familiar dark.

CHAPTER FORTY
Many Flames

From the darkness emerges light. A single light. It pierces the black veil like a pinprick star in the heavens. The light wavers and dims. I think for sure it will disappear, but it grows in strength and brightness.

I focus on the flame. The flame burning inside of me, which has transformed to an inferno. I stare deep into the heart of it, and in its dancing red fire, a face emerges—a round, caring, and loving face with wrinkles and small ears all framed by dark black hair.

Sister Maria Luisa smiles at me. Her expression conveys the everlasting love fueling the flame. Our eyes meet and I find all her secrets and stories. I understand the heartbreak of leaving her parents and the city of her birth. The pity she felt for the indigenous tribes of the jungle and how they were abused by the conquistadors. I experience the love for the native peoples—for their traditions, stories, and lives.

In a blink of an eye, the flame splits in half like a single cell organism. Now there are two flames. My eyes focus on the new flame, and in its glare, another face appears. A bearded man with green emerald eyes, rough skin, and a muscled neck. In his sad eyes, I watch his entire life on the Eurasian steppes. The fruits of his meager harvest of barley. He hopes the cows will be fat enough for winter. There is the petite and pretty aristocratic wife he loves. The two children he adores and for whom he makes small toys out of twisted dry hay. The wars against the barbarians he fights, and his cold death in a faraway land.

I cry out when the two flames split into four.

A Patrician woman of Carthage. She sails across the Mediterranean in search of a lost love. A Roman ship attacks them, and she dies at sea. Her lover never learns of her true fate.

Another flame shows a beautiful woman with dark black hair, an angular face, and a smiling mouth. It's the woman who I first saw during the Ascension ceremony in Salem. She works in sub-Saharan Africa as a rural nurse vaccinating children against polio. She falls in love with a man. She's pregnant and gives birth to a beautiful boy. She loves him.

Four flames multiply to eight. Eight becomes sixteen. Over and over again the flames increase until I can no longer keep track of the different lives that flood my mind.

Soon all I observe is a great endless ocean of flames. Thousands of lives; thousands of stories. They come to me as a wild river. They come to me in a whisper. Some are noble, great, and long lives. Others are brief, anonymous, and insignificant. Some are kings and queens, nobles and baronesses, while others are merchants and farmers, beggars and slaves. Men and women. Girls and boys. Lives from across the world and from every part of the planet. Some from cultures that have disappeared and some that speak languages that are now extinct.

I recognize them all. The realization takes my breath away. I've been all these people. Sometimes I've been souls whose lives were turned into songs. Some changed history. Most died forgotten.

As I stare at the ocean of flames, I realize that I haven't lived thousands of lives. I've lived millions. Some of my past lives are so primitive that the people couldn't write or even speak. But I know what they felt, what they wanted, out of their brief time on this planet.

They come back to me in a great flood. They are me. Their hopes are my hopes. Their fears are my fears. My dreams, my marriages, my loves, my children.

So many times I have relived the same emotions and experiences. The great circle of life repeats itself infinite times. The one thing that connects them all is the everlasting love. The essence of the Mother Goddess. I can identify that thin connection in all the past lives. They've all loved unconditionally. They would all sacrifice themselves for the innocent.

The past souls stretch back to the beginning of time. The Ascended have always been there. They have been guides to humanity. Marker posts that edge along time's great continuum.

My final true purpose comes to me at that moment. I am the light and the love that is humanity. I am the good to counterbalance the evil. In that moment, I remember it all. There's no longer fear, only exultation. I know and believe.

The flames whirl and spin around me like a cyclone. Millions of lives. All these dancing flames converge on me. I join this tornado—spinning and swirling. At long last, I am changed. I've come home, and I am no longer alone.

I am Ascended.

CHAPTER FORTY-ONE
The Gift

The roar of the voices flares up and disappears. The silence is complete, and nothing stirs. It takes me a moment to realize that I'm back in the small church with the little girl in front of me. Gurzil holds me with a tight grip. His hands on my hips and breath on my neck. It seems that no time has passed.

Everything is the same, except for me. I hear their voices whispering to me, urging me, warning me, converging on me.

I inhale sharply, and it's as if someone pushes the play button on life.

Gurzil senses my hesitation, and with a swift move, he presses his body close to mine. His hand finds my hand, still holding the blade to my throat, and pulls it away. "Not so fast," he says into my ear. "You're not going to get out that easy."

The voices grow louder in my head. The flames blaze up. They tell me of my gift.

While still holding my hand, he brings the knife back to the little girl's throat. She stares up into my eyes—full of incredible fear.

"You're going to do this. Whether you like it or not. I command it because I am a god."

I can't help but smile. Fear and worry are gone. A self-confidence that I never knew was possible burns inside of me. Gurzil thinks he moved my hand. But it's I who has allowed him to move my hand. It is my will, not his.

"There's no easy way out," he hisses, a triumphant tinge in the back of his throat. "You're going to do exactly as I say. Do you understand?"

I do understand. I understand that gods like Gurzil have been in control for too long. I understand that they abuse the balance in the world. I understand the pain and suffering that their power unleashes on the world.

Turning my head and facing him, I see Gurzil flinch and hesitate, his confidence faltering for a second. He still thinks that I'm the scared and uncertain woman I once was. He doesn't realize I am something new—something he should be scared of. Our eyes lock.

I nod, and his mouth parts to a smile. He thinks he has me under his heel. "Good. Repeat after me." His voice rises as if he were a priest intoning a sermon, "I make this sacrifice—"

I repeat his words in a steady voice. "I make this sacrifice."

One of his eyebrows lifts. He senses that I'm different, but his hubris blinds him. He's so close to his prize that he's incapable of realizing the truth staring at him. He bristles with excitement, thinking that he has won the great game. "—To the glory of the one true god—Gurzil." His grip tightens on my hand, and I know that in the next second, he will force me to slice the girl's throat. He will force me to kill an innocent and commit me to a Descended state for eternity.

I don't hesitate nor do I intend to obey. "To the glory of the one true goddess—Gaia."

Gurzil tenses with rage, his muscles ripple up his arm. His hand tightens on my hand, holding the knife. But before his brain can send the signal to pull my hand, which will kill the girl, I reach through his skin and enter his mind.

A thousand images fly through my consciousness as I enter his soul.

Oscar Diamante was an orphan boy—unloved and oppressed. Growing up on lonely streets, he was taught to be an animal from a young age. Fear, hate, and anger are the only realities he's known throughout his life. A life of crime was the only way for him. The cold steel of a gun felt comfortable. Drug deals, the murder of a family as retribution, the enslaving of girls to do favors for rich men. His life has been lived deep in the gutters of humanity, and his Ascension caused a greater imbalance in the world.

I push him aside and dive deeper into his past, reviewing the hundreds of lives he has known before. Each one worse than the one before. His entire reincarnated life, both Ascended and Descended, has known only death, violence, and pain. A SS commandant in charge of a concentration camp. A rapist in Victorian England. A marauding Cossack. A thief and livestock stealer. The older souls command him. The old demon from Greek mythology—the Minotaur; he who demands blood sacrifices. These old souls are Gurzil's true masters.

I search deep into his memory, searching for his creator. The god who Ascended him, but I only find shadows of the maker— nothing that names him. He is a Father God—an Ancient. A god that has never known a Descended life.

I pity Gurzil. He's a lonely child. A scared thing that doesn't know what to do or how to act without hurting others. I know him and love him because even the most evil need to be loved, but I also know that being loved doesn't give one the right to hurt others.

Gurzil is still frozen by my touch. Time has stopped again as our minds meld.

There is only one thing I can do. Gaia has a gift, which is hers alone. I remember what Caishen said: I Ascended him.

I have the power to Ascend others.

And the reverse side of this is the power to Descend.

I reach deep into Gurzil's twisted soul, finding that which gives him the power to be a god. It is a burning ember of hate, a red coal that has fueled him for millennia. It's not a beautiful flame. It's a blistered and deformed slug of molten evil. In my mind's eye, I grasp this burning ruby of hatred. It doesn't burn. Once I have it in my hand, I yank it out of him and hold it before me. The burning ember loses its luster. It dims and dies, now only a blackened and charred husk. It disintegrates into dust which disperses into the air.

Time resumes its normal course. Gurzil's hand falls off of mine, and I drop the knife from the girl's throat. It clatters to the ground. His energy drains from him. I have taken away his soul and the ability to reincarnate. I turn and find Gurzil's eyes, which still retain a brief spark of life.

In that second, he knows that I have fully Ascended. He realizes that he has Descended, that he'll never come back. The hate burns up one last time, but his eyes roll back, and his face assumes an emotionless and deadened stare. His knees lose the strength to keep him upright, and he collapses to the floor.

A dead silence consumes the room. It is as if an evil air has been sucked clean out.

Tatiana screams, shattering the silence. "What did you do to him?" She fumes, red in the face. Her eyebrows arch in a demonic accusing stare. The servant of the Shadow God, Gurzil's maker, is not happy.

"I Descended him," I reply.

Her cheeks puff, and she bares her teeth. "You killed him?"

"Killed?" In my core, murder of an innocent is not possible. My past lives and souls would never allow such a thing. But there are other ways to punish gods that abuse their powers. "No, I took away his soul. I extinguished his flame of Ascension.

The spark that fueled his reincarnation and connected him to his past lives is no longer."

Tatiana shakes her head. "You made him into a goddamn vegetable. That's what you did!" she screams, pointing an accusatory finger at me. "You're going to die." She spins to one of the guards, who still have their rifles aimed at me. The guard shakes his head as if waking from a bad dream. "Give me your gun, you goddamn savage." As Tatiana screams at him, his eyes open wide as if seeing for the first time. The confused guard takes a step back.

"My brothers, I implore you," I say to the guards in Spanish. "Do what is right. The evil is gone. You don't need to fear or hurt anymore."

The guard nods toward me, swings the gun, and points it at Tatiana. At that moment, both Malachi and Brutus reach for their guns, but the guards are faster. Their gun butts strike them on the back of their heads. They collapse unconscious to the ground.

"What are you doing?" Tatiana screams. She reaches out for guard's gun, but he pushes her back. She flies across the room and slams into the wall. Her eyes land on me while she rubs her shoulder. "What did you say to them?"

"Only the truth."

Tatiana shakes her head, and her evil eyes narrow on me. "You're going to pay. We're going to make you pay!"

I stare her down. "Go back to your master. Tell him that things are no longer as they were. Gaia has returned."

Tatiana shoots me one last nasty expression. She spins and runs out the door.

"Please release the children," I say to the guards. "They've done nothing wrong."

One of the guards nods, and he tells the children to go home. The children run out, and the guards exit as well. In the end, it's only Jared and I. Whichever past life had occupied me leaves, and I am back to my old self.

I rush over and undo the restraints on Jared. "Are you OK?"

"Mattie . . ." he groans. His whole body is a wreck.

I get his legs undone, noticing that he's bleeding from his stomach and leg. His injuries are bad. "Hold still. We have to get you to a doctor."

"Wait . . ."

"No, we need to get you to a hospital," I get his arms undone, and he falls forward into my arms.

"Mattie, listen. I want to say this in case . . ." I hold him in my arms like a child who has fallen asleep. He pushes back. With a strained cry of pain, he lifts his head and looks into my eyes. "I love you," he says.

I choke up, remembering the revelation from my Ascension. My voice catches, but I force myself to tell him the same. "I love you too." Our lips find each other, and there is nothing more glorious than that one kiss.

Because I know it will be our last.

CHAPTER FORTY-TWO
Healed

"You don't need to leave like this," Jared implores. He's weak but alive. He looks small in the large hospital bed. "We still can be together. I don't understand why you're leaving."

Part of the reason I'm leaving now is that I know Jared will be OK, but he is still to weak to follow me. I shake my head. I've been worrying about this moment the entire week since we arrived in Cuzco. "I need to understand who I am and my purpose."

He shakes his head and turns away.

I can't believe how close I'd come to losing him. After my Ascension, we were able to convince some people in the village to drive us to the nearest hospital in Cuzco. The drive took eight hours, traveling over hilly and mountainous roads as Jared's condition worsened. By the time we arrived at the hospital, Jared was near the edge of death. He was brought immediately to intensive care, and his heart even stopped at one point. But he was strong; Jared pulled through in the end. I never left his side.

He's been in recovery for the last week, and I have been

avoiding having this talk with him. I know I have to leave, but I wasn't going to tell him until he was almost healed.

It's hard for me to look at Jared, so instead, I stare at the muted television hanging from the ceiling. The mugshots of Malachi, Brutus, and Oscar Diamante flash on the screen.

The news channel replays the same story it has for the past week. On an anonymous tip, the FBI discovered the bodies of the murdered women in Salem, buried in a hasty grave. They found that the guns used in the murder matched those of the women murdered in Peru. Further investigations revealed that their guns also matched the one used for the murder of Patrick. The infamous drug and human trafficker Oscar Diamante, now in a vegetative state, along with his top two lieutenants, Brutus and Malachi, were awaiting trial in both countries. It is a small measure of comfort that justice will be had for the deaths of Patrick, Gertrude, Alice, and the other priestesses.

"What do you mean?" Jared finally asks. "You're Mattie. You're the same person you've always been."

I shake my head. He doesn't realize how untrue that statement is. "I need to go because I can't grow into who I am unless I'm alone."

"What are you talking about?"

"I'm Ascended now."

"But you're still Mattie."

"No, it's not like that. It's like I have a thousand voices in my head, and they're all trying to tell me different things at the same time. I don't know who I am anymore, and that is why I need to have time to myself."

"But you seemed like you had control back at the church."

"That's the thing. I have these past lives, which are chomping at the bit to take control. The times in India, in the Amazon, and in the church. Those people were me, but in a way, they weren't. They were past lives, but they are also now my lives. I need to be alone so that I can figure out how to live with all of them."

"But I'm your protector," he says. "I'm supposed to be with you, and my job is to protect you for life. You don't need to leave because we can work together. I can help you and support you," Jared replies, his voice sending bolts of longing through me.

"But that's the thing. I need to do this alone. There are so many things that I can only understand by myself. Heck, it's like my real self has been asleep for two thousand years. Like I haven't really been awake since my last Ascended state. I have to go and sort through my issues."

"What about what you said to me?"

I pause and am unsure what to say. "I know . . ."

"You said you loved me." He bunches his hands into tight fists. "I love you. Doesn't that mean anything?"

I sigh and weariness hangs on me. "It does, and I do love you, but I can't completely love you until I can understand myself first. Can't you see? I'm leaving because I don't want to hurt you."

"Interesting way of not hurting me. You leaving."

"Jared, please try to understand."

"No, I do," he says cutting me off. "Go, I'll be fine."

"Don't be this way, please."

"I don't know how you want me to be."

"I want you to understand that I do need you."

"Well, when you're ready, I'll be here."

New tears fill my eyes, but I know now is the time to leave. I turn away and rush out of the hospital before breaking down.

But to where I am going, I don't know.

CHAPTER FORTY-THREE
The Final Prophecy

The warm waters of the Pacific wash over my feet. Perfect blue waters. The sun blazes, and I pull my beach hat down farther on my head. I scuttle a few feet to the side to take advantage of the shade of a palm tree.

I don't need to feel alone anymore because I'm not. I have thousands of voices inside me who constantly remind me of this fact. I'm not weak or powerless; I'm something different and new.

I'm not sure whether I should be proud or terrified of this.

A boy comes up to me and offers me a shell necklace. I buy it. He smiles and walks off.

After he leaves, I close my eyes. The voices rise up in my mind. One by one I ask them to be quiet until there is only one.

One life, one past soul. It's the last Ascended life I knew. The Goddess Gaia.

An image appears in my mind, and I realize again the horrible truth of what will be. It's the truth I discovered when Jared and I kissed that last time.

I now know the third part of the prophecy.

I will kill the man I love.

Acknowledgments

Writing is hard, but these people made writing this book easier. Forgive me if I forgot to mention you, but know that you helped to shape this book, and for that, I am eternally grateful.

Firstly, I want to thank you, reader. You decided to read through this book and follow Mattie's adventures. I truly hope you enjoyed them. If you did, please share this story with others either through social media or word of mouth. Books live and die by reviews, so if you can post one on Amazon or Goodreads it would make a real difference.

My huge thanks to those of you who read through early drafts and gave invaluable feedback including Tracy Costa, Thomas Finan, Emily Frongillo, Cheri Scotch and Louise Place. Thank you also to the members of the North Shore Writers Group for their incredible edits and critiques.

My deep appreciation to the Mystery Writers of America, New England Chapter for providing great community, learning, and fun times. In particular, Jay Shepard, Don Kaplan and Ray Salemi, who taught me how to order an Old Fashioned.

I would be remiss without mentioning the many fine authors who provided me their time and advice including Dale Phillips,

Jerri Ledford, Matthew Quinn Martin, Chris Holm, Jane Haertel and Jamie Schmidt. Buy their books!

Lonely as writing may be, good friends made this endeavor more enjoyable. Thank you to Axel, Peter V, Wiley, Jake, Peter Swedish, Sanjeev, Adam, Chris, Rami, Aaron, Pete C. and the Cocca-Bateses.

Thank you to the fantastic team at Spirit Warrior Press for believing in Mattie's story and helping it come to fruition.

I'm lucky to have some of the best siblings and close family imaginable. Thank you Ariel, Leif, Noah, Josh, Abigail, Caryn and Meyer for reading over early drafts, being there to pitch ideas, and being great. I love you all.

Mom and Dad, you taught me to love books, so I guess you are partially to blame for this whole affair. I love you both.

And lastly, to my two true loves—Drappie and Lala—you are my everything.

About the Author

J.R. Walcutt is a former microfinancier, chicken farmer and tarot card reader. He's searched for lost Native American tribes in the deserts of Mexico, traveled extensively in the south of Spain, worked as an aid worker in Mumbai, lived on a sinking boat in the port of Jaffa-Tel Aviv, and started an export business in Beijing. He lives on the North Shore of Massachusetts.